D0210922

THE
WOLVES
OF
FAIRMOUNT
PARK

ALSO BY DENNIS TAFOYA

Dope Thief

THE
WOLVES
OF
FAIRMOUNT
PARK

DENNIS TAFOYA

 MINOTAUR BOOKS NEW YORK

THE WOLVES OF FAIRMOUNT PARK. Copyright © 2010 by Dennis Tafoya. All rights reserved. Printed in the United States of America. For information, address St. Martin's Press, 175 Fifth Avenue, New York, N.Y. 10010.

www.minotaurbooks.com

Library of Congress Cataloging-in-Publication Data

Tafoya, Dennis.
    The wolves of Fairmount Park / Dennis Tafoya.—1st ed.
        p. cm.
    ISBN 978-0-312-53116-4
    1. Drive-by shootings—Fiction.   2. Witnesses—Fiction.   3. Fairmount
Park (Philadelphia, Pa.)—Fiction.   4. Pennsylvania—Fiction.   I. Title.
    PS3620.A33W65 2010
    813'.6—dc22

                                                            2009047490

First Edition: July 2010

10 9 8 7 6 5 4 3 2 1

For my children

ACKNOWLEDGMENTS

Writing is a famously solitary occupation, but the truth is it takes a ton of help to get to a finished manuscript. I want to say thanks to my agent, Alex Glass at Trident, my manager, Brooke Ehrlich, and to my editor, Kelley Ragland, and her assistant, Matt Martz, as well as Hector Dejean, India Cooper, and everyone at Minotaur Books.

Deep appreciation goes to my developmental editor Laurie Webb, who was with me every step of the way, as a sounding board, a first reader, and a wise friend; to August Tarrier, gun moll and intrepid navigator, who read the book in early drafts and made invaluable suggestions. To my excellent friends in the Liars Club, Jon McGoran, Ed Pettit, Jonathan Maberry, Don Lafferty, Kelly Simmons, Greg Frost, Marie Lamba, and the rest of the gang, for camaraderie, endless support, and invaluable advice; to Scott Phillips and all the other writers who have become my friends and guides in the last two years. To Rachel, Shilough, Lauren, Julian, Greg, Scott, and dozens of other independent bookstore owners and workers who went out of their way to support my work and give it a home. To Karen, Peter, Marie, Dick, Olivia, Dan, Christine, Jessy, Lucy, Maria, Bren, Cori, and Anita for their patience, wit, and friendship; to Shannon and Patrick from the Other Side, for

ACKNOWLEDGMENTS

generosity above and beyond the call of duty. Lastly, I have to thank my family, especially Elena, David, and Rachel Tafoya, for the inspiration to write this book. You make me proud every day.

I am the son
and heir
Of nothing in particular

—Morrissey

THE
WOLVES
OF
FAIRMOUNT
PARK

CHAPTER

1

When Michael Donovan and George Parkman Jr. were shot in front of the dope house on Roxborough Avenue on a Thursday night in June, Mia and Tisa were standing on the stoop at Pechin Street. They had some time, a little break before the next johns— the fat, shy Jewish kid who always brought blow and the old Polish guy from the neighborhood who smiled wide and told dumb jokes and kept his money in one of those little plastic things that you had to squeeze to open, like Tisa's grandmother had to keep her nickels and dimes in. It had the name of a bank on the side of it, she remembered. So on nights when the old man came by that was what she thought about, her *abuela*, a nice old lady from Ponce who always smelled like baking.

Tisa moved to the edge of the porch and lifted the hair off the back of her neck because it was hot inside and she was sweating a little, and Mia followed, digging in her bag for her smokes and bringing out two. A single moth ticked against the porch light. Tisa watched Mia screwing up her face to see the end of the cigarette, and it always made her laugh when she was high, which she was a little.

Mia lit her cigarette and then Tisa's and then waved out the match, leaving blue trails of smoke, and because she was high,

Tisa had to watch them curl and dissolve in the hard white light until they were gone. They picked up their conversation from earlier, talking about how Mia's man was getting out again and how did she feel about that? Mia said he was so good to her when he wasn't loaded, and Tisa gave her a look and said, "Yeah? When was that?" With that look like *will you please?* That was when they heard the shots, like popping noises from up the street, and saw the black car go by, the radio blaring and a girl screaming, "*No, no, no.*"

Michael Donovan's father, Brendan, was getting in his car at the Roundhouse at Eighth and Race, the Police Administration Building that was supposed to look like a big pair of handcuffs, and wondering if he was doing the right thing asking to get off the street. He sat in the car and watched motorcycle cops come and go and thought about his own father standing on a chair at the Shamrock and toasting Brendan in his new uniform the day he graduated from the academy. The only time he could remember the old man really drunk, his eyes shining and rimmed pink. The place was full of cops, the guys the old man had worked with, the stone-faced Irish and Italian guys who voted for Rizzo because he was one of them, the guys Brendan thought of as his uncles.

He was sitting in the car and lost in his head, remembering the bitter shellac taste of the Scotch and Patsy McDonnell's sister Iris pulling him to her in the corner by the big old Rock-Ola jukebox all those years before. He was thinking about those days, when women were mysterious and unknown to him as visitors from another country, then the radio made its hissing squeal and reported shots fired on Roxborough Avenue, and Brendan had the thought, *Someone else's problem now.*

Asa Carmody and Detective Danny Martinez were down at a strip club on Front Street. Danny was on the edge of getting hammered, feeling the vodka starting to work in his blood. His eyes shining, he was watching a red-haired woman dance while he was trying to sort out fives from ones on the bar in front of him. Asa was buying rounds and calling attention to himself like he was wearing a sign, *I'm here. Remember me here.* Wearing a green T-shirt with a yellow shamrock from a bar on Ridge Avenue, and the leather vest that was the only thing his father left for him when he disappeared down a rabbit hole when Asa was nine. Looking at his watch every few minutes and making a circle in the air with his finger for Doreen to set them up again, Danny and him and a couple of rummies from the neighborhood. One more round, the night was young, yeah? Danny was trying to put this all together in his mind, but he was slow tonight. He watched Asa peel off bills and stick them in the girl's G-string and whisper something and point to Danny. Asa with his stiff ginger hair and his hooded eyes, all business all the time. Thinking he was looking like a guy having fun at the bar with the friend he grew up with. Danny knew Asa, and knew he wasn't ever having fun. It wasn't in him.

The woman's eyes were guarded, hard to read, but she nodded. So then Danny knew she was his to take home with him, and something wasn't right about that. The woman was tall, and her hair was a hard, opaque red, like plastic, and she smiled shyly at him, but it wasn't like she was attracted to him. It was more like she was afraid. Danny was wondering how many more vodkas it would take for him not to care, how many more to shut off that voice in the back of his head that said he was being played. Being moved as if by magnets under the floor. When the cell phone went off, he was relieved. Now he could make excuses and get away from Asa. Get his head straight and get back in the game.

George Parkman Sr. was leaving his girlfriend's apartment on the river, wiping his mouth compulsively like he always did, trying to erase the perfumed waxy residue of her lipstick and wishing the wind would pick up and blow the smell of her out of his suit jacket. Telling himself he'd stop coming here. Call her and end it. Give her a few bucks, help her get set up with that store she was always talking about opening, Jesus, whatever, he had too much at risk to be so fucking dumb.

It was just that out on the floor at the plant, the metal stamping shop out on Rising Sun Avenue he had inherited from his father, he could feel his life going by in a rush. That green light that made them all look like they were dying, all the guys in their blue shirts and safety glasses and the smell of the cutting fluid that used to smell like money to him and now it felt like he was drowning in it. Home was no better, with a strange, deli-

4

cate son he didn't know and Francine telling him the same story every night about her mother's cataracts or some shit. So he needed something real in his hands, someone he could hold on to who looked back at him with eyes that weren't lined with disappointment at what the money never bought. Was that a crime? Was that a sin? Was it?

Orlando Kevin Donovan, Michael's uncle, Brendan's half brother, was nodding, lying on a tattered couch on the roof of his girlfriend's house, a needle in his slack white fingers, his eyes opening and closing, opening and closing, the orange light from the street caught in the mist blowing down Green Lane toward the river.

He was still new with the needle, getting used to the hard rush of light into his head. He was carried along in a warm current and he had a lurching sensation of motion in his stomach and he remembered the first time he went on a real roller coaster. Dorney Park, somewhere up in the country, it took forever to get there. It was summer and Brendan had taken him and brought a girl and Orlando loved it all, being with his older half brother and the shy, pretty girl and eating hot, greasy funnel cakes white with sugar and the crush of people all around. He remembered sitting in the rigid bench of the coaster and the bar going down in front of them with a hard clank and the feeling of the chain catching under the car and the long ride up into the cloudless sky. The feeling in the pit of his stomach now was the same as that day when they crested the rise and teetered on the summit, Brendan grabbing his hand on the bar and saying, *Are you ready? Are you ready?* and Orlando shrieking and shaking his head and laughing.

Now, on the couch, the dope blowing up in his head, he was thinking that summer was coming, July was coming and another birthday and he was still alive. Still here, the blood tunneling through him and the lights pulsing in his eyes, red over green over white, the city coming awake in the dark and the faraway popping of guns a signal, a salute to him. The black sky was an ocean and he was suspended in it, the winking lights all around like the glow of phosphorescent life pulled in the current, and the echoing rumble of his heart resonating with the crack and shift of the plates in the earth.

Dogs began to bark then, first one, close by, then others, blocks away, and he remembered his mother telling him when he heard the dogs at night it was the wolves, the wolves in the park that had never been caught and never would. She'd lean over his bed, her breath sweet with wine, swaying drunk and her eyes on fire, and afterward he would lie awake for hours and listen for them, see them moving in a line down the trails in the dark woods, silver and black under the moon and their teeth snapping, bone white.

An hour later, Orlando was on the street, watching the frantic light show of ambulances and cop vans, the families clumped at the curb (ready to go at any hour, empty eyes drawn to the dancing lights, surging at the TV cameras like fish hoping to be fed). He hung back, wanting to observe but not be observed, still rolling with the dope, the dwindling chemical jolts becoming a music that moved him along the river of black road.

He had been a student at Temple, but he floated away from that like the last man from a sinking ship. Let it all go when his mother, Maire, turned up dead, wedged behind a Dumpster off Oregon Avenue. His mother finally gone, he walked the streets and fed his growing habit, bumped along in the current like a stick in the black rainwater, and wasn't it all so terrible and grand? Some nights he could hear the throb and hum in his legs and chest, while he stood under the last working light on the block, his slight black form outlined in white.

Now he stood and watched the uniformed cops clumped by their cars, the detectives with their badges out and huddled by the bright splash of blood on the steps of the house Orlando knew was a dope house run by some Dominicans from Kensington. As he got closer he saw the bullet holes in the front door and a kid in a blue jacket using chalk to circle a bright shell casing in the street. Another cop, a young Hispanic guy in plainclothes, bent close over a bunch of glassine bags and frowned, then looked up and said something to an older guy wearing nylon gloves and working a pen in his hands, clicking it, twirling it in his fingers, clicking it again in a way that Orlando found hypnotic. There was a low, buzzing hum and one of the TV crews turned on one of those intense blue-white lights that Orlando knew was called a sungun, and he fished in his leather jacket and put on his shades.

He saw one of the uniformed cops narrow his eyes and then bend to the ear of the young Hispanic detective and point out

Orlando and whisper something. Shit, what was that about? He turned then, slowly, as if his attention had been caught by something back up the street. He began to wander away, his head down, when he heard someone shout behind him, and then he started to run.

He kept close to the line of cars, running hard for the dark at the end of the street, whipping off the sunglasses and holding them in one balled fist. The circling lights of the ambulances and cop cars played in the wet trees and across the houses, the world going red and black, red and black. He hadn't run flat out in a long time and felt it as a burning in his chest and a hot line in his flank, and his jaws hung open and wet like a dog's.

He had loved to run as a kid, but that was a long time ago, and he didn't seem to be getting anywhere. He felt every step, his boots hitting the street with a painful smack that rattled his knees and jarred his head. At the end of the street he grabbed the bumper of a sagging Olds, bent double, and vomited hot bile into the shadows, hearing now the easy stride of the young cop, the tap, tap of his small feet, and he braced himself for the flashlight so when it snapped on he was ready, a grimace pressed into his face and his eyes screwed up, and the cop said his name while Orlando waved the light away and nodded, thinking, *Shit, shit, it was going to be a good night, and now what?*

Now the cop was saying, "Orlando, man, why you running from me?"

Orlando heaved, his throat too burned to talk, but he stood upright and managed a shrug, like what else was he going to do? It was the game, like cowboys and Indians. Junkies and cops. You chase me and I'll run.

"Orlando, isn't Brendan Donovan your brother?"

"Why?"

"What do you mean, why? Is he or isn't he?" With that exasperated cop voice, tired from listening to dipshits lie all day. His brother had it, too, that voice.

He began to put it together, the lights and the splash of blood. "Did Brendan get hurt? Is that what this is?" Making a big sweep with his hands, taking in the lights and the cop cars and the news vans. Feeling guilty now he had run. And his brother (half brother, Brendan was always quick to say) lying in a hospital, or worse?

The cop cocked his head, moving the light over him, and Orlando wondered how he looked. Black leather jacket, black jeans hanging off his skinny ass, his pale skin even whiter now than usual. His pupils tiny as pinheads in his face, his white-blond hair growing out in spikes and barbs from when they'd cut it when they had him up at PICC, the prison in Northeast Philly.

"No, Brendan's okay," the young cop finally said. "His son's been hurt."

Orlando's mind raced, picking things up and dropping them. Trying to remember the last time he'd seen his nephew, Michael, thinking of him as a little kid, but he'd be what, a teenager now. Fourteen? Something. His face was hot, processing all the guilt of being banished from his brother's life since the second time he'd been arrested, coming out of a store on South Street where he'd shoplifted a dozen hats while Zoe flirted with the kid at the counter. Having trouble even calling up his nephew's face. His nephew. Jesus.

"Michael? Michael was hurt back there?" Knowing he must sound like the dipshit junkie he'd become. His head steaming with the effort of calling up his own family, the gears and belts in his brain slipping while he blinked into the flashlight.

The cop shook his head, and Orlando dropped his gaze. He wanted to say, *I'm not just this. I wasn't always this.* He said, "Get that fucking light out of my face and tell me, is Michael okay?"

Kathleen Donovan sat in the chapel, balling Kleenex in her hand and looking at the tiny stained glass window, wondering at the compact, utilitarian version of faith represented by a chapel in a hospital. A couple of benches that stood in for pews. On the blond paneling in the front of the room, a design like a star that might suggest a cross. The same scuffed linoleum that ran through the corridors. What kind of generic God would hear your prayers here? Faceless, nameless, demanding nothing, offering some kind of bland good wish for a speedy recovery, maybe. This was not the God she knew from grade school at Holy Cross. The God of Holy Cross was a jealous and an angry God, full of judgment on the unrighteous, or even the lazy and unwary. His agents were bitter and frustrated nuns and snarling priests whose hands were stony and quick to mete out punishment. Whose tongues were as sharp and wounding as their hands.

Whose presence did she wish for now? From which God did she seek mercy for her son, bleeding down the hall in the

ER, his face swollen, his eyes blackened? Dear God, she pleaded, dear God, but who was watching? The bland and nonspecific deity of this small room off a busy hallway, or the wrathful ghost of the hard stone church at Holy Cross? She worked the piled Kleenex in her hand like a rosary and thought again that she had always expected this night, the emergency room vigil, the tense faces of the cops, the practiced concern of the Captain, but in her mind it had always been for Brendan. She had spent so much time and imagination on warding off the image of Brendan shot down on some North Philly street, she felt blindsided by the news that it was Michael. She had wanted to argue with the cop who had called the house, say, no, it was Brendan found unconscious on the curb on Roxborough Avenue, surrounded by broken glass and cellophane wrappers, like something thrown away. No, not her son, Michael. *You mean Brendan, my husband,* she told the kid who had called. That's what she had been preparing herself for all these years. Then it was Brendan ringing through, and when she heard his voice she screamed.

They had had to get someone to unlock the chapel, which wasn't usually open unless the priest from St. Josaphat was there to say Mass. Brendan's partner, Luis, had looked at the Dominican janitor when he'd said that, and said to him in Spanish that he could get the goddamn keys or pack for fucking Santo Domingo, forgetting as he always did that Kathleen spoke Spanish, too.

Wedged into the narrow pew now, she looked over at Francine Parkman, the mother of the other boy shot down on the curb on Roxborough Avenue. She was small and dark, with a brown line for a mouth and eyes with shadowed lines under them. Italian, or Puerto Rican, Kathleen thought. She had a trim waist, an expensive sweater that looked like cashmere. She looked, Kathleen thought, like money. Did that matter now, in the weak green light of the chapel? Were they supposed to be sisters now their two boys were shot down on the same street corner in the middle of the night? Already she had seen the way George Parkman had looked at them when the Parkmans had come in, their faces white, their eyes wild. Something ungenerous in the line of his mouth. Suspicion that Michael had gotten George Jr. into some kind of trouble?

The door opened and they both turned to look, their bodies as tense as if they were condemned prisoners, wondering which of them would be the first to be taken out to some bullet-pocked courtyard. There was the doctor, his hair prematurely gray, his eyes infinitely tired, and behind him George Parkman, his expression blasted and empty. Kathleen turned to look at Francine Parkman, who threw up a hand in self-defense as they got closer. That's what she would remember later, that small hand, sprinkled with minute brown freckles, the nails dark as blood, shuddering with the effort of holding back the terrible thing coming.

Kathleen watched them go, their wracked bodies bent, their shoulders heaving, and wanted to ask, *Is he your only child?* It was insane, she guessed, but it was in her mind that they should have had more children, she and Brendan. That having one child had been a mistake. That to have one child was a kind of bet with God about the goodness of the world, a hope too fragile to hang so much happiness on. Hadn't Brendan come home every night, his eyes full of the ways that people let each other down, slid backward into darkness? Their terrible needs and endless rage and desperation imprinted on his face, a terrible bone-deep knowing that soured his expression, rearranged his features so that when he walked in the door at the end of his shift, sometimes for a moment she didn't know who he was.

Brendan Donovan couldn't find any place to be. He couldn't stand to be in the room with Michael, hearing the buzz and clack of the machines and wanting to touch his son's swollen face and trying to keep from breaking down. The place was full of cops, his friends and guys he didn't even know, and there was comfort in that, but already there were questions about what Michael and the Parkman kid were doing in front of a dope house, and if there was one thing Brendan did not want to be it was the cop with the bad kid. He'd seen it, they all had, but that wasn't how it was, and if he tried to tell them, grab one of the detectives and put him straight, he'd just get pissed off and forget himself and want to put a fist in someone's eye.

He paced, getting to know a little route from the ER to the front desk to the vending machines. He had just turned to walk back down the quiet hallway from staring at the candy bars he didn't want when he saw the Captain moving up the hallway, nodding at him and talking out of the side of his mouth to a young Spanish kid in a rumpled suit who was carrying a notebook, and Brendan had to think about that, about his kid's name and his name and Kathleen's in the chicken scrawl of a homicide cop's notes stuffed in a file somewhere, and their life reduced to a shorthand narrative passed from the cops to some bored ADA and then the newspapers and TV to circle back to him through family and friends.

"Brendan." The Captain put his hand on his arm, and Brendan nodded but couldn't say anything. "I'm so sorry. How is Kathleen?"

He cleared his throat and pointed down the hall toward where he'd last seen her, in the chapel with Francine Parkman. "She's hanging in."

"I can't imagine." The Captain was tall, big across the shoulders, going bald now. He was a tough fucker, and the guys all liked him. A Jew among Irish and Italian Catholics, a guy who almost never raised his voice, almost never sounded like brass usually sounded, like they were trying to shut you down before you got a chance to say anything.

Now the kid was putting his hand out. Brendan wondered if he was Dominican—he reminded Brendan of guys he knew from the neighborhood. Wide but not fat, muscled in his arms, with skin the color of milky coffee and the close-shaved head all the young guys had now.

"Danny Martinez."

"Brendan Donovan."

The Captain put his hand on Martinez's sleeve. "Danny is Violent Crimes. He's the guy who put that Derrick Leon and his friends away." Brendan remembered Derrick Leon, one of those scarred, wild-eyed gunmen who came out of the drug trade once in a while, moving up fast by killing everyone he knew, and Brendan remembered he'd been locked up but didn't know who'd done it. This Martinez kid looked about twenty-two, and something about him was more bookworm than street cop. Little wire-rim glasses and a way of taking the room in from the corner of his eyes, though you never knew. The Captain turned back to Brendan.

"What are the doctors saying?"

"They're waiting on X-rays. He's in, he's unconscious, but they're saying he's got eye movement and that's a good sign. He's got a . . ." Brendan had to clear his throat again. He tapped his right temple. "He got hit in the temple, but it looks like the bullet didn't penetrate the skull."

Martinez cocked his head. "Small caliber, like a .22 or something?"

Brendan shook his head. "Haven't seen the slug, but maybe. Maybe it was a misfire or ricochet or something."

"Yeah, the stuff we recovered at the scene looked to be all nine mil." He flipped through the little book, checking. "'Course it could have been two guns, and we haven't found all the slugs."

The Captain grabbed Brendan's hand. "Michael's a strong kid. And whatever he needs, you know he's got it." He looked at his watch. "I'll be back later. You need anything, you call me direct." He let go of Brendan and touched Martinez on the sleeve. "We're getting these guys. There's no question about that. None. Danny is the best guy in Violent Crimes, and this is our first priority."

For today, Brendan thought. Today and maybe tomorrow and then some other piece of unsupportable horror would come their way and then that would be the priority and this would all fade. It would matter to his friends, to Shawn and Luis and the guys he knew and worked with. To him and Kathleen and whatever was left of Michael.

He heard a strangled wail from down the hall and all three of them turned, watched as Francine Parkman bent double, ripped at her husband's coat, her mouth wide. A line of spit hung from her lips, and for a minute Brendan thought she was going to sink her teeth into her husband's arm.

The Captain and Danny Martinez looked down, but Brendan kept watching. In uniform he'd have turned away, too. Left them in their terrible moment, averted his eyes and looked at the floor or just walked away, but this was different, because they were here together, him and Kathleen and these strangers and their dead son. What was happening was happening to them all.

When they were done, the Captain off to wherever brass was always on its way to, and the kid back to the crime scene, Brendan went back into the chapel and sat down next to Kathleen and she picked up his hand and squeezed it and he nodded. He looked at her then and she raised her eyebrows and he shrugged. There was nothing to report, nothing to tell her. He didn't know anything.

It was the most profound truth he had picked up all those years riding in a Radio Motor Patrol car going out into people's houses in the middle of the night or the middle of the day and listening to them tell their stories. Nobody knew anybody.

Nobody knew the first goddamn thing about their wives or their husbands or their kids or their friends. He'd look at Luis and they'd laugh or shake their heads or just stare into the middle distance and wonder at what people were capable of.

To be fair, maybe he'd already known it. It wasn't some cynical thing he'd broken his head against, this knowledge of the strangeness of life. It wasn't like he'd gone out the first day starry-eyed and full of hope and he'd been blindsided by the terrible things people did to each other. He'd grown up with Maire and knew how she was and how no one had ever stepped in to stop her until his father had finally gotten him out of the house. They left Orlando there, all of four years old and already a sensitive and sad kid who knew too much about madness and fear and disappointment. Brendan would ask his father if they could go get him, but his father had tried to explain about the judge and custody and that Orlando wasn't theirs to take, but it all confused him and he'd wake up in the middle of the night and listen to the quiet and think of his little brother, trapped in a haunted house with a mad drunk.

CHAPTER

2

When Danny went to the station house off the river drive he'd been up twenty-four hours. His eyes burned, his mouth tasted of acid and coffee and mints, and he had stopped taking new facts in and was chewing on what he had learned. He hadn't been pressed this hard in a long time, not since the last couple days he'd spent working Derrick Leon, and he sat down on the hard bench outside the Captain's office while the old man finished a phone call. The sun was going down, and the house was fading around him. The place was hot as a sauna, and the pipes rang and clattered like it was an old submarine going deep.

Danny remembered Derrick Leon and the high he'd gotten off those last hours and sticking a shotgun in Leon's face in the garage on Thompson Street. The terrible parts, the crime scene on Second Street where Leon did his girlfriend and his mother or seeing the dead patrolman down on Oregon Avenue, the kid who had pulled Leon over and gotten one in the face—those things didn't hit him until later. It was the parts that worked, getting the tip from Asa about the kid from Leon's crew who had fucked up one too many times and was ready to give Leon up, all the parts fitting together and that sense of momentum. Getting the kid, DeAngelo Barnes, to point out the garage where Leon was hiding, Danny picturing him in there pissing in Coke cans and doing lines off the snapped-off rearview mirror from a junked Gremlin to keep his edge.

Danny remembered the heat, even at four in the morning when they went in. The two of them bulked up in vests, him and John Rogan, standing in that strange, gauzy light from the sodium lamps that made everything on the street a sickly chemical orange. Blinking sweat out of his eyes while they stood at the side door and waited for the SWAT guys to give them the high sign. A three-legged dog loping across the street like some kind of omen. Then the locker room stink of the garage, Leon passed out on a wrecked couch, shirt and pants off, one hand jammed down his underwear. Danny didn't handle a gun much, and when he did he was usually tense, but that night he'd felt bulletproof, untouchable. Big John fucked with him later, called him the Mountie, out to get his man. He had felt different that night, though, felt things he couldn't say, even to John. Not even drunk. He'd felt like something wielded, something moving under power, an engine of justice setting things right.

His mother had a picture of Danny walking out with Leon in cuffs that somebody from the *Daily News* had gotten. Leon's head was turned, saying something to Danny, and Danny was smiling.

The Captain motioned Danny in and hung up the phone as the younger man dropped heavily into a cracked wooden chair. The furniture at the station was ancient, crossed with red scars and scabbed with cigarette burns. Sometimes he'd try to conjure what the place must have looked like when it was first opened, but couldn't get it clear. It felt like it had already been faded and misted with cobwebs the day they'd turned the lights on, like a reopened tomb.

"Coffee?" The Captain pointed to a carafe on a low table against the wall, but Danny waved him off.

"I haven't had anything but coffee to drink in about a day. My ears are starting to ring."

The Captain sat down and lifted his hands. "What do we know?"

Danny flipped through his book. "The kids were standing in front of the place on Roxborough, which the Fifth District had got numerous complaints about in the last two months. People coming and going at all hours, arguing, music, blah, blah."

"Dope."

"Fits the profile. Front windows boarded up. Front door reinforced. Anyway. Nine o'clock, give or take, a black or dark car goes by, make unknown. One of the neighbors, a guy just got back from Fallujah, says automatic weapon, but the other neighbors just say they heard a lot of shooting."

"From the house, or just the car?"

Danny shook his head. "We're still looking at the scene, but it looks like all the shots came from the street. There are casings only in the street. Bullets and holes in the house, plus a blood trail, inside. Two guns recovered from a bedroom on the second floor, but neither one looks to have been fired. Place was a mess.

White residue on the kitchen table we're having tested, but I'm betting comes back dope."

"Any chance the kids were inside and dragged out to the curb? Like they got hit inside when they were buying and the dealers don't want them found in the house?"

"Nah, no sign of that. The blood trail goes from one of the front windows out the back. The kids, I think they fell where they were hit." He closed his book and looked off. "Couple weird things, though."

"I bet."

"Yeah. George Parkman, the kid who didn't make it?" Danny frowned down at the Captain's desk. "He had two handprints in blood on the sides of his face."

"Jesus."

"Never saw anything like that before." He lifted his slender hands and laid them alongside his face. "I got a photo from the ME."

"The shooter? Touched the kid's face? For some fucked-up reason?"

Danny shook his head, widened his eyes. Who knew? "The car didn't stop, that we know about anyway."

"So another person on the scene? Someone comes out of the house?"

Danny screwed up his face. He didn't like that.

"Tell me what you're thinking, Danny."

"The kids are standing there on the stoop. Maybe working up the courage to go in."

"Maybe just came out?"

Danny closed his eyes. "There's nothing in their pockets, so no, they haven't gone in yet. Money, but no dope. If you haven't done it, I'm thinking it takes a lot of working up to knock on a door like that. While they're standing there, here comes a car. Guy across the street says he can hear the radio in the car." He lifted two fingers, the kids standing on the steps. His other hand slid by. The car. "The guys in the car come by, spray everything. The kids, the house, they don't give a shit. Someone in the house gets hit. They grab everything, pick up whoever got hit, run out the back." He opened his eyes. "Then the guys in the car throw a handful of bags out the window, like a calling card."

"Bags?"

"Baggies. Decks." The Captain nodded. The tiny glassine bags of heroin that got dealt out every day. In their hundreds, in their thousands. "These have a little gangster with a tommy gun printed on the side. Al Capone, they call it."

"Who deals that stuff?"

"John Rogan says that's Green Lane. So, if it's all what it looks like, it was Green Lane who shot up the house." The Green Lane crew. More dealers, bumping up against the Dominicans for the neighborhood, maybe.

"Tell me about them."

"Green Lane is Ivan and Darnell Burns. Ivan's locked up now, but his halfwit brother's running everything. Him and a crazy kid named Trey King from West Oak Lane."

"You see them doing this?"

"I wish I could say no. Ivan, at least he had some sense, but his brother?"

"Great. The other guys, Tres Nortes?"

"Yeah, that's Juli Mir, his cousin Teyo. Juli's got connections with African smugglers. Everyone else is moving Mexican heroin these days."

"Does that matter? Is this about connections?"

"Maybe. Probably, though? It's just about the same old crap. Territory and customers. Money. Only the dealers use the word 'respect' a lot."

"So we're going to see more of this shit."

"Yeah, that's likely."

"And the kids?"

"Wrong place, wrong time. The one kid—" Danny looked at his notebook. "Parkman Jr. Something like a thousand bucks in his pockets."

The captain cocked his head. "Jesus. So he was there to buy something. And the handprints?"

"Someone else. Someone who saw it, standing there when the kids got shot." He fished in his pockets, first one, then another, came out with a grainy print of a digital photo. He handed it to the Captain, who looked at it and gave the smallest shake of his head and seemed to Danny to slump a little more into his seat. The picture was of the slack white face of George Parkman, his hair rucked and red with his own blood. The colors exaggerated, the way they were in digital. The red bright and lurid, the one open eye a brilliant, unreal blue. The kid's features were somehow both delicate and not wholly formed, the face of an adolescent boy. His eyes canted down, as if finally the dead are disinterested in life, or maybe embarrassed to be seen. On his cheek, a long, slender handprint in rust.

The Captain did the same thing Danny did, and Danny could see that anyone who looked at the picture would do the same. He put his hand on his own cheek, a delicate gesture like someone feeling for his own temperature. The Captain took his hand away and looked at it, then at Danny.

"Yeah," said Danny, reading the Captain's eyes.

"That looks small. That hand. Or thin."

"Yeah, for what it's worth. Someone standing there when the kids got hit." He took the picture back from the Captain. "See, that's the other thing. One of the neighbors, a retired nurse, she said that right after the shots she heard screaming. A girl, she said."

"So why is she there? Was she a third? With the kids?"

"That's part two, right?" Danny stood up, fanned himself with his notebook. "I gotta sleep a couple minutes, then it's out to find out if the kids were there alone."

"Brendan's kid?"

"Still out, but the doctors are saying he's got eye movement, responsive pupils, so it's not all bad, I guess."

The Captain nodded, then stood up and walked around to put his hand on Danny's shoulder.

"This is our family, Danny."

Martinez knew that, but he was smart enough to let the Captain do his thing and say his piece. He didn't need anyone to light a fire under his ass, but he held his tongue. He had been letting older cops do that since he got out of the academy. They had things they needed to say, and he figured it was worth it to listen and maybe learn something. At least it showed some respect, and Danny knew cops well enough to know that respect was the real currency. At some level it was why you became a cop.

"You're young, but when you get older and have your own kids, you'll know. We go out and wade through this shit night and day, and we need to know there's a bubble around our wives · and kids. That they're looked out for. Protected." Danny nodded, and the Captain went on.

"It's been a long day, and it's going to be a long night, but I need this done. I need a head on a pike outside this house." He pointed out at the street, at the river, the neighborhoods, and his eyes were shadowed. Danny could see a puckered white scar between two rocky knuckles. "This has to be answered, and I mean right fucking now."

CHAPTER

3

It was dusk and turning cool. Orlando paced on the street near Brendan's house, looking up and down the narrow road and rubbing his hands together, a nervous habit that had gotten worse lately. He wished Brendan would come home so Orlando could say whatever it was he came to say and get away, out of this neighborhood of old ladies looking out at him from between the drawn blinds.

He lit a cigarette to have something to do with his hands and then tossed it away, walking down the sloping street past a blue Dumpster where one of Brendan's neighbors was renovating a narrow house, guys going in and out carrying loads of pried-up woodwork and speaking Polish to each other. They eyed him as he walked by craning his neck to see inside, and a big guy with a shaved head and a hooked nose cocked his head and said something that Orlando didn't need translated. He held up his hands and kept moving, but made a note that the place was empty and when he'd looked inside he'd seen an opened wall and the warm red glint of copper pipes. He kept walking the narrow, canted street, tucked his head down.

. . .

Brendan was standing in the kitchen listening to phone messages, his keys still in his hands. Kathleen had gone right up to get a shower and a change of clothes so they could get back to the hospital. There were voices from outside, and through the shades Brendan saw the red crawl of lights from an RMP in the street in front of the house.

He was moving toward the door before he heard the knock. Standing on the porch were two young guys from the Fifth District. One tall, black, with the trim body of a runner, the other pale white with freckles and broad across the shoulders. Both had shaved heads, the way they all wore it now, so many of them coming out of the service. The shorter one pointed a metal clipboard toward the car where a pasty kid with blond hair stood with his hands in his pockets, and it took Brendan a minute to recognize his half brother.

Orlando moved to stand at the periphery of the porch, looking down the way he always did, one arm cocked over his face and the hand touching his hair. The same stance Brendan had seen a thousand times when his brother was in trouble. With the old lady, or at school with the nuns. In police stations and courtrooms. Hiding behind his pale hand, his eyes flicking up. Poised for the blow.

"Sir?" The young cop looked apologetic. They'd know, of course; every cop in the city knew about Michael by now. "This individual says he's—"

"Yeah." Brendan waved a hand, cutting him off and showing his teeth in something that wanted to be a smile. "Yeah, he's with us." He waved, one quick, sharp flap of his hand. "Get in here."

The kid tucked his shoulders in and skirted the cop and slid past Brendan and into the living room without a word. Brendan stepped out to the porch, smiling again to show everything was okay. The two cops looked at each other; then the taller one came up and shook his hand and said he was sorry and they were all pulling for his son. The pale, black-haired one looked sheepish and said he was sorry to disturb him and Kathleen but an elderly woman down the block had called them when she'd seen . . . The cop motioned with his head past Brendan toward the inside of the house. Brendan told them he appreciated their coming and keeping an eye on things. Cop to cop, the way he talked to the guys on the job. His face burned red, and he wiped at his mouth and nodded to them as they got back in the RMP. At the door he turned and looked at the blank faces of the houses up and down the narrow street and wondered how many of his neighbors had seen what happened. Great, he thought. Just what they needed now.

Brendan came back in and shut the door to find his half brother standing in a corner of the living room, his hands in his pockets, his eyes flicking around the room. He had always been a good-looking kid, but now he looked tired and maybe sick. His eyes were red, his skin pale and blotchy. His leather jacket was scuffed, and his jeans looked unwashed and greasy. Brendan let out a long breath. He was trying to remember the last time he'd seen him. It was at least a year. Maybe it was the time he'd seen Orlando coming out of a social club on Broad Street that Brendan wouldn't have gone into with a shotgun and a dozen friends. The Tip-Top, that was it. Jesus Christ.

He'd almost called Orlando by his middle name, Kevin. It was something he'd begun doing when his younger brother had started to seriously fuck up, in high school. The name Orlando was ridiculous for a grown man. Something their crazy, drunken mother had named him in one of her moods. A weightless name that seemed to pull his brother away from normal life and into the dark corners where she'd lived. Where she wandered until she died, frozen solid behind a Dumpster, shaped to the hard ground like a bundle of rags.

So let his junkie friends call him Orlando, or Little Brother, he'd heard that, too. Brendan wanted to hug the kid, and smack him hard on the side of the head. Both feelings working on him at once. And of course it wasn't just his brother and the mess he'd made of his life. It was Michael lying unconscious in the hospital. From standing on the steps of a dope house. Someplace his brother, God help them all, had probably copped.

"Yeah," said Orlando, and Brendan came to himself again. "I know. I'm sorry. I just heard and I didn't . . ." He shrugged. "I didn't know what to do."

Kathleen started down the stairs, and they both watched her come, her hair wet and lines like bruises under her eyes. Brendan caught his brother's eye and pointed toward the door silently, his eyes hot and white. Orlando put his hands up, placating. He got it.

Kathleen looked lost in her head and it took her a minute to see Orlando, but when she did she ran to put her arms around him.

"Orlando." She held him close, and he looked over his shoulder apologetically at his brother, his eyes sorrowful as a dog's. Kathleen stepped away. "You heard about Michael. Thanks so much for coming." She seemed genuinely glad he was there.

"He just came by for a second."

"Yeah, I just wanted to see if, you know." Orlando shrugged. "There was anything I could do. And to say I'm sorry."

"Thanks. I wish I could make you something." She swiveled toward the kitchen.

Brendan said, "But we gotta get back to the hospital." His eyes were lifeless, and Orlando looked down, rubbing his hands on his pants.

Kathleen touched his hand and looked into his face. "Come by and see us sometime. When Michael's home." She moved away, touching her wet hair, and Orlando moved toward the door.

Brendan followed him out to the porch, and Orlando turned. It was full dark now, and they were just shapes to each other, blue-black figures of men. A car went by, and they watched it go, Brendan waiting for his brother to speak.

"I know you don't want me here. I just didn't know what else to do." He looked blank and defeated, which just made Brendan angrier somehow.

"Jesus, Orlando." He shook his head. "Are you eating? Do you have a place to live?"

"Yeah, I'm okay. I'm right down the street from, you know."

"From what?"

"From where Michael—" He shrugged. "From where Michael was last night."

Brendan took two quick steps toward him, and Orlando closed

his eyes and stood straighter, as if expecting the punch that Brendan had had coiled in him since he had first seen his half brother on the porch, but Brendan just grabbed the loose sleeve of his jacket and twisted it, bringing them closer.

"Christ, was he with you? Was he coming to see you?"

Orlando opened his eyes. "No, Brendan, no. I haven't seen Michael in, I don't know." It came out in that tone, that whining schoolkid tone that junkies used with cops.

"The detectives said the boys had a thousand dollars. Was that to buy drugs? From you?"

"No, Brendan. No. I don't know what they were doing. I don't know anything about it."

Brendan released his brother and held his hand out. "Give it."

"What?"

Brendan snapped his fingers twice and flapped his hand in a "gimme" motion. "Whatever you took from the living room."

"Jesus, Brendan."

"Don't even." His hand went up fast and he slapped his brother. "Don't even fucking start."

Orlando didn't flinch, but looked down and put one hand into his jacket. He came out with a small picture frame and handed it to Brendan, who took it roughly.

He had to hold it close to see it on the darkening porch, some kind of phony silver frame with a faded picture of Maire that Kathleen had found among Brendan's father's things and put out on the bookcase near the TV. Brendan had thought about making her get rid of it, but for reasons he himself didn't understand he let it stay. Though he had moved it back behind

31

some other pictures. Michael in his hockey uniform, Brendan and Kathleen on their wedding day, impossibly young. Other, better memories from the family he made, not the one that made him.

Brendan shook his head.

Orlando kept his eyes down. "I wasn't going to sell it."

"Yes you were. You might tell yourself something else standing here now, but you were." His voice was quiet now, and his eyes flicked around the street to see if anyone could see them. "Don't come back here. I know you mean well or whatever, but you're not . . ."

"Not welcome here. I know."

"No, it's that you're not *you* anymore. You're just this collection of urges and twitches, and I can't have that around my home." He didn't raise his voice, and when he said it he patted his brother on the arm. No hard feelings. "I don't know you anymore. I know what happened to you, about Maire and how she got. But I can't help that now, and I can't help you."

Brendan heard a noise from inside and turned to see Kathleen moving in the living room. When he turned again, Orlando was gone.

Kathleen came out, her head down, distracted. She looked at him, narrowing her eyes in the dark. "What's going on? What's that?" She pointed to the frame in his hand.

"It's a picture of my mother."

There was a small buzzing noise and a faint click as the streetlights came on, and it was night.

· · ·

Orlando walked up the stairs of the boardinghouse off Green Lane, moving slowly, listening to the hollow sound of his feet on the stairs and thinking about his brother and his mother and trying to remember when he wanted to be something. Trying to remember if there was a time when there did seem to be a way forward.

He was on the clock. It had been most of the day since he'd fixed, and he needed to get high. He should eat, he knew, and he was thirsty, but that could all wait. Right now there were pulses of electricity shooting in his arms and legs and a hot line running from his temple to his jaw that was his jones waking up.

When he got upstairs, the door was ajar and Zoe was inside. There was music on, old Interpol she loved. "Turn On the Bright Lights." She was dressed from the restaurant in the black skirt and the bright orange shirt she hated because it made her skin itch. He put his arms around her without a sound and she stiffened at first, saying his name like it was a question, and then falling into it, pressing her hands into his back and letting his head fall to her shoulder.

"What's wrong, babe?"

He thought about what to tell her, and she drew back to see his eyes. He lifted a shoulder, let it drop.

"My brother, Brendan, his son got hurt. Shot, up the street at the place the Nortes run." The Nortes were the Tres Nortes, Three Norths, a mostly Dominican crew from up in Kensington.

"Jesus, Orlando, is he dead?"

"No, but he's in a coma."

"Did you see your brother?"

"Yeah." He almost never talked about his family to her, and they were just names. She had a big family out on the Main Line that she hadn't seen in a year. He sat on the edge of the bed and pulled open Zoe's purse. "What do you have? Do you have anything?"

"Yeah, baby, but we got to talk about that."

He rifled in her purse for a minute, then dumped it out and picked through compacts and lipstick, keys and loose coins, and worked two tiny glassine bags out. He held them up and one was ripped and empty and he looked at her darkly.

"No," she said, "I didn't."

"We talked about this."

"What did I just fucking say? I didn't shoot, I just snorted it, Jesus. Fucking Julian was in my shit all day, I couldn't do nothing right. It was just to take the edge off, you know? Motherfucker thinks being manager makes him God. So I couldn't wait, okay? I didn't know when you were fucking coming home."

Orlando shucked off his jacket and pulled his works out of a hole in the lining. He opened the nightstand drawer and took out a bent spoon and got a book of matches out of a white box and went to work. When he was ready he tied himself off, and Zoe paced and shook her head.

"I'm just saying what the fuck, though, right? I mean, you can use a needle and I can't?"

Orlando banged up the vein in the crook of his arm, the needle in his teeth like a knife.

"Gimme two seconds, then you can add to my fucking misery, Zoe."

She stopped pacing and watched. "You suck."

He pulled up some of his own blood into the needle, then fired into his vein, his hands beginning to shake. He untied, then grabbed her and pulled her into his lap while she lightly smacked at the top of his head.

"I hate you pretty bad, you know it?"

"No, you don't. You love me."

He held her thin body to him with one hand and with the other dumped the rest of the dope out of the small bag and pushed it into lines on the top of the dresser with the edge of a snapped-off CD. He made a small noise in his throat, an animal moan that was the dope beginning to land. Zoe bent to the dresser and inhaled the lines and they both fell back as if from a fire, lost in their own bodies for a minute. Listening to that faint hum, like for that moment you could hear your own electricity, the circuits and wires that carried the current giving off sparks that snapped and rang inside.

After a while she folded herself into him and he said her name and breathed into her neck and she rocked in his lap to make him hard.

"I need you on this side of things," he said into her hair. Her eyes closed and opened and she smiled at him and shook her head. He said, "I'm going down into the caverns, into the caves, and I need you up top, holding the rope, right?"

"You talk such shit."

"Yes, but you love me."

"No." She moved against him and he cupped her small breasts with his hands and she turned and fit her mouth on his. She was beautiful and her skin was creamy white so that when he touched it he always expected it to be malleable, to give in his hands like butter.

"I'm the man in the dark, with just a little flashlight, going down and down and seeing everything, all the ice and the rocks and the bones, and I need to know you're there, you're holding me up. I'm going to see things. All the things that no one has seen for a thousand years. All the world left underground."

"I want to go where you go, I want to see." Her whisper was fierce, and her hands moved on his jeans and inside his shirt. She loved him, loved the lean arc of his body, his hot, skittering gaze and his mind that moved so fast, so fast, twisting and surging ahead of him into the world to find each thing and know it, like he was being pulled along by tethered dogs that strained to be away.

He said, "If you let go of me, I'll just drop and be gone. I need to know I can get back."

She stood up and pushed him back down on the bed and straddled him, reaching between her legs to open his jeans, holding him in her hands while they kissed, mouths open. She pushed his shirt open and sat back, seeing his thin torso, the ropy lines of muscle, tattoos of crude black demons taken from Mexican broadsheets on his arms and leering red devils he'd had copied onto his chest.

He reached under her skirt and pulled her panties down onto her thighs and touched her lightly while she said words he couldn't understand that might have been Spanish or just sounds. She was hot where he touched her, gaping, and he caught small, slick drops on his hands and touched each fine hair with the tips of his fingers, and when she pushed down onto him she said, *"Ruin me. Ruin me."*

CHAPTER

4

Danny stood at the bar in the little place on Ridge Avenue where Asa Carmody held court. He fucking hated waiting for Asa, but it was standard, and Danny got that it was part of the game. Carmody letting Danny know he had status. He might set things up for Danny, put him onto people or point him one way or another, but it was on his terms and it wasn't because Asa was a fuckup who needed to snitch his way out of trouble. It was for his own reasons and in his own time.

Danny nursed a Coke and watched the arms of the neighborhood rummies going up and down like pump handles. Getting those first drinks of the night to stop the shakes. Danny had on a decent suit, an Italian he'd gotten at the Gallery downtown, and kept his elbows off the greasy bar and looked at his watch. The place smelled like stale beer and fried food and smoke, and the small TV had ESPN going. There was a little hole in the wall above the chair nearest the door that looked like a bullet hole and probably was.

It was a little after eight thirty when the door opened and a big kid from the neighborhood came in and looked at every face in turn, like the Secret Service, before he went back to the door and opened it, motioned for someone outside to come in. The kid was big across the shoulders, and Danny chewed an ice cube for a minute and finally came up with the name.

Chris Black, that was it. Christ, Danny had forgotten how big the kid was. His massive head stubbled with black hair, a muscle shirt showing the tattoos. Irish crosses, Celtic knots. The inevitable leprechaun with his fists up, ready to fight, on his right bicep. Danny had locked up his older brother, Shannon, twice before he was found in a car off Kelly Drive in Fairmount Park with a dark hole in the back of his head.

Now Asa came in, and Danny got that Chris Black was some kind of half-assed bodyguard. That was new. A step up for Asa Carmody, he guessed. Asa nodded, then crossed to a booth, and Danny left his Coke and came to sit across from him. Before he got to the table the door opened again and another guy came in, this one wearing a black leather jacket, and Danny didn't have to rummage for the name. He knew that one. Angel Riordan.

Asa put out his hand, and they shook and sat, Chris Black standing near the door and Riordan going to the bar to sit and watch the room. Asa Carmody wore a belted leather coat and a white collarless shirt, and Danny saw he was growing a beard, the hairs wispy and red.

"What's all this?" Danny waved a hand toward the two behind Asa. "The Praetorian guard?"

Carmody shrugged. He dropped his key ring on the table, a shamrock in Lucite, and a book that Danny angled his head to see.

"*Public Enemies*. What's that about?"

"Dipshits." Asa held up a hand, and the bartender nodded and began drawing beers. "The 1930s, John Dillinger, Bonnie and Clyde, all them, yeah?"

"Why dipshits?"

"I mean, it's interesting as history. J. Edgar Hoover and how the FBI modernized and all that, but the criminals?" He made a face. "Morons, mostly. Hillbillies, for real. From the actual fucking hills, yeah? I know plenty of morons with guns."

Asa was a self-improver, Danny knew. He was always reading. Mostly biographies of larger-than-life types who made it big. One week it was Howard Hughes, the next it was Pablo Escobar. Danny saw the thread of need in Asa to be something, to own something and be seen. It had begun to make Danny nervous, but he didn't see the whole of it, the full shape. On some level Asa was just a neighborhood character who had gone to Roxborough with Danny and kept him in touch with what was going on.

Like tonight. Danny was here because Asa had someone he wanted to put with him, he said. Something, he said, that would help the investigation of the two kids shot down the hill. Danny knew there was some angle for Asa. No one told the police much unless there was an angle for them. It was one of the first things Danny had learned on the street, but seeing the two pistoleros with Asa made him think a little harder about what the angle was. A Get Out of Jail Free card? Asa had been in minor scrapes when he was a kid, but only really locked up once for a month, and that was a long time ago. Whatever he was into now, he kept it a lot quieter than the bunch of mopes Danny usually ran across.

He watched Angel Riordan drinking at the bar. He was small

for someone in his business, shaggy black hair and pale skin. Sunglasses, now and every other time Danny'd seen him over the years. He was older than Asa and Danny, in his late thirties, and he'd been killing people since he was a teenager. Asa knew that under the black jacket there'd be a gun, and out in his car more guns.

Asa said, "A couple of minutes my guy'll be here."

"Who are we talking to?"

"One of the Green Lane bunch, they call him Soap. Or Soapy, or some fucking thing."

"I know Soap." Danny remembered him, one of those un-likely gangbangers who seemed too delicate for the life. Just a get-along, go-along, the way Big John called them. Guys who fell into the gangs and drugs because that was what was around, in the air they breathed, on the corners where they hung with their friends. If people in his set had gone to school and gotten jobs, that's what Soap would have done, but they didn't. They got jumped in or they started doing errands and lookouts for the local drug operations, and they went in and out of jail until they died or got too old for the game. They became jugglers, the kids who handled the drugs on the street, and if they lived long enough they might bump up a rung or two, but most of them were never going anywhere but jail.

Chris Black opened his cell phone and listened for a minute, then put the phone in front of Asa, who took it without looking at him and listened for a minute, then hung up without saying a word. He nodded at Chris and then turned to look at Angel Riordan, who was staring into the middle distance, seeing God-knows-what.

"Angel," said Carmody. "Angel." Then Angel Riordan turned and saw him and came back from whatever dark hole his mind was in and nodded and walked outside, pulling a cell from his pocket. Which answered a question that had been in Danny's mind. Not a bodyguard, Angel Riordan. Danny had trouble picturing that, and the exchange seemed to confirm it. Riordan wasn't a guy who would look out for you or watch your back. You pointed him at someone. He was a shotgun that walked and talked.

Asa said, "When Soap gets here, I'm not in it anymore, okay?"

Danny nodded, sure. "I appreciate this, Asa."

"It's cool, Danny. We go back, you and me. We have to do for each other 'cause no one else is going to, yeah?"

Danny said yeah, but he was wondering what he was doing for Asa, exactly. People began to drift in, the beginning of the crowd that would fill the place until midnight. Kids from the neighborhood, working guys and their girlfriends. The guys they'd grown up with, who said "wooder" for water, and during football season bet the Eagles. The "Iggles," the way it came out.

They'd drift home around twelve, that crowd, and then for the last couple hours it would be the mopes. Friends of Asa's, hijackers and dope fiends and second-story men, people who were dangerous, or who wanted the vibe that came off of dangerous people. They'd drink hard, stun themselves with it, do lines off the bar to keep the party going as long as possible and then stalk off into the night, reeling with the effort of standing upright.

"I can't be seen to be in this thing, you understand, right?" Asa looked at Danny, dropped his chin to show his serious intent.

"Sure," Danny said. Here they were, though, in the bar Asa

spent most of his nights in, where he was known. Danny was chewing on all this when the door opened again and Soap came in, his eyes down like he was being called to the principal's office. He was half a step in front of Angel and another big, tattooed mope from Fishtown that Danny recognized but couldn't name. Soap had on a loose black T-shirt and a do-rag and heavy boots that looked like they cost a lot.

Asa turned and smiled and waved him over like they were old friends, then got up and waited while Soap fit himself into the booth, his head down, not making eye contact with Danny but looking at Asa out of the corner of his eye. He didn't look happy to be there. The guy with the tattoos waved at Chris Black and then disappeared back outside.

Danny looked back and forth between the young black kid and Asa, waiting. Asa finally touched Soap's arm, making him flinch a little.

"This is Detective Martinez, Soapy, man."

"How you doing?" the kid said, but his eyes barely flicked up.

"Good, Soap. How's your sister?"

"You know Jelan?" He picked up a little then, raised his head and took Danny in.

"Yeah, she was at Roxborough with me and Asa, year or two behind us. She works at the nail place down by Ripka?"

"Not no more. Them Vietnamese women treat her like shit, she moved on up out of there, doing hair and nails in her living room, making twice as much as she did working for them damn Vietnamese. Going to school at night."

"That's cool, Soap. She was a nice lady." Danny looked at Asa, who tapped Soap again.

"Tell Detective Martinez what you told me and Angel, Soap."

Danny watched Soap's eyes, flicking over Asa once more and then around to Angel, who had moved to stand at the bar again.

"Yeah, you looking for the ones shot up that dope house where the Nortes were doing business. Killed that boy."

"That's right, Soap. Lots of people want that closed, right? A cop's son was hurt. You don't want that mess on your hands, do you?"

"No, you don't." Asa being helpful, leaning in close to Soap. The kid said, "Nah."

"You don't like to talk about your friends, I get that, no one does. But you got to think about this, Soap. This is going to be bad, and it wasn't like your friends went out of the way to keep it quiet, huh?"

"My friends." He looked out of the corner of his eye again. Maybe at Angel Riordan, maybe at nothing at all. "Friends got nothing to do with it. That mess was all Darnell Burns. He wanted them Nortes out, and he sent somebody, I bet that crazy Trey from down 19th Street, to light up that place. Them kids, too. All that mess."

"You bet it was Trey, or you know?"

"Since Darnell's brother Ivan got locked up, Trey's been pushing up, you know? Darnell wants things to get done, but he ain't hands-on, not like Ivan, you know."

Ivan Burns was the real power in the Green Lane crew, Danny knew, and he made a note to talk it all out with Big John. Big John had worked the Criminal Intelligence Unit and was the encyclopedia of gang life in Philly. Who was coming up or going down, who was expanding and who was being pushed out of the way. Nothing was ever static in the drug business. You were either getting squeezed out by competition or getting locked up or harassed by the cops. Or you were going big, pushing hard at the boundaries around your turf and making new connections. That drew action and money, but also heat. The game was constant motion, cycles up and down. The players came and went, but the game was always there, twenty-four hours a day.

"So how do we know it was Trey? How do we prove it?"

A long pause. Soap shifted in his seat like he couldn't get comfortable. He looked up and down, everywhere but at Danny. "They got the gun."

"Who?"

"Darnell got it. It's in his mother's house, down off Sixty-ninth Street." He held up his hands. "I can't say more about this, you understand? I can't even be here."

"I understand, Soap."

"This is rude, all this shit. I know people break out, come and do business where they shouldn't, but you start shooting people all up and down Roxborough Avenue? You start shooting children? There are things a Christian does not do." He shook his head, looking as sage as any nineteen-year-old drug dealer could. "Ivan ran things tight. Darnell? He wants the money, he wants the respect, but he's, you have to pardon me, he's a goddamn idiot."

"You saw the gun?"

"Yeah, it was right out on the table in the dining room. A MAC-10, little thing but with that long clip." Soap shook his head. "Darnell likes machine guns. Seen *Scarface* too many times."

Then Soap was gone and Danny was on the street talking into his cell. Setting things in motion. Later he'd think about this last couple of minutes, try to remember Soap leaving, Asa walking away. They must have said good-bye. He'd have told Soap thanks, said something to Asa. Later all of that would be important, but in the moment he just lost track of them. He was standing on Ridge Avenue, hunched against the noise of the traffic, talking to Rogan about wiretaps and surveillance, and when he turned around he was alone on the street.

Michael wouldn't wake up. The doctors said all the signs were good, but he still wasn't coming around and it had been two days. Kathleen held her son's hand and told him about everyone who had called and everyone from school who asked about him. The room was crowded with flowers, and Jeannette Sullivan from Michael's class came and stood shyly in the door and said she was praying for him, then walked down the hall in tears while Kathleen smiled and Brendan shook his head.

Brendan went to the door to watch her go, her shoulders heaving, strawberry blond hair shielding her face. He looked to Kathleen.

"Did you know about that?"

"I had my suspicions." She got up and straightened two flower arrangements on the sill, pulling the cards to read the inscriptions. "She was the one he bought the pendant for, when we were in Cape Cod."

"Right, the mysterious pendant."

"You gave him such crap about that."

"I don't like secrets."

"Teenagers need secrets, Bren."

He nodded, then came back in and forced himself to look at his son's slack, pale face. He took a tissue from a box and dabbed it on his tongue and wiped a fleck of white crust from the corner of Michael's mouth.

"What else don't we know?"

Kathleen straightened things on the night table. "Hon, he's a good kid. He's not into drugs."

"Did you know he hung out with little George? I thought that kid was gay."

"I know the two of them talked once in a while. Michael has a lot of friends. People like him and he likes everyone."

"It doesn't take a bad kid to make a mistake, Kath." He slumped in a chair and looked at his hands. "Someone says, let's try this, and they do, and then it's anything goes. They could have been just curious, or stupid, or there because they dared each other."

"When he wakes up, he'll tell us."

"There's nothing, nothing on earth as dumb as a teenage boy."

"He's a cop's kid, Bren. He's your kid. He knows right from wrong." She went over and touched Brendan's hair and he caught her hand and kissed it. She was thin, red hair to Brendan's black, with full lips that always drew his eyes. He knew that people fell out of love, but he knew it the way he knew people could eat insects or speak Estonian. Luis, his partner, had been married and divorced twice. Maybe it wasn't luck, though, maybe, he thought, he was just too stubborn to change his mind about anything that really mattered. You loved someone, you loved them, and how was that ever not true? His father, he knew, had loved Maire till the day he died, even though he had to leave her and get Brendan away from her when she went downhill, and in dying cried not for himself but for the loss of her.

"When he left the house, he said he was going to help little George with a project?"

"That's what he said, and Francine said George told her they were going to the coffee shop on Main to work on something for school."

Michael's chest rose and he gave a strange, keening sigh and they both looked up, but there wasn't anything more and he settled back down. His head was swaddled in bandages, and his black hair peeked out from beneath them, sticking to his cheeks.

They both got up and stood over their son. Kathleen touched his forehead, as she had done a thousand thoughtless times, and Brendan fought to remember a prayer, any prayer from all those years at Father Judge. What he got finally was the Policeman's Prayer, which had been shellacked onto a piece of dark wood in his father's living room and which was somewhere in Brendan's attic now. *When I start my tour of duty, God, Wherever crime may be, As I walk the darkened streets alone, Let me be close to thee.*

Jesus, he hadn't thought of that in years. It was the kind of weepy nonsense that kept him away from church, but when he was a kid he used to get a secret thrill from reading it, and every time he did, he'd known he'd become a cop.

CHAPTER

5

Chris Black sat next to Angel Riordan in Angel's car, a beat-up Accord that Chris was embarrassed to be seen in, his long legs jacked up under his chin. Soap sat in the back firing up a joint and saying didn't they have some decent music, cause KYW Newsradio wasn't doing it for him. Mostly Chris wished he could get out at the next light and away from Angel Riordan, who creeped him out with his quiet way, the man like a black cloud lurking all the time. Said almost nothing unless you asked him a question, and even then he'd just stare at you from behind his shades, the little machine inside his head clicking away until he finally gave up an answer, weighing everything he said like each word cost him money.

Right now Soap thought they were taking him home, which was cool 'cause you never knew how people were going to react when they finally got what was going on. Though man, anyone who got in a car with Riordan had to be either stupid or not paying attention. They were moving along the river, Angel with someplace in mind, he guessed, 'cause he didn't ask Chris anything and he drove like he knew where he was going.

Soap sat with his legs splayed in the back, singing along with the KYW news jingle, then asking them if they wanted to come with him to the club, meet some people, get some drinks. "Man, I knew your brother, man."

"Yeah?" said Chris, not really interested. He had been hearing Shannon stories for years and was sick of it, like Chris never did anything and his older brother was a legend.

"Yeah, man, he was cool. I mean, he was crazy, all due respect, but he knew how to have a good time." Soap laughed, and here it came. "I remember him down that strip club used to be down there off Front? Motherfucker gets up on the stage with the girls, starts taking off his pants, grabbing his johnson. The owner wants to get up in it, till he seen it was Shannon. Then it was cool."

"Yeah," says Chris. His brother was a borderline retard, truth be told, but he let it go 'cause pretty soon he wasn't going to be hearing any more stories from Soap.

"Hey man, where the fuck you all driving me to?"

Angel just turned his head to look at the kid, so Chris said, "Man, this is for your protection. Last thing you want is to be seen coming right from Asa's place and meeting with a cop, yeah?"

"Okay, yeah," said Soap, and pinched off the roach and put it in his coat. "I get you, yeah, this some Wile E. Coyote shit."

Chris nodded, but couldn't guess what the stoned kid was trying to say. Angel came to a turnoff near Fairmount Park that put them along the creek and drove down into the woods a ways, moving slow.

"Now it's the woods, huh." Soap sang some more, his high voice filling the car, "KYW Newsradio . . . Ten Sixty." He closed his eyes. "Man, I didn't realize, this stuff is harsh, man, like getting hit with buckshot in the head, you know?"

Chris turned and said, "What?" and almost laughed. "Is it?"

"Yeah, I got this weed off my sister's boyfriend. This shit is powerful."

Ahead of them the rear end of a car came into the headlights, a beat-up white Buick with its front end stuck in the weeds.

Angel spoke for the first time. "Come on, then."

Soap roused, gathered himself up, and slid over to get out. Chris got out to stand by Angel, his hand making the unconscious gesture of touching the hard butt of the pistol through his shirt.

"This is better, yeah? We'll get you home in this other car, so no one sees anything, gets nervous?" Chris working it maybe too hard, not knowing how the man could be so dense to what was happening. Soap made a gesture, throwing up his hands like okay, whatever.

"Yeah, sure, we change cars. This is how they do it in the big leagues, huh?"

They were in a small clearing in the woods between the river drive and the water. There was the constant hissing susurrus of the cars going by behind the screen of the trees, and to their left was the vast black space in the lights that was the Schuylkill River at night. Across it they could see the expressway and the lights of the cars going by, bumping along in a stop-and-go stream like in something Chris had seen on TV about blood cells moving in a body.

They turned to look at it, Soap and Chris and even Angel. The river and the expressway and the trees, and behind that the city and the lights. Chris was talking again, saying how Asa thanked him for coming out and helping with the thing with the cop, but Soap waved him off.

"Fuck that, he going to leave my sister out of it?"

"Yeah, Soap, that's right, man, you got no worries."

Chris moved ahead to stand by the car, and Soap followed, still talking.

"Asa Carmody is a freak, and you all freaks for working for the man. Motherfucker smiles but don't mean it. Bring family into business like that? Threaten my sister?"

"Nah, man." Chris was heated, forgetting himself for a minute. "Nah, it ain't like that, it's just he thought you were cold, man, when he asked you for help. Asa's the kind of guy—"

The shot made him jump a little, a flat pop that hurt his ears, and he froze, his hand still out in front of him. Making some kind of point to Soap, who went down on his back, eyes open, his string pulled forever. Chris turned to Angel, who was already putting the gun away, bending to drag the kid by the foot to the edge of the water.

Chris said, "Jesus. What the fuck, man?" He held out his arms. "I thought you'd throw me a sign or something. That's uncool, man, I thought I was the one getting shot."

Angel stopped in the action of dragging the body, bent to the task, one of Soap's oversized boots in his hand. He straightened and looked at Chris, said nothing, but cocked his head a little, like a dog. Like he didn't know who or what Chris was. He went back to it, shifting to get leverage on Soap's right leg and then making a quick jerk that let the momentum of Soap's body carry him down the slope of the last few feet to the edge of the water.

He got down on one knee over the body, fished in his jacket, and came out with the longest knife Chris Black had ever seen. Some kind of dagger, speckled with rust and as long as his forearm. Angel paused for one second, drew a breath, then placed the tip of the knife between two of Soap's ribs and pushed down. He pushed it hard, cords in his pale neck straining, working the grip in his hands until the hilt hit the kid's chest.

Chris stood, transfixed, saying, *Jesus, Jesus,* in his head. "What the fuck," he said quietly. "I don't, um. What the fuck."

Angel pulled the knife out, and it made a long and terrible noise as he worked it free. He set the tip against Soap's abdomen again, this time lower down, and pushed it hard. There was nothing in his face, no rage or disgust, nothing at all that Chris could see. It was just work.

There was an exhalation from Soap's body, a breathy hiss that made Chris jump.

"It's nothing." Angel tugged the knife up again. "Just air." He lifted the tail of Soap's shirt and wiped the blood off the knife in long smooth strokes. "See? You make some holes they go down and don't come up so fast. Otherwise he's there floating for all the world to see." Chris caught the faint accent then, the hard, clipped tones of Northern Ireland. Chris had an uncle that sounded like that. Like the old man was working stones in his mouth when he talked.

Angel stood up again over the body and made the knife disappear into his coat again, then stood back and pushed the dead boy into the water with his foot. He pushed at his feet, then at his shoulders, the body rasping over the lip of river stones. When he was done, one of the kid's hands was still in the mud at the

54

lapping edge of the water, as if even in death he didn't want to go that way, and Angel toed it gently with his boot until the kid floated away toward the city and the lights.

Chris opened his cell phone while Angel stood still on the riverbank and watched.

Chris said, "Yeah, we're all done." There was a pause. "Yeah." He closed the phone, waited a minute.

"Angel, man, we got to go, we got things to do." He shuddered a little, he couldn't help it. To see the kid's face go slack, his eyes go blank and dry. To know it again, that we're machines that can get turned off. And the other, Angel working like a butcher on the kid's chest and stomach. Hard not to cross himself, ward that off somehow.

He got back to the passenger side of Angel's car, wanting him to hurry up but not wanting to get into his shit when the man was in his shooting mood. Eventually, whatever Angel was doing was over and he came back and opened the door, looking over the car roof at Chris in the dark.

"You talk too much."

"What? I talk too much?"

"Alla you people," he said and got in. Chris got in, too, his mind going, chewing on what the fuck that might mean, hoping it would never be just him and Angel down here on the river.

The moon was a perfect white circle of ash, and Orlando and Zoe were laced together on the couch on the roof, her skirt around her hips, hair wild on her shoulders, both of them breathing hard as winded sprinters. She dropped her head to his chest and he twined her hair in his fingers. She fished in her purse for her cigarettes and put one in her mouth. He took one from her and stuck it unlit in his own, felt the expansion of her lungs through his own chest as she pulled the smoke in, held it, let it go.

"I saw Mary from Conrad Street today."

"Yeah?"

"Yeah, she was in with her baby. Getting dinner for her and Marty."

"Man, I ain't seen Mary in, I don't know."

"Yeah, she looked good."

He kissed her along her hairline, watched her eyes. "Tell me."

"That baby was so pretty. Just couldn't stop looking at it, you know?"

Mary and Marty were a couple that used to hang out with them when they first started up together. Marty had gotten caught with a loaded gun the year before when he and a couple friends from East Landsdowne had staked out a liquor store in Atlantic County, down the shore. The DA had dropped the case, but it scared the shit out of him and he had gotten cleaned up and out of the life. Got a job detailing cars and married Mary.

Orlando talked around the unlit cigarette. "Mary's pretty. I guess Marty's a good-looking kid, too, so . . ."

"Yeah."

She let the smoke go in billows from the side of her mouth, squinting, seeing things that were only inside her head.

"You want a baby, hon?"

"No." She flicked away ashes. "I don't know. I want both, I

guess. This life and that one. Other things. I don't know. What do you want?"

The wind moved, and he reached under the blanket and snapped his jeans, then touched her tiny, rounded stomach where she was slick with sweat.

"To know, I guess. To know everything."

"Everything you can know if you never leave East Falls?"

"Isn't that everything?"

"Seriously, have you ever been more than five miles from the Schuylkill River?"

"I was down the shore with my mom a couple times. Before she lost the house."

"That doesn't count. Everyone's been down the shore."

"You want to leave?"

"I don't know, Orlando. Some days I just want to know where we're going, I guess."

"We're going down the Wawa on Ridge Avenue."

"Do you promise?"

"With all my heart."

He thought of his brother and the picture of Maire. He remembered standing in a closet with Brendan, a line of white light falling across his brother's face as he angled to see if their mother was coming. Orlando was pressed back into the darkest part of the closet with the empty luggage and some blankets with a camphor smell that burned his eyes. He could hear his mother stomping from room to room, raging. Slamming a book on a table, breaking things. He tried to guess what was being broken from the sound. A porcelain angel holding a violin, a lamp that was a hugely pregnant Mary on a pale donkey.

After a while it got quiet, and his brother held up a hand to Orlando to be still and slowly opened the door and stepped out, his eyes wary as an animal's, lifting his feet with silent, exaggerated care like Elmer Fudd in the cartoons sneaking up on Daffy Duck. He shut the door behind him, and Orlando burrowed deep into the junk in the back of the closet and listened hard for every squeak and rattle from downstairs. After a while Orlando got tired of waiting, of listening for nothing, and fell asleep.

George Parkman Sr. was drunk. He had carried a Scotch up to get dressed for the viewing and had barely touched it, but with nothing in his stomach and not enough sleep he realized the couple of sips had pushed him over the edge into that place where he seemed trapped in a heavy column of air that made his movements clumsy and slow and pushed down on his face so that he was afraid to speak for fear of slurring his words and drawing attention to his impaired state.

He sat there half-dressed, hating the thought of going to Donahoe's, but it was the funeral home his family had always called so there it was. The place was ancient, owned by aging bachelor brothers whose florid pink faces radiated a practiced and unnerving sincerity that George found it difficult to be in the same room with, never mind to negotiate the details of his son's viewing and funeral.

Christ, a viewing. That was Francine, to want the boy's ravaged body on display. When they were dressing, the silence punctuated only by the occasional strangled exhalation from Francine,

as if she were getting the news again and again, every five minutes, he had wanted to grab her arm and say, *Let's not do this.
Let's just,* he'd say, *let's just take him out to Fernwood and put him
in the ground, you and me, and leave the rest of them to go sit at the
funeral home and talk to each other,* which was what they were
there to do anyway. He remembered his old man stretched out
at Donahoe's, couldn't stop staring at his father's sunken, waxy
cheeks while his aunts chatted away with cousins they'd hadn't
seen in a year and he didn't know what any of it was for.

He heard Francine stand up in a rustle of clothes and listened
to the hollow clacking of her heels on the stairs going down and
he realized he wasn't nearly ready. He was sitting on the edge
of the bed with his tie crumpled in his fist and suddenly came
to himself and looked down at it, the gray silk crushed in his
hand. One shoe off and one on. He bent down and fixed his
shoes, stood up and left the tie and went for another one, nearly
identical to the first. He stood and looked at his side of the
closet, hung with more than a dozen suits, a cashmere coat he'd
bought six months ago and never worn. Business was good; the
money rolled in. Francine had wanted to send George Jr. to a
private school in Newtown, but George Sr. had said no. St.
Vincent's was where he'd gone, it was good enough for his son.

He went to stand at the mirror and looked at his own hard
face and broad shoulders and narrow eyes. He dropped his tie
again and went quick into the bedroom and got a picture of the
three of them that sat on Francine's dresser. He went back into
the closet and stood still in front of the mirror, holding the
picture up and scrutinizing George Jr.'s face and then peering
over the picture at his own reflection.

The kid had one of those unformed teenage faces that made his father nervous. There was something so tentative about the kid, the way he walked and talked and sat on the corners of seats, his body bent toward the door and escape. It provoked George Sr., that way of being. *Sit still,* he'd wanted to say, as the kid jiggled his foot, *sit up and be here. Be a man,* that was what he'd finally say, when the kid would come to him with some fucked-up concern that he couldn't understand. George Jr. was always trying to explain some subtle problem about the way other kids looked at him or expected him to act that he didn't feel, and it bothered George Sr. to think his kid wasn't popular or good at anything physical and it made him nearly insane that somehow the boy thought his father wanted to know or could help, as if they were allies, when it was all George Sr. could do to keep from smacking the kid.

What he'd wanted, when he was honest, was a kid like Michael Donovan. George Sr. would sit in the stands at the hockey games, his own son nowhere in sight, off somewhere with that crowd that wore pale makeup and black lipstick, which at least George Jr. had enough sense to keep off his face. Michael would come off the ice and high-five his father and grab one of the other kids and bang on his helmet, his face open and good-natured and comfortable with being the kid everyone liked. The kid they looked to.

What were they doing together on that street, in front of that house? Was it some game, some taunt to his narrow-shouldered artsy son to be somewhere dangerous? Was it finally George Jr. trying to be in with the cool kids, and buying dope from a boarded-up crack house was what the cool kids were into?

He'd smoked dope when he was their age, everyone he knew had smoked dope except some of the Catholic girls, and some did pills, but mostly they'd all drunk beer, which he couldn't see George Jr. doing.

Now he held the picture up, tilting it one way and then another. He searched his son's face, traced the boy's slim hand where it lay across his chest, looking for himself. There was Francine's aquiline nose, a fullness in the lips that might have been from his mother, but where was he? Where was the evidence that at last this was his son? He got down on his knees and propped the picture against the mirror, trying to somehow get both his image and the picture of his son in front of him. He was sitting like that, pushing his eyebrows up and down, squeezing the bridge of his nose, his eyes streaming, when Francine finally came back in and found him there. She took the picture from him and stood him up and picked a tie out of the rack and put it in his hands. She looked at him and he looked down and wiped at his nose with his sleeve.

"You're crying for yourself." She shook her head. "Jesus."

"Why did this happen to us?"

"You never looked at him, practically. The whole last year, what did you ever do with him or say to him?"

"I didn't know, how could I know, Francine?"

"You wanted what? For him to be captain of the team? That wasn't George."

"These are the things a man wants for his son. I don't care who you are. You want to see him out there, in front of people. Standing up."

She shook her head and her eyes flashed and she slapped him.

He shook his head as if it didn't register, and she lifted her hand again but dropped it.

"You didn't deserve him. That's why he's gone."

"A mother and her son and a father and his son, that's two different things. You can't know."

She closed her eyes, the muscles in her face working, and then opened them again. "Get dressed."

At the funeral home there were crowds, more than he expected. Teachers and kids and parents, clogging the narrow street in front of Donahoe's and standing silently in the back of the room, and George Sr. wasn't prepared, kept wishing he'd either stayed sober or kept going, pouring the warm, bitter Scotch into himself until he lay obliterated at the foot of the bed.

He had thought of his kid as an oddball, a loner, but there were a lot of kids there and only some of them were obvious losers. A girl with a shaved head and a fringe of hair at the front sat next to a big kid in a leather jacket and gripped his hand while tears rolled down her face. When he stared too long at them, the big kid looked in his eyes and cocked his head, calling him out. Jesus. Was this red-faced slab of a kid friends with George Jr.?

There were also nice-looking kids with open faces, though, kids who could be cheerleaders or jocks and who wore dresses or jackets and ties, and he wondered how they knew his son and why they were there. Was it some kind of admission of guilt, the cool kids having somehow gotten George Jr. into something that got him killed on the steps of the dope house?

When he couldn't stand to be out in front of everyone anymore he walked back through to where there was an old-fashioned drinking fountain and conical paper cups, and he filled one and stood looking at some ancient print of Cork that was so dark all he could make out was there were cows in it, or maybe small, misshapen horses. He became aware of someone standing at his elbow.

He turned to see a big man in an ocher sport coat holding out his hand, and he stood for a minute before taking it. The man had red hair that curled in on itself like cheap carpeting and a pink face with broken veins across the bridge of his nose, and he smelled like something sweet that might have been wine.

"Mr. Parkman. I'm Abbott Collins."

George stood there for a minute, trying to remember, and it came to him in a rush. The private detective his former partner Joe Reese had recommended.

"Right, right, sorry." He shook the man's hand, his grip too tight. Something his father had passed to him and automatic now. The detective nodded.

"No apologies, Mr. Parkman. This is a black day." The man had a strangled voice, as if he'd burned his throat. "All my sympathies, sir."

"Thank you." He wondered what was next. Joe Reese had said he'd put the guy in touch, but George hadn't expected the man to show at the viewing, for Christ's sake. "Joe said you helped with something. Employee theft or something?"

"Yes, that's one thing I've done. I guess he thought you'd want someone looking into George Jr.'s death. Someone besides the police."

"The police."

"Yeah, they're working it, to be sure, but there are so many rules for them, you know?" He moved in, too close for George, who retreated toward the wall and almost unseated the picture. "A cop, he has to ask permission for everything. Things that should take a week take two. Things get lost in the shuffle, in the paperwork."

"You don't like the police?"

"No, no, not at all. I was a cop, eight years homicide. The cops are good, they just don't have, you know, the freedom of action that a professional would have."

George pronounced his words with the drunk's exaggerated care. "Freedom of action." He liked the sound of that. It called up images of this hulking fucker in his cheap coat slamming some smart-aleck kid against a brick wall in an alley and cutting off his wind until he told them who did this to his son.

"Can I ask, sir, what the detectives have said? What they've told you about Brendan Donovan, for instance?" The man turned and George turned with him to see them, the Donovans, Brendan and Kathleen, coming in now from the entryway and talking softly to some people they knew in the back of the room.

"They haven't said anything. I talked to the one guy, a detective, I can't remember his name. He wants to talk to me again. He didn't really tell me anything."

"Nothing about Brendan Donovan, or his brother?"

George turned to the man Collins, had to keep himself from

grabbing his sleeve. "Tell me." He searched the man's face with his eyes.

"Abbott," said the man. "Call me Abbott." He took a card out of his pocket and gave it to George, who crushed it in his hand.

"Tell me what about Brendan Donovan." He let that get out louder than he intended, and the larger man took his arm and led him into a darkened corner. George craned his neck to keep an eye on the Donovans. Collins leaned in and cocked his head.

"Brendan Donovan has a brother, a junkie. They didn't tell you that. The kid's been arrested a half-dozen times. They pick him up, he skates. Because someone steps in for him." Collins pushed his head over twice, fast, pointing out Brendan. "The kid, they call him Little Brother on the street, 'cause he's a cop's brother."

George's eyes narrowed, and he drew his mouth down. "You'll look into this for me, then?"

"Of course."

"A junkie."

"Yes, sir."

"Find out. Do what you have to do." George wiped at his face, feeling the booze sweat at his hairline. He had failed his son, had failed to toughen him to the world, to drive a steel spike through his center so that he could stand up for himself, and he had been caught up in something, driven to his death somehow, and this, this was what George Sr. could do now.

He could bring rage. He could let this man loose on the world to bring whoever had brought his boy low to some kind of rough and terrible justice. The alcohol worked on his head and he wanted to shout, to raise the detective's hand and point him out to the milling, aimless crowd of mourners. *This man is my champion.*

"And the junkie brother?" Collins smiled, his teeth uneven, crowding his mouth.

"What about the brother?" George watched Brendan, his mask of concern looking more and more like a smirk to the mourning father.

"He lives two blocks from where young George died."

George opened his fist, took the card and smoothed it in his hands, stared at the type, saw the perforated edge where it had been torn, so he knew it had been printed at home. A cheap card for a cheap, thuglike detective who would be his device, the mechanism that would transfer his fury to the world and make it pay for everything that had gone wrong.

"Two blocks."

"Not even."

George stepped back into the room, and everyone turned to him. Francine narrowed her eyes at his dry, appraising stare. He looked from face to face, and they all seemed unconscious, their gazes slack and sorrowful. He was aware of Collins standing beside him, and they were hunters together. He wanted another drink, would have it.

He went to his son and looked down at the slight reed of his body. A blue blazer and tie he'd have never worn in life. The boy's slender hands now carved from pale wax. George Sr. turned and looked out at the crowd with something that was forming into hate. He kept one hand on the lip of the box, as if it helped him to claim his place in the chapel. He wanted to tell them something, make a speech, declare his intent to find and punish. *Someone in this room,* he wanted to say. *Someone in this room.*

CHAPTER

6

It was quiet on the street, and there was a haze that obscured the end of the block and muffled faraway sounds, gave Orlando a feeling of being on a stage, even walking down Cecil B. Moore to Mexican Bob's house. When he got there he waved at the camera at the top of the door and LaDonna buzzed him in.

Mexican Bob was sitting in his chair, a red leather chair that he loved, that made him feel, he would say, like a Captain of Industry, which Orlando said he most definitely was, there being no one more industrious than the working thief with a jones. He was bleary-eyed and quiet this morning, and LaDonna took him coffee and pointed at the cup to offer Orlando some, and he smiled but waved her off.

Mexican Bob grabbed at her and she danced away into the kitchen, a red knit dress and perfect hair, despite it being so early in the morning when the streets were full of zombies clutching coffee cups and marching in their grim trains of the near-dead to work in the mausoleums down on Broad and JFK.

Orlando loved to watch them, Mexican Bob with his limpid eyes and the cascading mustache of a nineteenth-century cavalryman, his wasp-waisted love hovering at his shoulder. They had met in prison, when LaDonna was Levar and using all her guile to stay ahead of the tier gangs, and he wooed her and brought her home and paid for her surgery. It was one of those stories, beautiful and strange and transgressive, that cracked him open and made him love all of the doomed strangers in his world, even the ones that pointed guns at him or beat him with pool cues when they caught him unawares, nodding in the street on his way home in the middle of the night.

They were waiting for Arthur, an Afghan vet who came home from Parwan with metal in his knees and a drug habit. Arthur was supposed to have the keys to a warehouse on Front Street with a bunch of snowmobiles, and Bob said they'd go look and see what could be done. To move them meant borrowing or stealing a truck and he wasn't sure, but if they could bring it off it'd be a couple thousand apiece and would take the edge off for a few days.

Orlando didn't really know Arthur but had seen him around, and he seemed put together, his shit still relatively squared away for a full-on junkie, maybe the residue of the military. Tall, broad-shouldered, with short hair and a lot of bad road and long nights stored up in his eyes.

Bob's cell buzzed on the table, and when Bob just stared at it, Buddha-like in his chair, his arms holding his cup on his chest, LaDonna came in shaking her head and picked it up. She started to say hello but whoever it was cut her off, and she listened intently for a moment, then passed it to Bob, who frowned and fit it to his ear.

"Go."

He looked up while he listened, then hauled himself up out of his chair. He went to the front door, parted the curtains, and looked out at the street.

"Yeah, I see him." There was more talk from the other end that registered as a buzzing noise for Orlando. "Yeah, he has the look. Shit." He closed the phone.

Orlando raised his eyebrows.

Bob threw the cell phone onto the seat. "That was Arthur, there's a cop outside. Maybe a cop. He looks the part, but I don't know."

Orlando went to the window, hanging back but angled to see the street between the parted curtains. He tracked slowly parallel to the glass, seeing the street in little slices until he came to a battered Volvo station wagon with a wide swatch of duct tape over the rear bumper. In the driver's seat was a big man with short hair, sipping coffee. He was too far away to see much, but Orlando got the vibe off him and shook his head.

"Shit."

"Yeah," said Bob. "Well, discretion is the better part of not getting sent to the can."

"Okay, you got warrants out?"

"LaDonna?"

She leaned her head in from the kitchen. "No, hon. No paper out on you now."

Orlando looked philosophical. He squinted an eye at the floor. "Okay, I'll go down and cut up Ridge, you come out and go back, hook around Montgomery. He'll follow one of us if this is anything."

"That's it? One of us gets picked up?"

"You don't want him coming in here." Orlando swept a hand around the apartment. A long row of radios sealed in cartons, boxes of sneakers, three televisions taken from a motel in Pennsauken, the cables still hanging where they had been cut.

"No."

Orlando raised his eyebrows.

"LaDonna?" Bob waited by the door, got a reversible jacket from a peg on the wall. "Hon, you got my bail money?"

"Always."

"Okay, I get picked up, I'll call you." She came out, gave him a peck on the cheek. "And call Tricia, tell her she'll have to pick up Patrice at day care."

"She'll love that."

"Well, she is the boy's mother. If I'm under charge it will be every woman for herself."

Orlando went out first, watching the guy in the Volvo for any sign that he was interested in them. When he hit the street he heard the door open again behind him, and Bob moved fast to his right. Orlando took his time, meandering along past the shops, looking in the windows.

Orlando hummed to himself as he made his way past the parked cars. "Transatlanticism," by Death Cab for Cutie. It gave him a cadence, let him borrow the measured pace of the music to keep himself from running. He tried to see the car with the cop in the reflections of windows, but he couldn't get the angle, and he just paced off the steps until he thought he must be even with the car and turned away from the buildings on his left and set out off the curb, as if he were just heading east across the street.

He had time to take in that the Volvo was there, parked at the curb in front of a record store he'd been in a few times, and that the guy wasn't in the front seat anymore. He slowed and crossed the street, stepping up onto the curb and trying to look back down the block toward Bob's, and when he snapped his head forward there was the guy.

He was big, wide across the shoulders and with a paunch and loose skin around his jowls, crazy red hair that was wires and spikes, and that was as much as he got before the guy clocked him, hard, with an elbow that caught him across the windpipe and doubled him over with no air in his lungs and a bright pain across his neck and chest so intense he felt like he must be giving off sparks.

He went over hard and opened his mouth, trying to drag air into his throat, but it was like dredging mud and nothing would come. He put a hand out and the guy took it, as if for a second it was a misunderstanding or an accident and he was going to help, but the guy just jerked his arm out straight and used it like a lever to push him back against the passenger door of the Volvo.

Orlando straightened up and the guy opened the back door and shoved him in, holding his head down the way cops always did, though up close this guy didn't seem like he was actually on the job, and Orlando had never been thrown into the back-seat of a Volvo station wagon by a cop. There were beer cans on the floor that rolled under his feet and a smell of mildew as if the windows had been left open in the rain.

The guy crowded in next to him, Orlando massaging his

throat and finally getting a rasping gust of air into his lungs. The guy watched him choke for a minute, breaking off to look up and down the street, to see if they were being watched. His eyes were bright, the skin of his brow beneath the red hair a stark white, and the guy was nodding, as if he were having some kind of dialogue in his head.

"You're Orlando Donovan."

It wasn't a question, and Orlando backed up against the door and nodded, coughing and rubbing at his neck.

"Brendan Donovan's brother." The guy cocked his head, appraising. "Yeah, I can see it. They used to call you Little Brother, right? That was your name?"

Orlando extended his neck, opening his swollen airway. "Yeah," he croaked. "Some people used to call me that."

"Your brother keeps you out of the shit, huh?"

Orlando made a face. "What? Brendan?"

The guy shook his head, then gave Orlando an open-handed slap that caught him across the temple and rang in the car. "Don't lie to me."

"Shit. I'm not lying. I don't even know what the fuck you're talking about."

The detective raised a fist this time but telegraphed it, and Orlando could roll with the blow as the guy tried to hit him hard in the chest. It hurt, but he let himself bounce off the door and it didn't land the way it might have if the guy weren't so wired that Orlando didn't see it coming. He had been hit before, by people who knew what they were doing.

"You're a junkie, and your brother keeps you from getting locked up for all the shit you do."

"You're out of the loop, man. I don't see Brendan anymore. I just did a month in Northeast Philly. If anyone's looking out for me, they suck at it."

"You cannot lie to me, understand?"

"Okay, okay." Orlando held up a hand and looked around, watching people go by on the street. If he just pushed open the door, would this lunatic chase him down? "You're not a cop, are you?"

The guy leaned in and squeezed Orlando's knee hard. Orlando screwed up his face and leaned into it, trying to give the guy nothing.

"Close enough, shitbag. Close enough." The detective went into his jacket and came out with a small black gun. This time he was fast. The gun was out, and Orlando had the time to think *magic trick,* and the guy backhanded Orlando across the temple and he went out.

When he came to himself the car was moving and his hands were cinched together with flexcuffs in front of his chest, the whiplike ends smacking his face when he lifted his hands to touch his forehead and find the tender egg-shaped lump there. He was jammed down onto the narrow floor space and he tried to pull himself up but his body was slow and his head pounded in a way that made sparks and lines arc across his eyes.

"Don't move around too much, you'll puke." The guy turned his head slightly to talk to him, and the car swerved and then took a hard left that pinned Orlando against the seat for a minute.

Orlando slowly pulled himself up, using his pinioned hands and grabbing a frayed seat belt. There were cans and bottles beneath him that matched sore spots on his legs and hips.

"Yeah, sorry I gave you that smack, but that's what happens."

Orlando didn't know what he was supposed to be doing or saying to the guy, but he worked on clearing his head and getting up high enough on the seat so he could see where they were.

"When I ask you questions, just answer, okay? Don't fuck around or back-talk." The guy sounded like he was trying to be friendly, warning him about some situation that was beyond his control. "That's what happens. People want to act up and things get out of hand. I just, you know," the guy went on, looking back over the seat again. "I'm Collins, by the way." He sounded so normal now, Orlando half expected him to reach around to shake hands. "Anyway, it doesn't matter who I am. It's the people I represent you have to worry about."

"Yeah? Who's that?" Orlando finally rolled himself onto the seat, breathing through his mouth and fighting the urge to vomit. The guy had been right about that.

"The kid that got killed, he was the son of a very rich and powerful man. Someone's got to answer for that, right?"

Orlando could see what was around them now, and he saw that they were moving east and south, toward the Delaware. A couple blocks from the circle that would lead to the Ben Franklin and Jersey beyond. He didn't know what this crazy fucker wanted from him, but he didn't want to find out, either.

"Those kids were like a block and a half from you when they got shot. You see how it looks, right?"

"How does it look?" He could see the doors were unlocked,

the guy maybe depending on speed and reckless driving or just sheer force of personality to keep Orlando from bolting. Then the guy lifted his right arm and laid it over the top of the seat next to him, and there was the gun again. It was pointing down along the seat, not directly at Orlando, but the guy was idly fanning the hammer with his thumb.

"You got a couple of kids scoring dope, no offense to the dead kid or his family. You got a known dope addict, the uncle of one of the kids, a block away. So inquiring minds want to know. Did those kids come to you? You knew those guys and told the kids where to go to cop?" Collins's hand tensed and he cocked the gun and Orlando sat back straight and focused on the hand and the heavy black pistol until the guy thumbed back the hammer and let it slowly down. Jesus Christ.

Orlando looked down into the mess on the floor and saw a thick green empty beer bottle. Moosehead. He looked up and saw they were moving down Race toward the bridge and he wasn't going over any fucking bridge with this lunatic and whoever else was in his massive, red skull.

He bent over and reached down into the pile of cans and bottles and his left hip ached and he retched a little, looking up at the pistol a couple of inches from his face, but his hands closing on the bottle and bringing it back up with him as he sat back.

Collins turned. "Are you puking? What did I tell you, man? Sit still." They were coming to the light at Eighth, the Volvo out in the middle lane. The light was red and the guy slowed but didn't stop, letting the car coast toward the bumper of a Wawa truck and then cutting right into a gap behind a black SUV. Orlando pitched forward again and the guy lifted his gun hand

and began to turn and Orlando hit him as hard as he could across the side of the head, swinging his tethered hands in a clumsy side-arc swing. The first time the bottle bounced off his skull with a hollow ringing noise and the guy swung the car hard right and it bounced off the curb so Orlando wound up again, half falling off the seat as the car swerved, but focused on putting everything he had into one more hard swing and this time the bottle broke and the guy screamed and dropped the gun and clutched at a bright ribbon of blood at his temple.

Collins lost it, howling and pawing on the seat for the gun, and Orlando let go of the piece of bottle still stuck to his hand and grabbed the handle of the door and was holding it when the car stopped hard so that he was thrown forward, his forehead painfully connecting with the back of Collins's head. Collins moaned and slumped.

Orlando pushed at the door and had it half open, his left leg out, when there was a loud pop that he felt through the frame of the car as a green and white PECO truck slammed into the back of the Volvo. He bounced forward off the door and smacked down into the street, trying to catch himself on his cuffed hands, and then rolled with his hands pinned beneath him as more cars and trucks stopped short, rocking on their suspensions, and he heard a woman scream somewhere nearby.

There was a quiet moment, a little pause, and he could feel cool air on his bruised face and grit from the street under the backs of his hands. He rolled onto his side, then drew himself up onto his knees. Finally, he rocked slowly onto his feet and turned to see Collins slumped over the steering wheel, and he took off, running slowly and then faster and faster, heading west back up Race and cutting between the stopped cars while two guys piled out of the PECO truck and hollered at him to stop. Already he could see cop cars coming out of the Roundhouse parking lot with their lights on, and he picked up speed, running flat out past people who took him in, his cuffed hands and bloodied face, and they looked surprised and some looked angry, the way people could get when something was so unexpected and strange and upsetting that it was out of the realm of what they could hold in their heads on a Monday morning on their way to work.

Orlando ran hard for a couple of blocks, uphill past a mural of smiling Chinese kids, then cut right over the expressway, slowing when he made the turn and trying to fold his hands against his stomach while he limped along, breathing hard and occasionally spitting to keep the nausea down.

He zigzagged across the lanes of traffic on Vine, keeping his head down and moving north past a church covered with ideograms that looked like a secret message from an unknowable God. At Nectarine he spotted a ripped poncho lying in the gutter and picked it up, draping it across his cuffed hands. The effort of bending down as he walked filled his throat with a hot bile and he spit into the street to keep from being sick. His right eye was half closed with blood, his temple throbbed, and he could feel road dirt and glass in the backs of his hands as he moved.

He walked blindly for a block, his head down, adjusting the frayed blue poncho over his hands. At the corner he stopped, looked back down Thirteenth toward Vine Street, watched an ambulance make its way down from Hahnemann along Vine. Turned and got his bearings, headed for home.

. . .

Danny Martinez sat in a van at the end of Lamport Road in Upper Darby, watching a house in the middle of the block with a pair of binoculars. It was a quiet street of cramped row homes backed by wide alleys. His dad had gone to St. Cyril's, a few blocks away, and his grandmother had lived just off Long Lane in East Lansdowne and he could still see the kitchen of the tiny house in his mind's eye though he hadn't been near it in years, not since she'd died and they'd buried her at Holy Cross, out in Yeadon.

Next to him sat Big John Rogan, folded almost double into a small chair, wearing a pair of headphones. Big John squinted with the effort of trying to hear the conversation going on in number 76, where the mother of Ivan and Darnell Burns lived. Ivan was the head of the Green Lane crew, and he was locked up on weapons charges, pulled over for driving drunk and high when it turned out he had an unregistered Glock on the seat beside him. Being too fucked up at the time to remember to cover it.

Danny dropped the binoculars and rubbed his eyes. "What do we hear?"

"Darnell wants breakfast from the Caribbean place up on Sixty-ninth. Trey wants Burger King."

"They getting into it?"

"Nah, Darnell's still playing boss and Trey's pretending to get along. There's no respect there, that's all for Ivan. But Trey's smarter than Darnell, so he knows how to play."

"Anything about the shooting, the kids, anything?"

"Nah. Breakfast. Who's driving the mother to lunch with her church friends. They're talking about someone's coming by for something they're holding, and who they'd rather get next to from that show, *Lost*. Trey says Michelle Rodriguez, Darnell likes the tall girl."

"Michelle, definitely."

"I don't know, she's got problems."

"Yeah, but I got that rescuer complex. I think I can straighten her out." Danny looked through the binoculars again. A gangly kid lounged on a folding chair on the front steps. He had a black muscle shirt under a red jacket and kept touching his stomach, where, Danny figured, there was a pistol stuck in his jeans. "They all got problems, those Hollywood girls."

Big John closed his eyes. "They're too pretty. All pretty girls are trouble. I think they go crazy from not knowing anything except everybody wants to get with them."

"Yeah, it's a burden. When does SWAT get here?"

"Nine forty-five. They're serving a warrant in West Oak Lane, then we're next."

"What if Trey goes out for breakfast? We're going to miss scooping them all up."

Big John held up a finger. Danny watched him, his eyes raised.

"Darnell's mom is going to make pancakes."

Orlando stood at a corner on North Broad, watching the front of R and R Service. He lounged against the sign at the corner and tried to look normal, but a woman waiting for the bus caught him out of the corner of her eye and shook her head.

"You run, baby. Don't let them get you standing still." She walked away down Broad, probably not wanting to be around when whatever trouble was chasing Orlando finally caught up.

Orlando watched the attendants working the place, all suited up in blue coveralls with pinstripes. Calling to each other, giving each other early morning shit. Drinking coffee, orange and white cups from the Dunkin' Donuts up Spring Garden. After a few minutes he made his way up the south side of the open lot in front of the garage and waited for one of the guys, a tall kid with shaggy black hair, to move closer to where Orlando stood.

"Marty."

The kid jumped a little, took in Orlando standing there, the ratty piece of plastic over his folded hands, his face bloodied and his clothes torn.

"Jesus. What the fuck, man?"

"Marty, it's me."

The kid stood with a lug wrench in his fist, moved back a couple of paces, but Orlando just raised his covered hands.

"Orlando?"

"Hey."

"Fuck, man. You scared the shit out of me."

"Sorry, man." He looked over his shoulder at the street. A cop car went by, cruising slowly up North Broad, and Orlando canted his body slightly to give it his back.

Marty watched the car go by, turned back to his friend. "You're in trouble." It wasn't a question.

Orlando shook his head. "Tell the truth, I don't even know."

Marty cocked his head, and Orlando snorted.

"Yeah, okay, I'm in trouble, I guess I don't know with who. Some guy picked me up, but I don't think he was a cop. He was just some pissed-off asshole."

Marty pointed at Orlando's hands with the wrench. "What's going on under there?"

Orlando stepped closer, trying to shield himself from view with the side of the tool chest. He flipped his hands up, caught the scrap of poncho, and showed his wrists to Marty. The plastic had bitten through the flesh, and there were long tracks of blood disappearing into the cuffs of his jacket. Marty looked at Orlando's hands for a minute, then lifted the poncho and dropped it back over them. He looked hard at Orlando's face, too, at the bruises and cuts there, then back over his shoulder into the garage. He stood there for a long time, then dropped his head like he was praying.

"Marty."

"Go up around the corner to Sixteenth Street." He dropped the lug wrench and turned his back. "I'm on my break in a couple minutes. Go up there and I'll be up in a minute."

Orlando stood against a chain-link fence and moved his arms and legs against the cramps that were starting to form at his shoulders and knees. The bruise at his right eye had drawn up into a hard knot, and his stomach twisted, telling him he needed to start thinking about dope.

He looked up in time to see Marty rounding the corner, the

metal beak of the tin snips sticking out of his coverall pocket. *He's straight,* Orlando thought. It was something you could see in the lines around his eyes, a flatness and a distance from the world that he recognized.

He thought it was something like the look that he'd heard vets talk about. The thousand-yard stare. They'd seen something, the ones who'd kicked, and it was always there forever in their eyes. They'd been where Orlando went every day and it changed them, but now they were on the other side of things and it wasn't there for them anymore except as an image burned onto their retinas like the floating red ghosts of bright lights that had been turned off.

Now he smiled at Orlando and held his hands out for Orlando's cuffed arms under the parka, but the look on his face was the tolerant and sorrowful gaze of an older brother whose wild days are long over. Orlando stood patient as a child while Marty fit the snips around the cuffs and worked them back and forth, the plastic turning a hard white before slowly giving up and parting.

Orlando grimaced and worked his wrists in his hands one at a time while Marty looked up and down the street, flinging the plastic wraps over the fence into some weeds.

"Thanks, man."

Marty shook his head, no problem, but looked like there was more he wanted to say.

"What?"

Marty just looked down. "Take care of yourself, Orlando."

"How's Mary? Zoe saw her with the baby."

"She's good, man. You should . . ." He shrugged.

"Yeah." Do what? Come by? Come have dinner? Or talk over old times? When they'd walked the lines of parked cars on Frankford at three in the morning, trying doors to find one open? Not even to steal, some nights, but just to find a place to sleep? Or the time they'd rolled a drunk behind a bar on Girard, the guy's smell bad enough to make them gag while they poked through his pockets for a couple of dollar bills soggy with urine?

Marty fished in his pocket and came out with a crumpled ten and folded it in Orlando's blackened fingers. Orlando nodded, looked up the street and said, "thanks, man." Wondered what Marty saw when he looked at him.

Marty turned away, and Orlando said, "What's it like?"

The big kid turned back, threading the snips into his pocket. Orlando tried to remember how old Marty was. Twenty-three, twenty-four? There were white wires threaded in his black hair and deep hollows beneath his cheekbones.

"It's okay." He lifted one shoulder, let it drop. "It's okay. We eat breakfast on Sundays, up at Bob's. I talked to my mom last month. She's coming to see the baby. Maybe she is. I did so much stupid shit when I was high, I wouldn't blame her if, you know, she was done." He smiled. "It's not jail. I don't feel sick in the morning. I read a fucking book last week. Some days everything looks like shit, food doesn't taste like anything. I don't know. But it's not prison and I go home every night." He was talking to himself, too. "I just got to believe this is better, you know? Staying alive is better." Marty shrugged again, that was all he had. He turned away.

Orlando watched him go. He got his bearings off the street signs, stretched, struck out north.

There was a shot. Danny heard it, out in the world and then in his earpiece a half second later, the stony pop ricocheting around the neighborhood, and his heart did that thing in his chest like it was turning over, registering that things were going wrong and he wasn't in control of events.

Danny crouched at the edge of a stone wall at the foot of Lamport Road. He had on a Kevlar vest and held his pistol between his legs, pointing down. It was a good pistol, an H&K USP .45 he'd gotten the year before when his mother had given him a couple thousand dollars of the insurance money she'd gotten when his father had died of a stroke at the side of 95 during rush hour.

He'd been on his way to teach a class in HVAC at Bucks County Community College. He'd lived long enough for the medics to get him on the ambulance. To see his face while he tried to say whatever was in his head. He'd opened and closed his mouth, crying with frustration at whatever was stuck behind his thickened lips. His father had always been quiet, the kind of man who observed things from a wry and considered distance, and it bothered Danny for a long time that he'd held on to something he'd wanted to say and never got it out at the last.

Now Danny tensed and dropped a little lower. So did Big

John, but he was already so exposed it hardly mattered. They both looked up reflexively at the door two houses up the street where the SWAT guys were standing over the kid with the red jacket sprawled half in and half out of the chair and someone on the radio said, "Shit."

The SWAT guys Danny knew were good guys, careful and rehearsed and economical in their movements and when they were involved things usually went well, but they were there because sometimes things went wrong and people didn't always want to go quietly, and once in a while someone reached for his waistband instead of giving it up and things got bad.

Now the people in the house knew they were there and the guys at the door yelled *go, go, go,* and the door was breached by a short guy with a shaved head who swung a squat battering ram that popped the lock.

Danny got up and ran up the walk and took the stairs two at a time, Big John loping after him on his bad knees. Martinez reached the top of the stairs where two SWAT guys were hunched over the kid who'd been shot, one of them pushing a compression bandage down on the kid's chest and shouting into the radio, but the other one was looking over his shoulder at Danny with pursed lips and *no fucking way* in his eyes.

Danny went in, his pistol up, touching the back of the last SWAT guy to tell him he was there and watching them clear the rooms. His heart was beating hard, vibrating in his chest with a fast pulse so that he could feel the blood jetting out to the ends of his arms, and he knew he could never do SWAT because he'd become addicted to that feeling, that rush of going heavy through barricaded doors and pushing the shotgun out in front of him to get them down on the floor, and then he'd be no good for anything else.

In the living room he saw Darnell go over, pushed down on his face and his hands jerked behind him by two black helmets working with a furious economy while his mother moaned, a shrill, oscillating whine that leaked around the hands she had clapped over her mouth, fat tears standing on her cheeks. Another tall kid dropped wearily to his knees, his hands splayed across the back of his neck. Shaking his head, *shit, not again.*

Danny heard more shouting from overhead and went back toward the front door to get a view of the stairs leading up to the second floor. He heard the deep voice of one of the SWAT guys barking orders and then saw Trey King back to the top of the stairs with an expensive-looking Mossberg shotgun that was too big to swing in the little row house, trying to cover all the SWAT guys that were no doubt arrayed against him. He was a big kid, bulked up from jail and wild with the coke they'd been doing all morning. He was stripped to the waist, wearing only low-slung, baggy black shorts, and his back was slick with sweat.

Trey pulled the trigger once, a detonating crack and a flash of light that lit the hallway and the top of the stairs stark white for an instant before the SWAT team answered fire and there was the clattering of the small H&K submachine guns they carried and the pinging of brass as a rain of empty shells ejected onto the hardwood floors.

Trey tripped trying to back down the stairs out of the line of fire, and the shots from the cops perforated the old plaster walls of the stairwell, missing Trey but dumping dust and bits of lath down on Danny and on Trey as he fell hard on his ass and skittered down the dozen stairs to come to rest at Danny's feet. The shotgun cartwheeled out of the kid's hands, clipping him on the head and clattering out into the entryway. Big John picked it up while Danny pointed his pistol at Trey's face and the kid lifted his hand to touch a smear of blood on his forehead and said, *ain't that a motherfucker.*

Danny went back into the sitting room where one of the SWAT guys pointed a gloved hand down at the coffee table. There between a pizza box and a street copy of a monster movie on DVD was a black TEC-9 with a matte finish. It was old and scuffed up, with dull white metal showing through where the paint was worn through. Darnell and his cousin Pook were on the floor in handcuffs. Danny bent over the gun and inspected it, sniffed at the barrel. He could hear Pook swear under his breath.

CHAPTER

7

Orlando raised one eyebrow to look at the camera over Mexican Bob's door.

"Bob."

There was a long silence. Orlando half-turned to watch the street.

"Bob."

There was a click from the intercom, and he could hear breathing.

"Bob, man, I'm on the clock here."

"Lift up your face."

Orlando looked at his shoes.

"You heard me, man. Lift up your face."

Orlando worked his tongue in his jaw, then finally lifted his head and looked at the camera. There was another long pause.

"You get picked up, cops throw you a beating, and you do what?"

"Bob, man."

"You come right the fuck back here?"

"It wasn't a cop."

"Orlando."

"It wasn't, it was something else."

"That supposed to make me feel better? The man knows your business, he knows you got business with me, he knows whatever else."

"Bob, man." Orlando looked into the camera, held up his shaking hands. "Don't just cut me loose."

"Go home."

"I'm in trouble."

"Yeah, Orlando, you are."

The street was bright now, and Orlando stepped to the curb and tried to think what to do next. He rubbed his face, and his hand came away with blood over the black grit in the heel of his hand. He stepped nearer to a storefront with a plate glass window and angled his head to catch his reflection, licking one grimy finger to try to wipe off the blood at his temple and running along the hollow of his eye.

He became aware that he wasn't alone in the reflected image and turned to see a slender girl standing at his elbow, swaying slightly. She was staring at him, or staring at the blood on his head and in his hair, and her face was empty, her mouth moving. Orlando had seen her before but couldn't place her, a skinny girl with caramel-colored skin, a girl who had been beautiful before whatever had gotten to her. Her lips were full and dark and her eyes were large and blue, but there was grime at the corners of her eyes and her hair was lank, and something stained her dress dark in circles and blotches. Over the dress she wore a jacket with crossed hockey sticks that didn't go with her once elegant outfit, except that the jacket, too, was stained and ripped.

She reached out one small hand to touch his face and he caught it and tried to catch her eye, but she was focused on the damage to his face and as he watched she began to cry. Her expression didn't change, but clear lines of water ran from her eyes, making clean tracks in the sooty grime on her face. She pulled her hand back from his, but then again she reached for his face and he turned slightly to let her, ready to recoil if she tried to scratch him. He had seen enough street-crazy women, even beautiful ones, to know they were unpredictable and sometimes dangerous.

She touched his temple gently, and the crying intensified. She looked down and let her mouth open, working silently, her breath feeding a sort of muted, barely audible howl. It was crying the way kids did it, inconsolable, bottomless, as if nothing could ever be right again.

"Sienna."

That was her name. It came to his lips, somehow bypassing his brain, the way it sometimes worked. He had seen her around the neighborhood, in the bars and on the street. A party girl, maybe a hooker. He had taken her in on the periphery of things without registering her before. People moved through the scene, sometimes up and out, sometimes down, like now. The drinking and copping stopped being a party and became a job, a life, and people emptied their lives into the street and wandered, stunned and broken. It happened. It was where his mother had gone.

She turned away, not answering, looking at the spot of blood on her hands that had transferred from his face, and talked fiercely to it, words he couldn't catch or understand. When she turned, though, he saw the distension in her short dress, a swelling that might have been anything but that he was afraid meant she was carrying another burden. Looking past her now, he saw a white police cruiser slowing on the street, the driver looking his way, and he turned his head and looked back into the shop window, his head down until he was alone on the street.

When Kathleen and Brendan came home there were two dozen messages. Friends and news reporters and kids from school. There were a few hangups, one with the breathy sobbing of a young girl. Kathleen came down from her shower to find Brendan playing it over, his lips pursed.

"Listen to this."

"Why?"

"Does that sound like Jeannette?"

He pushed the PLAY button again, and they listened while Brendan moved the volume slider. Kathleen shrugged.

"I don't know, Bren. One young girl crying sounds pretty much like another, I guess."

Before the phone hung up, they heard another voice for a second, an older woman in a distant room asking what everyone wanted for dinner.

Kathleen shook her head. "I don't know, Bren."

He opened the machine, pulled out the tape. "I'll give it to the detective, what's his name. Martinez."

"Put another tape in, Bren. People need to be able to reach us."

"Are you pissed at me?"

"No, I just want to get back to the hospital in case Michael wakes up."

"If it was Jeannette with them, if she knows something about what happened—"

"I don't care what happened. Get dressed, Brendan."

"You say that now, but I want to be able to tell Michael . . ." He lifted his hand and made a fist, a dark look on his face.

"What, what can you tell him? You think this is ever going to make sense?"

"I need to understand this."

"You need, that's right. You. You think a world where someone points a machine gun at children can ever make sense?"

"I want to be able to tell him I did what I could. To know the truth of it."

She saw he was upset and put her hand on his neck, the way she did when he'd had a shift so bad he couldn't talk about it but sat in his blues in the kitchen looking out the window while a cup of coffee went cold on the table.

"I don't believe in truth, Brendan. I believe in you. And Michael. This house and work and dinner together most nights. The rest of it is the world going by and I don't care about it. Even if you find the man who did this? What will you know, really? And how many more people will be hurt in the finding out? The truth? The truth, you can have."

. . .

Orlando walked stiffly up Ridge, feeling the places where his abraded skin was being rubbed by the rough fabric of his jeans. His head throbbed and his stomach lurched and he knew he'd have to score or he'd get weaker and dopesick. He walked past storefront churches with names hand-painted or sprayed on like graffiti. The Triumph Apostolic Church of the New Age, the Starlight Holiness Church. He walked past Chinese takeouts fortified like Ulster police stations with bulletproof glass and barbed wire. Men and women sat on lawn chairs on the street in front of their houses or their shops, hair places and unlicensed notion stores, and everyone had something to say, some wisdom to offer, seeing him lurch up the street with blood in his hair and one closed eye. They told him to get along home, to run and hide, to get right with Jesus. At Thirty-third he turned north and caught the bus for Roxborough.

The time had passed to be discriminate in his choices. There were people he'd call if he needed dope, and then there were places he'd go when he really needed dope. It wasn't all the same. The quality of the dope, the vibe off the dealer, it all mattered when he was thinking straight, but when he was in a bad way it mattered less, and then not at all.

Near the hospital he turned south and found a three-story white frame house that leaned, canted toward the street like a drunk heading for the gutter. He tried to make himself inconspicuous, smaller somehow as he headed up the walk to the front door. He knocked and waited.

There was some rustling inside, some discussion, then he heard someone say, "We're closed," but before he could walk away the door opened and a young guy with red hair stood there, waving him in and shooing away a lean Puerto Rican kid who was shaking his head and pointing at Orlando.

"I told you, just don't say I didn't tell you, right?"

The red-haired guy smiled and propelled Orlando with one hand into the living room, which was stripped bare except for a sprung green couch and a chipped Formica table. The place smelled of burned dope and scented wax from a half-dozen candles stuck to the fireplace mantel. He could hear soft music from somewhere and voices upstairs and remembered that there were still people for whom dope was a vacation. Fun.

Orlando finally pointed at the red-haired guy and smiled. "Asa, right?"

"Yeah, that's right." Orlando knew him vaguely from the life, had heard his name, seen him pointed out by Bob or someone but couldn't think where. Asa didn't look particularly pleased to be recognized, but he put out a smile and invited Orlando to sit down with a wave. "Benigno thinks we ought to discriminate against you, given your brother's a cop."

Orlando counted out a few bills and held them in his fist. Asa pointedly walked away, looking at Benigno, the Puerto Rican kid, who took the money and vanished into a back room. After a few minutes a young girl with a sweet face but ancient, guarded eyes came out of the back and waved Orlando into a darkened room off the empty kitchen.

She carried in a tray and set it down on a scarred table while he sat in a plush chair under a ratty green slipcover that glowed slightly in the dark room. The girl shaped her mouth into a smile that carried nothing, but set up a candle that she lit with a wooden match. She lit a second match and ran it over the butt of the candle and stuck it to the table, then pulled a length of tube off the tray, set it down in front of him, then pulled out a bag, a needle, a spoon.

Orlando, who noticed such things, lifted the glassine bag to his face and saw the logo, a green skull surrounded by lightning bolts and the word RADIOACTIVE in block letters. He looked around him into the dark room, and the weak yellow light of the candle showed he wasn't alone. In what looked to be an identical chair across the table there was a humped shape that revealed itself to be a man when he put a cigarette to his mouth, the end glowing silently as he pulled on it.

"Don't mind me," the man said, his voice quiet, rolling with dope and drink and a soft Irish accent so that his words seemed to curl in on themselves. "You go ahead, man." Orlando sat for a moment, gathering himself, then lifted the spoon and opened the little bag.

He cooked up, tied himself off, and found the vein with his finger in the dark, a humped, sinewy wire at the crook of his elbow. When he fired the dope into his arm the man across the table lifted a bottle of Irish whiskey from the floor and slid it across the table. Orlando lifted it quick and put it to his lips, feeling the astringent burn of the liquor on his swollen lips and taking a quick swallow before the dope landed hard in his heart and he had to put the bottle down and roll back in the chair, his eyes drooping.

"There you go, yeah?"

Orlando couldn't speak, but nodded, his head falling off the stalk of his neck as if unmoored. He saw the man reach to the floor again, and he must have turned up the volume on a CD player or a radio, because now there was music, louder in the room. A song about wolves in the snow, with a strange and high and reedy sound that drifted in Orlando's head and set up vibrations in the echoing dark of his brain.

"Beautiful," Orlando said, or thought he did, and the man nodded but said nothing. The song ended and another came on, something very different. Violins, arcing and keening in a way that suggested sleek and shadowed things moving in a black sea, so much that Orlando peered around him in the dark, half expecting to see long shapes curling around the legs of the table.

"This music," he said, shaking his head.

"Oh, yeah," said the man, reaching to grab the bottle and taking a long pull so that Orlando could see the hard knot at his throat working in the dark. He put the bottle down again, lit another cigarette. "It makes me see them," he finally said. "Calls them to mind."

Orlando shook his head. "Who?"

"The ones out there, in the river. The ones moving in the river at night."

Orlando said nothing, watching the cigarette glow and fade, glow and fade in the dark.

"Do you think of them?" The man moved, and Orlando could see he was wearing dark glasses, even here. The man lifted a hand, held it in front of his face in the near dark. It glowed white in the flickering light of the green candle. "I think of them. Moving, slow, down the bottom of the river. Nothing to stop them, nothing to hold on to. Even if they could reach out, what would there be? Just the silt, that slick black silt? The smooth stones and cold water and nothing to stop them till they come to the sea."

Orlando stared, straining to see the man, part of him there in the room and part of him in the river with the blue, drifting bodies. The man moved his hand, and Orlando could see it there in the space in front of him. The darkness and the mud. Smooth stones below and the cold river all around. The moon overhead, bloated and misshapen by the view from the river bottom. A body, twisting slowly, arms wide, hands empty and luminous in the black water.

Danny Martinez sat with John Rogan in a bad room that hadn't been painted in so many years he couldn't say what color the walls were anymore. The furniture was ancient dark wood and steel speckled with rust, and there were posters on the walls going back years—public service posters and wanted flyers and interoffice memos taped and tacked over each other like sedimentary deposits on the walls of some lost cave of the civil bureaucracy.

On the table between them was the gun that had been used to shoot George and Michael. Ballistics would take a while, but that's what Danny believed the tests would show. Handcuffed to a ring on a chair nearby was Darnell Burns, the star of this play, though he didn't know it yet; his head up, looking defiant in the chastised schoolboy way of low-level criminals.

"Darnell, tell us about the Nortes." Danny squared off a stack of files on the chair. They were arrest reports he'd grabbed from John's desk, but they made a large pile and Danny would pat it while they talked, letting Darnell think what he would about what was in the files.

"They ain't shit to me." Darnell thrusting out his chin.

Big John raised an eyebrow at Danny, turned away to hide his smile. This wasn't even sport.

"But they come to Green Lane, disrespect you, disrespect Ivan . . ."

"Let them come, see what happens."

"We know, don't we, John?" John Rogan turned back, working his pen in his hands the way he did. Clicking, twirling, clicking. "We know they came down, and someone had to do something. Set up on one of your blocks. Act like Green Lane don't mean shit."

"Ivan says, never let them think they can move, or they will."

"That's right, that's right. You had to head it off. You had to send a message about what's what. Who runs what. You had to let them know that they had crossed the line. So you sent Trey to do something."

Darnell's brow creased. "Trey?"

"See, we got Trey's fingerprints on this gun, and we know this gun did the murder at Roxborough Avenue."

"I don't know nothing about that business. That gun showed up—"

"Yeah, we heard that story before. That the gun was thrown in with some dope you bought yesterday."

"Yeah, I told you—"

"Darnell. You got to think clearly now."

John leaned in at Darnell and spoke for the first time, the squared-off plain of his giant forehead looming. "The clock is ticking."

Danny nodded and pointed at John. "See, there you go. You can sit there and say I don't know, and it wasn't me, but in another room just like this one, Trey and Pook and all of them are trying to explain why the murder gun is on your mother's coffee table. What do you think they're going to say, Darnell?"

"Bullshit."

Danny smiled. "The DA is coming, Darnell. And the DA is going to get a story and go see the judge. She ain't waiting on Darnell Burns." Danny got up, went to the coffeemaker and poured a few inches into a gritty foam cup, and set it in front of Darnell.

"This is a mess, Darnell. I don't know if you get it. A child is dead. A white child, and we both know what that means. Another child is shot, and that's the child of a policeman." He shook his head. "I know you know what that means, too. And we come to your house, and we bring the SWAT, and Trey comes out shooting, almost gets killed, and you have any idea what all that costs the city? It ain't cheap, a gunfight. Every single bullet they fire costs money, and all the paperwork and the time and all that."

"You bill me, I'll write you a check."

Rogan smiled, and it was a terrible thing to see. "The clock is ticking."

"Why you keep saying that? Why does this bighead freak keep saying that about the clock? Goddammit."

"'Cause it's true, Darnell. The DA is going to indict someone, and I mean right now, tonight. She doesn't play. She doesn't ask twice. Dead children and a gunfight and people known to be in the drug business? Meaning you, Darnell. Someone is going to jail." Danny sat back and pointed at the clock.

Big John said, "Tick, tock."

Darnell pulled up hard on the cuffs around his wrists, clattering the steel chain. "Get this big Irish mope the fuck out of my face."

"He's doing you a favor, Darnell. When Ivan sat in that same chair, Big John helped him, too."

"You know Ivan?"

"Everyone knows Ivan, Darnell." Danny lifted a file and leafed through it, pointing to things Darnell couldn't see. "You think Ivan only got fourteen months because the judge liked his face?"

"Now you are telling me some bullshit. Ivan never talked to no DA."

Big John leaned in again, even closer, so that his sour, coffee-tinged breath could hit Darnell square in the face. "Everybody talks."

Danny smiled, pointed at John again. "There you go." He tapped the open file as if it were proof of the truth of John Rogan's words. "Ivan gave up two guys from Kensington who were moving dope for the Nigerians." Who knew, it might even be true. "And whoever tells the story first wins, Darnell. That's how it works."

"You got the wrong motherfucking guy. You need to go out and talk to someone else."

"No, we don't need anyone else. We got a house full of

suspects. Between you and Trey and Pook and poor Marcus, shot dead on your mom's porch? We got plenty of suspects. So, no, we're not talking to anyone else. We got the murder gun, and you have some hard fucking choices to make now. Who is Trey to you? Not family. He's not even a cousin."

Danny slid closer to Darnell. "Man, whoever pulled the trigger on those kids is going away forever. For*ever*." Darnell Burns looked down, slumping, and John looked at Danny and waggled his eyebrows. He reached behind him and grabbed a yellow legal pad and put it on the table and uncapped a pen.

Danny was quiet, serious. "Was it a mistake? Of course. No one thinks those kids got shot on purpose. A couple of dumbass kids in the wrong neighborhood when those lowlife Nortes were being dealt with. By Trey King."

"Trey did that?"

Danny said, "You didn't send him."

"I never sent Trey to kill no Nortes."

John raised his eyebrows at Danny. Was this kid dense or honest-to-God confused?

"Then, man, your conscience is clear." He smiled and pointed at the gun. "This gun is in your house, but it's Trey's prints on it. Trey, acting on his own? Getting ahead of himself, maybe trying to impress you? Or Ivan? You can't be held responsible if someone you know does something stupid, right? We have a little talk, make everyone feel good about you cooperating—"

"I'm no snitch."

"No, no, no. Nobody is snitching, Darnell. But why take the weight for something you had nothing to do with? End up doing thirty fucking years? Just 'cause you happen to invite somebody into your mother's house for pancakes turns out to be the world's biggest dumb-ass? Motherfucker shoots two white children? Motherfucker shoots the son of a *police*? Motherfucker throws down on a SWAT team when they come? Like to get your mother shot?"

"If Trey shot them kids, it didn't have shit to do with me or my business."

"That's right. This ain't about loyal or disloyal, Darnell. This is about smart or stupid. Darnell, you're the smart one. Ivan might be the face, but you're the brain. Everybody in the neighborhood knows that." He had to keep looking at Darnell. If he'd looked up at John, he'd have had trouble keeping his poker face. "But maybe Trey said something to you? Gave you like an indication of his state of mind?"

Darnell Burns looked beat. He lifted his hands again futilely, the chain rattling. "Trey?"

"This is what it's like to be in charge, Darnell. You have to make the hard calls. You have to know when someone has to go down so the rest of the team can make it. Ivan knew, he made his choice. I know it's tough, 'cause it all falls to you. It's just you, and us, and the DA, and the ticking clock. 'Cause you're the *smart* one."

John reached one meaty fist down, holding the pen out to Darnell. "Be smart now."

Orlando walked Pechin Street like it was the deck of a ship in a storm. Headlong, he tilted in the direction of his movement, his heavy head pointing the way and somehow pulling him along toward home. The houses seemed to lean in and then away as he lurched, one hand cushioning his aching ribs as he squinted into the orange sodium night. The air was warm, the streets shining with a film of greasy water under black clouds that raced toward a thin blade of white moon.

He turned the corner at the end of his block and stopped, canted his head, and tried to count windows, looking for the lit shade that would tell him Zoe was home, which he both wanted and didn't. He wanted to feel her thin, hot arms around him, but he didn't want to see her eyes when she took in how beaten in he was. He forced his eyes open wide, felt the stiff resistance of his gummed, bruised lids.

He was afraid there was a calculus in the way she looked at him, measurement along the arc of his trajectory, and he felt there would be a point she'd pull back, float away as he picked up downward momentum. She'd retreat to some safer place, he thought, and he'd have to be ready for that. Maybe she'd go back to her parents out on the Main Line, maybe just on to someone with a less desperate need for the blackness at the center of everything.

At the same time he felt disloyal for even thinking she'd cut him loose. She was tougher than he was, harder, carried a straight razor and would step in, ready to fuck up whoever looked ready to get in his shit. He wandered the world and she backed him up. He'd get caught up in dreams, lose days in watching the movement of people along the blocks, the repetitions and codes of the jugglers and whores, the runners and bagheads. Collected the stamp bags, the little glassine decks from the corners that had intricate little logos in wild colors; something about the underworld expressing itself plain in the light of day that set off strange harmonics in his head, as if he'd found pieces of a wrecked UFO at Third and Indiana.

He was slowing, painfully lifting his head on his stiff neck, when he heard a car door open. He had time to wrench his head toward the street, to take in the big man moving fast, his face contorted with rage and seamed with livid cuts, the lines of the wounds on his temple and cheek black in the light from the streetlamps.

Collins lunged up at Orlando where he stood balanced on the curb, jamming the short-barreled pistol against Orlando's neck and tensing his finger on the trigger so that Orlando stopped, his body held in a stiff line that arced away from the outstretched arm.

"I wanted to ask you questions." Collins breathed through his mouth, his lips flexing as the air moved through so that he seemed like an alien struggling for breath in an unfamiliar atmosphere. "You could have been at least some help to that poor, bereaved man before you died curled up in some junkie squat."

Orlando said, "I don't know—" but Collins shook his head and pulled back on the hammer with a dull click that Orlando felt through his collarbone where the gun was jammed into a hollow at the side of his neck.

"I don't even care," said the older man as he looked up into the sky as if judging the lateness of the hour.

"A few years ago, when I was on the street with the other brain-dead cops? When they still thought I was one of them? There was junkies started showing up dead. From the fentanyl, remember that? Shutting down their lungs." He licked his lips.

"Me? I thought great, let them go. But the brass? They're going to do a public service, let the junkies know. Don't do the fentanyl. They show them. On fucking TV! On fucking TV they show the powder, show the labels on the bags, tell the dumbasses to stay away."

Orlando closed his eyes and tried to shift to the side so when Collins pulled the trigger, the bullet might pass through his shoulder. Collins reached out with his other hand and put it on Orlando's head and grabbed a handful of his short blond hair and pulled him forward, angling the pistol inward, toward the center of his body.

Collins kept talking, jumping back and forth between anger and a sad patience. "So what happened? Do you remember?"

Orlando shook his head, then angled it up to see into the mad, bright eyes catching the moonlight.

"I remember. They lined up. Around the fucking block."

Orlando could hear him panting, a whistling through the older man's thin lips, and he could smell the curdled sweetness of the wine on his breath and the meaty smell of the blood that ran down his ruined cheek into his collar.

"They wanted it. The junkies. They came from Jersey, from Wilmington. From fucking . . . *Scranton* in junkie caravans. They wanted it. They wanted it so bad the dealers couldn't keep up. They'd bang up in their cars and pass out. Run off the road.

Hit fucking trees half a block from where they scored. The dealers ran out of it. They were putting phony labels on the regular shit so the stupid bastards would think they were getting the poison." Collins moved closer, pulling Orlando's head down and moving close enough to whisper.

"Know what it was called, that poison dope?" Collins shook Orlando's head hard, pulling his hair, and Orlando grabbed at the muscled forearm. "Of course you do, you probably did some of it. 'Die Trying.' How you like that? How fucking perfect is that? That was when I saw it, the insanity of it. And I stopped being a cop right then and there. When people like you run toward their own death? Line up for it? What can I do but give them what they want?"

He started to pull the trigger. Orlando felt the increased tension in Collins's hand and grabbed the extended arm with both hands, and it was lack of balance and general weakness that saved him. He fell off the high curb as the pistol made its hollow, concussive pop under his left ear, the blast from the muzzle deafening him and blowing bits of his jacket and shirt collar over the sidewalk behind him.

He pulled desperately at the man's arm, clawing for the gun and screaming with the pain in his ear as he went down and Collins was pulled down with him as Orlando fell between the bumpers of two parked cars. Collins grabbed uselessly at the wet, cracked-open rear of the Volvo and went down hard, his arm pinned under Orlando and giving way with a hard snap as the bone parted between his wrist and elbow.

Collins screamed and Orlando grabbed the rubber bumper

of the car and pulled himself up, the pistol clattering out of the older man's useless hand and disappearing under a rusted-out Caprice with a bumper sticker that read FLYERS HAT TRICK '76. Lights had begun to come on, and Orlando saw some curtains opening to white, annoyed faces. Collins tried to sit up, moaning and cradling his arm while Orlando staggered back, trying without success to pull himself up straight.

It was then he saw the blood, a jet of dark crimson liquid that had spattered his hands and the Volvo's wet windows and left a dark streak in the ruins of his once-white shirt. He'd been shot. He put his hand over his shoulder and finally felt it, the adrenaline that had been protecting him from the shock of it leaking away and a dull ache at his collarbone under his left ear turning into an insistent whine and a bright pain flaring in his neck and shoulder.

He had time to take a few steps toward home, to register the whine of sirens somewhere, the sobs of the big man trying to pull himself up from the curb with one good hand. To think of Zoe standing at the mirror, putting on lipstick, running a brush through her black hair and smearing shadow over one brown eye. Wearing a red top, listening to a Cuban song, slow and sensual in a way that made her move her hands with an exaggerated, liquid grace. He saw more—Bob and LaDonna dancing in a dark space, holding each other and swaying; his brother and his wife in the dim lights of a hospital room. Machines humming and green LEDs, Kathleen asleep curled in an orange chair and Brendan at the window, staring out at the night. The Irish guy from the dope house standing at the canal in Manayunk and looking at the water, his hidden eyes blank with terror. Orlando dropped to his knees, lifting his bloody hands to see them one last time. Then he went over hard, skidding down into a widening pool of his own blood so that the last thing in his eyes was the bright slice of moon reflected, inches away, white against the spreading black.

CHAPTER

8

There was a press conference, with Danny standing by the Captain and pictures of Trey and Darnell and pictures of the murder gun and the crime scene splashed with blood. The Captain bounced his hand on Danny's shoulder and flashbulbs went off, and the city's children could sleep safe and order was restored. It all made Danny, sweating in the lights, unaccountably tense.

Worst moment: when they brought Francine Parkman in, and Jesus Christ, who would even do that? He put out his hand, her eyes bright with whatever they were pumping her full of to keep her upright and walking. He took her cold fingers and felt a repeating tremor, like she was being electrocuted, a shuddering he swore he could hear in her rattling bones.

Then someone walked her away and he didn't know where to look, but there was a hot sensation on the back of his neck, something he hadn't had since he was a kid and his father had taken him to some hobby shop out in the suburbs somewhere and caught him stealing a little plastic figure from a display. Danny had watched the tacky strings of separating glue lengthen as he pulled the fine, hand-painted man up to his eye and was wondering silently at the perfect little daubs of paint on the eyes and lips when he became aware of his father moving fast, crowding him, pulling the plastic man roughly out of Danny's hands and sticking it hard down in the oblong shadow where it had been moored. His old man didn't say anything, didn't make a face or shake his head—but the violence in his motions, the rough way he'd taken the soldier and quick, panicked way he'd pushed the little man back into the glue, made Danny back away, and the terrible feeling, that guilt, that spreading circle of heat on the back of his neck as if a feverish hand were placed there, that was the feeling he had watching the mother of the murdered boy being moved down the hall and away from the lights.

Brendan's partner, Luis, didn't like mess. He had been a cop for nineteen years and knew it wasn't about catching bad guys or pulling the gun like on TV; it was about keeping the noise down, moving people along, and cleaning up the damn mess. People called the cops when their neighbors came home drunk, when they locked their keys in their cars, when the UPS truck blocked their driveway again, when they couldn't handle their own god-damn kids. They called from vacation houses in Bermuda because they thought they left the gas on or a window open. People called cops the same way they called plumbers or locksmiths or doctors or their mothers. When they just didn't know what the fuck else to do.

So he had never liked any of this shit with Brendan's kid brother. His partner's brother was a junkie, that was old news now. Getting locked up for petty theft, for being on the nod in some nice store and generally freaking people out. Sure, at first Brendan would run over to see if he could help, get the kid out of whatever jam he was in and turn him loose with a kick in the ass. Come back to the car looking embarrassed and pissed off, and Luis would wave it off. What the hell could you do? That was family. Anyway it only happened a couple times and then Brendan stopped going. No one had to tell him anything; he just knew enough to know the kid was his own worst enemy and there was nothing to be done about it.

But now this thing was all blown up. Brendan's kid had been hurt, and now the brother was upstairs shot, and here they were, standing again in the fucking emergency room, Brendan hot, looking like he wanted to kill somebody, and that fucking lunatic Collins cuffed to a bed in an observation room while they waited to ship him out to Northeast Philly. In there raving and clanking his chains, one arm in a cast.

Luis knew who Collins was, remembered all the bullshit that had happened when Brendan had seen Collins tuning up some poor junkie on Indiana, hitting the kid over and over. Collins saying later the kid had gone for him, which was a fucking joke. Luis had looked the other way and kept his mouth shut, but it had bugged Brendan and he'd said something in the hearing of an inspector and the whole thing got out of hand and then Collins, the asshole, had gotten written up. It hadn't cost him the badge, not by itself. The fact that Collins was a nut, the fact that he came in drunk, *that* was the shit that got him yanked. The thing Brendan and Luis had seen—Collins banging the poor junkie's head against a parked car—that wasn't the first time or the last time Collins had gone off on someone.

It was the way things were. Everyone stood by and watched while somebody went off the deep end, everyone thinking, *Somebody should do something about this guy*, and then when somebody finally did, like Brendan, everybody looked sideways at him, and to Collins they all said, "Yeah, that was a bum rap," like Brendan should have kept his mouth shut. Even though they were all glad the crazy, drunk fuck was gone.

Not gone enough, of course. He had just moved to South Jersey and pretended to be some kind of private investigator, that's what the detectives told him and Brendan. Drank and got even more bitter, and if it was possible even more crazy, until he saw a chance to come back and fuck with Brendan and his family.

Luis watched Brendan standing with the detectives, his face all red and Irish-looking, his neck rigid with the effort of not cursing, and the Parkman kid's father, who was shaking his head no over and over and denying a lot of something. Luis was thinking, *Oh, boy*, as Brendan finally said something loud and made a gesture with his hands like *I give up* and walked quick toward the elevator to go up and check on his brother, who the nurses said was basically okay. Luis would stay down here, thanks.

He thought about one of the last times he was with his father, before the old man's heart attack and his mother bringing them all up here from the DR. Luis and his sister were going at it, fighting over a toy or something. He remembered being in the dirt yard, remembered the sound of his sister's voice calling him *chancho*, a pig, and poking him in his soft belly, and his father coming out of the house, shaking his head, a big cigar in his mouth. Holding up his hands like he was praying, saying, *Calma,*

113

Dios mío. Smiling, shaking his head. *Calma.* That was his old man. He didn't take sides, didn't give a shit who did what to who. He just wanted things to be quiet while he smoked his Partagas.

Luis looked around himself now at the chaos of the emergency room, at the detectives looking skeptically at Parkman, at crazy, ranting Collins with his broken arm held out stiff in front of him, telling his story to an empty room, and he shook his head and headed out to the parking lot, fishing in his pocket for a cigar.

Orlando sat on the edge of the bed, watching the nurses go by and wanting a cigarette. He was supposed to be lying flat, sup-posed to be letting the antibiotics work, drinking the apple juice they'd left for him, but he just wanted out. The hospital was bright, loud, crowded at all hours, and he just wanted to get out and into the street. Zoe didn't help, pacing the floor and looking at him as if he were guilty of something. She'd go to the door, look out at the hall, move back to the window and look out at the traffic on Ridge, her eyes sliding to him, until he said, "What?" She just crossed her arms and shrugged.

He said, "How many times I have to tell you?"

"He just shot you? No explanation, no nothing?"

"He was fucking crazy, I don't know." He reached out, but she did a matador slide and his hand grazed her hip. She held up her arms, like *don't touch me;* and he sighed. She went to stand by the window again, and he got out of bed, awkwardly dragging the IV pole and the clear tubes, the blue floor freezing under his bare feet and his shoulder already itching where the bullet had passed through the skin, leaving a bright furrow like a set of painted lips stitched shut.

He went to stand by her and watched the street, too. The headlights of the cars crawling from signal to signal, the streets bathed in a greenish glow from the streetlamps. He heard her breathing and looked over to see her head down, her hands over her eyes.

"What am I supposed to do, you get killed? Where do I go then?"

He breathed out, tried to think what to say. Then he saw a shadow in the door and it was Brendan. Shit.

"Orlando?"

He ducked his head, a reflex. Looked up at his brother as he resolved from a dark figure into someone recognizable. Saw for the first time the gray pasted into the hair at his temple, the deep cul-de-sacs under his eyes. Looked down again.

"You're out of bed? You're okay?"

Orlando couldn't think what to say, mumbled "sorry" under his breath, looked from Zoe's wary, foxlike eyes to Brendan's frantic ones.

"Jesus, Orlando. Jesus."

"I didn't do it. Didn't do anything. This crazy fuck tried to kill me."

"We don't have enough, me and Kath? Not enough to worry about? We have to hear this, too?"

"I swear to Christ, Bren." He held his hands up, empty palms catching the light, and the IV pole rattled. He felt like a ghost, a phantom festooned with chains. Not fully present in life, able only to horrify. Looking from one disappointed face to another. The fact of him an object lesson, a curse.

When he was alone he shifted in the hard, narrow bed, unable to sleep. The nurses knew dependency when they saw it and only gave him aspirin. The pain wasn't bad, but it sometimes flared in his neck and back so that he couldn't get comfortable, and he slept in short shifts and then woke up disoriented and stiff.

Toward dawn he lay watching the sky turning a hazy brown and remembered the day he'd met Zoe, at a used-book store on Richmond Street full of local characters who came to drink beer and eat meatball sandwiches from a place around the corner. It was snowing, and she was dressed in black and her head was wrapped in a dark scarf so that only her face showed, that buttercream white skin and her dark lips, suggesting something confectionary, so that he followed her through the dim confusion of aisles until he could work out something to say to her. He couldn't remember what it was he'd said, but she'd smiled and before long he was pulling her from shelf to shelf, getting books down to read her passages he loved. Tugging the sleeves of her coat that were glazed with broken bits of ice. He showed her the back of the store, where the aisles ended in a chaos of unsorted books and flickering lights that was like the entrance to a mine. He spent hours there every week, stacking up ancient hardbacks with pages gone a speckled brown like birds' eggs, or lurid pulps with half-dressed women whose green- or blue-tinged skin seemed to promise both sex and death.

When they left the bookstore, they got *paczki* from a bakery up the street and walked to an empty bar on Lehigh. They drank whiskey and the pale, watery beer he liked and kissed in a corner booth listening to songs in Polish, the singers sounding alternately angry and heartbroken while the music struggled to keep up. She pulled his hand into her lap and he got hard, touched his lips with a finger red with the sickly-sweet jelly from the pastries. He opened her pants under her coat and she breathed into his mouth, making small, dovelike sounds.

Remembering it later, he knew there must have been other people in the place, a bartender, some old guy drinking Pabst with his head down, but he remembered the two of them as alone in an empty room. The tiny barroom windows stingy with the failing afternoon light, the cold coming in waves through the thin plywood walls. Breathing on her small, white hands to warm them, putting each cherry-tipped finger in his mouth to taste it, and when she asked what she tasted like, he said she tasted like red.

John Rogan stood over Danny's desk holding a newspaper under his arm until Danny raised his head and snapped his fingers.

Rogan gave it up slowly. "It's probably nothing."

Danny read the article twice. Darnell Burns's lawyer claiming that his client was at SCI Chester, the prison where his brother Ivan was locked up, until the end of visiting hours at eight thirty.

There was a grainy picture of somebody the lawyer claimed was Darnell coming out of the visitors' room.

Danny shrugged. "Could be him."

Rogan made a face. "With the hood up like that? Could be anybody." He reached down and shifted the paper. "Reminds me a little of Wyclef, before he shaved his head?"

"And they had the gun."

"They had the gun. So they did it." A beat. "Or they know who did."

"You're not sure, now?"

Rogan looked away, scratched at his neck. "I'm sure Darnell Burns is a violent moron. I'm sure he's capable of it."

"And they signed the statements."

"Yeah."

"Do you think this is bullshit, John? Did we make a mistake?"

"I think these mopes locked up is a good day's work."

"That's not the same thing, is it?"

"Don't make yourself crazy, Danny. It's as close as we're going to get."

There was music playing, loud, from the house on Boston, and Freddie Castro looked up and down the street nervously before knocking on the door. The place was run-down, dark, and there was newspaper stuffed in the street-level window. He knocked again, louder, and finally Teyo opened the door a crack, saw it was him, then stepped aside, motioning him to get off the street, quick.

Teyo and Freddie were original Tres Nortes. They'd been in the Youth Study Center with Juli when they were young, the old one on Callowhill that the city finally closed after it got so old and fucked up that the city decided to turn it into a museum and send the kids to West Philly. They'd come up together, Juli and Teyo and Freddie. Now Juli was shot to pieces and the whole thing had turned to shit.

Teyo had been with Juli at the dope house on Roxborough when the place was shot up. He'd been calling Freddie all week while they moved Juli from place to place around the city, asking him what to do, where to go. Now they were here, in a derelict house on Boston Street, and Teyo asked Freddie to come because he thought Juli was dying.

Inside, the music was a roar of guitars and drums and the sound was like being beaten on the ribs, the lyrics about being down with the sickness. Teyo looked at him for a minute, his eyes wired open by coke and fear. He was sweating, the house closed up and stinking, and now that he was inside Freddie could hear someone screaming. The living room was almost pitch-black, lit by a few candles, and he followed Teyo, who just shook his head and pointed to where Juli thrashed on the couch, bleeding out of holes in his arms and legs, jamming his fist into his mouth in a vain attempt to shut himself up.

The place stank of blood and vomit and backed-up toilets, and there were bandages and water bottles stacked up on a packing crate they were using as a table. Pacho De La Rocha and Dippy from York Street were there, looking disgusted and sick, standing in the corner smoking and spitting in the heat. Teyo walked through into the kitchen and stood by a candle where he had an open bottle of rum and he took a long pull and waited for Freddie.

When Freddie gave up trying to understand whatever Juli was screaming around the fingers he had jammed in his mouth, he walked through into the airless kitchen and took the bottle from Teyo and sipped at it. Teyo couldn't stop shaking his head. His shoulders were glazed with sweat and his beater hung limp and wet on his body.

"I know, right? Could this shit be more fucked up? I finally told him Juli, man, you go to a hospital or you're going to die here, brother. He don't even make no sense now."

"Who's out doing business? Who's running the corners while you're in here watching Juli?"

"Fucking nobody, that's who. It took like three seconds for everybody in North Philly to hear Juli was down, and with Juli down, we're out."

Juli stopped screaming and started talking furiously to people who weren't in the room, something about getting ice cream, and that was even worse, Freddie thought. His mind was gone, even the pain, and he was spiraling down to nothing, and that meant the Nortes were done.

"And that guy, that African guy? Juli set that up like two months ago and the fucker is here, he's here right now, and without Juli out front, that deal is over. That's like a million dollars." He made a gesture in the flickering candlelight, kissing the tips of his fingers. Gone.

"You got the numbers for the guy? The African?"

Teyo shrugged. He started going through his pockets.

Freddie smiled and hit Teyo on the shoulder. "Let me see what I can do."

Freddie walked back up Boston toward Emerald, looking back over his shoulder at the house, still hearing the thump of the drums and bass, the noise they played to try to drown out Juli's dying screams. He took out the card Teyo had given him with the numbers for the African, thought about when Juli was strong and they'd been making real money and he'd been able to take Pilar down to where he'd grown up in the DR. Show her Playa Rincon and Santo Domingo. Lie on the beach and drink rum drinks and eat fresh fruit and snapper in coconut sauce by the beach at night. Jesus, he wanted to go back.

He finally came up to the Mercedes idling in the dark, and the window powered down as he got close. There was a snapping sound and Asa Carmody was working a Zippo, lighting a cigarette, squinting at Freddie and nodding his head. The man all tics and head bobs and edgy impatience. There was movement all around him now, Asa's guys coming out of two SUVs and moving back down the street toward the blacked-out Nortes house. One of them had a shotgun out already, working the slide, fishing in his pockets to come out with shells, dull red and gleaming brass under the humming lights.

Freddie reached out with the card, and Asa snapped his fingers impatiently and Freddie laid it in his hands, not sure what was going to happen next. Asa nodded and said, "Okay," just the one word, and Freddie nodded back and kept moving, walking fast, his head tucked down, hoping to get down to Front Street and the noise of the cars and the rumble of the trains to cover the sound of what was coming next.

He'd thought Asa would say something to him. Something about how this was the smart move, the Nortes were done anyway, Juli was done, and this was just what was coming, so what could Freddie do but be smart? He could be smart, or he could die with his friends in the little stinking house on Boston Street. The Nortes had their run, but now it was time for Asa and his guys, and all he'd done was see the truth of things. Asa hadn't said anything, though, had just stared at him, and there was nothing to do but walk away fast and cover his ears with his hands.

Danny Martinez was sitting at a little Italian place in Manayunk, on Main Street, and watching his phone on the table as it buzzed and skipped on the white tablecloth. He didn't know the number, and the wine was hitting him hard on an empty stomach. Rogan was late, and Danny ripped a piece of bread out of the basket and stuffed it into his mouth. The phone was still buzzing when his mouth was empty, so he finally picked it up.

"Detective Martinez?"

"Yeah, this is Martinez."

"This is Jelan Williams." The voice was hesitant, rising as if the statement was a question. "I don't know if you remember me." He remembered Jelan. She was a beautiful Jamaican girl from north of Ridge Avenue. Wide, almond-shaped eyes and a long body that seemed to curve like a bow drawn taut. Asa had gone out with her a few times, and Danny had always had a little pang of jealousy when he'd seen them together. Though they didn't last. It never seemed to with Asa. The girls were drawn to him—he was always a good-looking kid and put out that knowing vibe, a sense of power in the world, even when they were teenagers.

Jelan was one of those serious girls who seemed to have a plan, which might have been what brought her to Asa, the master schemer, when they were young. Of course, that was a lot of years before, and other than the occasional glimpse around the neighborhood, Danny hadn't seen Jelan since then. The uncertainty in her voice seemed unlike her, though. The way he thought of her.

"Jelan, sure, I remember. How are you?"

"Oh, fine, thank you. But I'm calling about Darius."

Danny's stomach grumbled audibly and he shifted the phone. "Darius."

"My brother, Darius. He was a few years behind us at Roxborough?"

Danny shook his head. Soap. She was talking about Soap. He had just seen Soap at the bar, when was it? Two days ago, three?

"Oh, of course, I'm sorry. Darius." He had to force himself not to use the name he'd thought of as pinned to the kid, and he tried to remember if he knew how he'd come to be called Soap. "How can I help?"

"I'm not sure what to call you these days. Is it *Detective*

Martinez?" A slight mocking tone, but with affection. It was the old Jelan, who had regarded him slyly out of the corner of her eyes as if she'd had his number, even when she was sixteen and he was, at eighteen, a shy, bookish kid unable to look at her with anything but hot need. A scene came to him, a flash of her in her blue and white cheerleading outfit, flitting by him as he stumbled out of the boys' locker room at the end of gym. A nearly imperceptible smile, a slight warp in her graceful neck that told him she knew everything that was in his roiling teenage-boy head. That's what he got, his awkward half-step, her eyes and knowing smile, and a flash of blue and white. One of those seconds that stick in your head and never come out.

"Danny. Call me Danny, Jelan."

"Danny."

"Is Darius in trouble?"

"He's, well. He's missing." Then it came out of her in a rush, the way it always did at first. This part was always the same, from the first time Danny had been in uniform and a frantic mother had grabbed his arm, near the art center on Allens Lane, to tell him her son had wandered away from the playground, her story pouring out, her eyes streaming. All of the worry coiled in them springing out when there was someone, finally, who might help. Someone whose job it was to find the missing one in that moment when nothing else was important.

"Darius always takes our mother to church. Always, and he didn't show up on Sunday. We called everyone he knows, and no one's seen him. I went to his apartment, I spoke to his girlfriend a dozen times, that brainless girl Bertrise from Ludlow. A more exasperating child I have never met. She's carrying

Darius's baby, for God's sake, but that girl has no more clue about life than a sparrow in a tree. She thinks I'm an idiot to worry, that he's just hiding because all his friends were arrested last week. She thinks he's some kind of secret agent, but I know what Darius does for money, Danny. I'm not stupid. He got involved with that boy, Ivan." *Bwoy,* the way she said it now, agitated and worried about her brother. "They deal drugs, and I've talked to him until I'm blue in the face, but he fell in with that craven bait."

"I'm sorry?"

She stopped herself, gave a laugh with nothing in it. "Bait." It sounded to Danny like *be-it.* "I'm sorry, Danny. I turn into my mother when I think of Darius and what he's made of his life. Bait, you never heard a Jamaican say that?" she said, and he heard it then. "It means scoundrel, I guess. Bad man. That good-for-nothing Ivan. His ridiculous brother, Darnell. Driving around the neighborhood in a stolen Mercedes. Carrying guns. Children, all of them."

"My grandmother used to call them *malditos.* The bad kids. She'd throw stones at them when they came near the house."

There was a long breath on the other side of the phone, and when she spoke again, Danny could hear she was having trouble holding it together.

"It's what I should have done. Throw stones. He's not a mean boy, Darius."

"No, he's not, Jelan. He's not a hard case."

He heard her break down then, a liquid rasp in her voice. "He threw in with stupid men, but he's just a boy. He can be sweet, he doesn't have that violence in him."

"Jelan, I'll look into this, okay?"

There was a long pause while she collected herself. When she finally spoke again, her voice was quiet, resigned. "Thank you, Danny."

"I'll come see you. I'll talk to some people I know who know Darius." He'd almost called him Soap again. "I'll come see you tomorrow, okay?"

"Yes, thank you. My mother is beside herself."

"I can imagine, Jelan. But I'm glad you called me." He stopped short. Where had that come from? He hadn't thought of Jelan in years before bringing her up to Soap the other night, and now there she was in his head and it made him feel strange. A little light-headed, aided and abetted by the wine and the lack of food and sleep. Well, at least she missed it. Whatever was in his voice.

"Thank you so much. You can't imagine what it's like for us to live with this worry."

Rogan finally came in, and Danny told him about the call. John squinted, shifting his eyes right and left while he thought. They went over everything again, Asa bringing Soap to Danny, the tip-off about the gun and Darnell and Trey and the Nortes. Danny was edgy, pissed off. This was supposed to be his victory lap for getting Green Lane off the street, but he had the feeling again he'd been caught in something.

"I didn't tell her I'd just seen him."

"No."

"This doesn't look good, John."

126

Rogan scowled, his heavy brows dropping until his eyes were slits. "I don't see it."

"It would have to be Trey and Darnell. Are they smart enough to have gotten to Soap that fast? Kept it this quiet?"

"When's the last time anyone saw him?"

"The sister says he didn't take his mother to church. Sunday morning. So, from Saturday night."

"When did you talk to him?"

Danny looked away. The waitress came, and Rogan ordered Jameson's and Danny got another wine. When she left, Rogan leaned in.

"Whatever happened to Soap, it was in process before you ever got involved. Either they knew he was going to the cops, or if they got to him the same night, they heard about it awful fast. Either way, not your fault, Danny."

"Yeah, maybe, but I never even thought about it. Never did one thing to make sure he'd be protected."

"First of all, we don't know what happened. He could be holed up somewhere. I mean, he came in and told you about his buddies, what they were up to. He should have at least suspected they'd be a little miffed. Fuck, he could be down the shore drinking Tanqueray while we worry about his scrawny ass."

Danny nodded, and they sat in silence while the waitress brought their drinks. They sat wedged into a corner with their backs to the wall, looked up every time someone walked in. Old instincts from their days on the street. Gunfighters.

Rogan looked at Danny. "Who set up the meeting? Asa?"

Danny nodded. "At Rodi's, that bar he hangs in, out on Ridge. What?"

"Nothing."

"Asa's given me good tips over the years. We go back."

"Yeah, I know you go back."

"What the fuck does that mean?"

"Nothing, Jesus." Rogan held up his hands. "You just gotta ask, Danny."

"Yeah, I know. I know. You don't have to tell me. I fucking ask."

"And?"

Danny moved his shoulders in his suit as if his clothes didn't fit right. "And I don't know, okay? I ask myself why he does what he does and I don't know. We were friends. His father took off and he hung around our house. He was always a schemer, but I don't hear his name around anything major. He's just, you know, in the neighborhood. Maybe gets a high off putting me onto these things."

Rogan sat and watched, holding his sweating glass in one pale fist. His face closed, his belly pressing the table. It was the pose Danny thought of as Irish Buddha.

Danny picked up his drink, put it down. He took off his glasses and rubbed his eyes. Looked at Rogan looking back at him. "Oh, you know? Don't fucking start with me."

Chris followed the Africans. There were two guys, a shorter guy, big across the shoulders with close-cropped hair who did all the talking, and a taller guy who didn't say much of anything but who had wild, long dreadlocks and a print shirt that made him

easy to pick out in crowds. Chris had followed guys Asa was doing business with before, mostly Mexican guys who hung around
Ninth Street in South Philly, but these guys moved all over the
city. He watched them talk to a bunch of tall, skinny guys on
Germantown Avenue, two of them with what Chris guessed
were Muslim robes. Then they drove down to University City
and ate at a restaurant with colorful paintings and posters for
Ethiopia on the walls. He walked by the door while they were
in there, thinking it would mostly be a black crowd, but it
looked like a lot of kids, probably from Penn, and the smell made
him wish he'd sat down and ordered something. The short guy
got into some kind of argument with the waitress, pointing to a
plate and maybe getting into how it wasn't like back home. The
girl just smiled and shrugged, looking over her shoulder at the
kitchen, and Chris felt bad for her, this know-it-all giving her shit
about the food.

The Africans had come to do business with the Dominicans,
the Nortes, but the Nortes were gone and they'd do business
with Asa now. Asa had gotten the number from Freddie and set
it all up, and in a few hours they'd be at some derelict hotel on
North Broad doing the deal. They might not like it, but what
were they going to do? They had dope and needed to unload it,
and the Dominicans were gone, gone, like they'd never existed.

Back in the car he followed the two Africans along Fairmount and hung back when they made a couple of quick turns
down Eighth and then east again on Green. The tall kid with the
wild hair went into a house and was gone for a while. Neighborhood boys began to congregate around the Navigator, trying to
get Chris talking and making motions for him to roll down the

window, so he pulled out and coasted down Green, circling back up Seventh and stopping at a corner in front of a mural of some guy with old-time clothes who must have lived in the neighborhood once. Probably a long time ago, 'cause the guy was white.

Chris watched the tall, skinny African guy talk to a guy wearing a desert camo jacket over unlaced Timberlands, his attention drifting to the weird-looking face painted on the wall. He tried to read the inscription out of the corner of his eye, but all he got was something about somebody called Hop-Frog. He thought the guy in the picture looked a little froggy and could see people calling him that. Chris had known a couple guys named Frog, one black and one white. He didn't know how the black guy got his name, but the white guy had got his by flipping out when somebody's boyfriend pulled a gun on him up in the Lucien Blackwell Homes and jumping right out of his sneakers trying to run away. Chris remembered the guy, Frog telling the story on himself, making them all laugh at some bar on Fairmount. Patting his chest to show his heart beating fast.

Up ahead the African kid walked with the guy from Seventh Street in the camo jacket, who looked both ways up and down the street while the kid counted off bills and put them in the older man's pink hand. The guy in the jacket made the money disappear and put his hand out again, and the African stood still for a moment before pulling more money out of his pocket. It made Chris think about money, about the scraps he got from Asa, and he got a strange, hollow feeling, knowing that whatever he was making was a tiny fraction of what other people were getting, of what Asa was getting. A fraction of what he'd been promised.

When Chris focused again, the guy in the jacket was opening the trunk of a beater Audi with holes eaten out of the rear bumper by rust. The two men stood for a minute by the open trunk; then the African kid nodded and handed the guy more money and they shook hands and everybody went away happy. Chris flipped open his phone and called Asa, who told him to come in and meet him. He started to say something else, but Chris wasn't listening. He was thinking about Frog, the kid, running hard down Brown Street in his socks, his ass clenched, his head low, waiting to get shot. Wondering, was it worth it? Wondering, how good-looking was the girl?

CHAPTER

9

Orlando stepped out of the hospital and into the sunlight and looked toward Ridge Avenue. He was wearing a green scrub shirt they'd given him up on the fifth floor under his black leather jacket. His shirt was gone, shredded and bloody, and they'd thrown it away when he'd come in the night before. At his neck the stitched furrow stung and itched, and he lifted the shirt from time to time as he walked, checking on the wad of bandages taped to his shoulder.

He stood at the curb for a minute and watched a big Lexus SUV idle at the curb, the driver lost behind smoked glass. As he walked south toward Ridge the car moved, keeping pace, and Orlando stopped after a few car lengths and turned, too tired and too sore to run. He could hear a song playing from inside the car, muffled, and it took him a minute to recognize the lyrics. Some group from long ago that his brother liked. *History shows again and again how nature points out the folly of men.* He remembered his brother singing it in his high, cracked voice, holding an empty Pepsi bottle to his pale lips like a microphone, making exaggerated faces, maybe like he thought a rock star would.

Orlando limped a few more steps, then sighed and turned as the smoked window opened, trying to prepare himself for whatever was behind it. He was tired, his shoulder ached, and he thought, *If this is it, okay. I'm no fucking good to another living soul anyway.* He watched the window go down, heard an electric motor whirring with its insect buzz. He almost closed his eyes, ready for the percussive slap of whatever bullet was coming his way, but at the end he just cocked his head and watched.

Asa and Angel were talking when Chris came up on them in a parking garage off South in Old Town. Chris could hear their voices and slowed as he went up the ramp, realizing they didn't know he was there and listening to the conversation echo off the cement blocks, the place cool and damp in the heat of the day. He dropped to one knee and listened, hearing his own name while he pretended to tie his shoe.

Angel was talking a lot, for Angel. ". . . not my kind of deal," he was saying. "You don't listen when I talk, do you? I tell what I do, and what I don't do, and I'm not after getting gummed up in some deal I don't know anything about."

"You know about it because I'm telling you about it." There was a silence, and Chris could picture Angel doing that stare, like you were too stupid to bother explaining things to, so Asa kept going. "I need you on this. This deal. This deal with the Africans is a lot of money. Think about it."

"What about the walthead with the muscles? He's the one you want for playing games."

"No, Chris isn't smart enough. He'll fuck it up without you watching."

"Right, so, why don't you watch him?"

There was a pause, and Chris heard a match struck. He heard Asa's voice, low, intense, but couldn't make everything out. He heard bits of it. The Irishman's flinty consonants, the rolling music of Asa's bullshit. His boss's voice going up hard over two syllables, punctuating each sentence. "Fuckup," Chris heard him say. "Fuckup."

The guy at the wheel of the Lexus said he was George Parkman Sr. and asked Orlando to get in the car. Orlando looked back at the hospital, shielding his eyes from the sun. Parkman shifted in the seat, but Orlando couldn't sort out whether it was embarrassment or impatience.

"Look, I just . . ." Parkman shrugged. "I didn't know Collins was crazy."

"Okay."

"Let me just, I don't know. Let me buy you lunch."

"Nah, we're cool."

Parkman opened the door and got out. He was tall, big across the shoulders. He put out a hand. "Just give me a couple minutes, okay?" After a minute he dropped the hand and looked down, stealing glimpses like a guilty dog. Orlando shook his head.

They went to Le Bus on Main Street in Manayunk, a place the older man had clearly been before. Orlando glanced at the menu and put it down, then turned his head to watch the street, keeping the guy in the corner of his eye. The guy put the menu down with a decisive slap, then watched the waitress as she moved around, snapping his head up to call her over, like *don't waste my fucking time.*

When she came over, the man pointed at Orlando and did the headshake thing again, as if he came from a planet where that was how they communicated their primary needs. Orlando shrugged and ordered tea, and the guy put in some kind of complicated salad order with dressing on the side. The guy kept looking around the room, as if for people he knew, and Orlando frankly watched him now, since the guy was looking everywhere but at him.

Finally the guy flicked his eyes over Orlando and then locked his hands behind the chair, pushing out his chest. The guy looked prosperous, with an expensive haircut and clear blue eyes and one of those watches that has a bunch of dials, but Orlando recognized the manner—guarded, surreptitious, impatient—as junkie, and wondered if he was an alcoholic or had some other jones that came out to play when he was alone.

"You know what happened." Orlando just stared, and the guy said, "To my son," after a beat, and Orlando dipped his head.

"I'm sorry."

"Well, yeah, thanks." Because what else was Orlando going to say? Parkman looked around the room, sheepish, like a kid caught stealing, and then he said, "You know, that guy, Collins? I didn't know he was crazy."

"Yeah, you said that."

"Well, I didn't. And I didn't send him to do, you know, *that*." Fast, like he was spitting, and his lips were twisted like the words were bitter in his mouth. Pointing vaguely at the hump of bandages on Orlando's shoulder.

"He said he'd look into it. I had no fucking idea he'd do . . ." He shrugged, waved a hand at Orlando sitting there in his mold-green OR scrub shirt. "He thought you knew something."

"I got that."

The waitress brought bread and the guy tore it with his hands. Took a long sip of red wine that left a dark mustache that the guy licked at.

"But, you know."

"What?"

"You know why we had to ask, right?"

And that was why they were here. Sorry my crazy fucker friend tried to punch your ticket, but, while you're bleeding, just what the fuck do you know, anyway? Orlando smiled, and the guy hung his head, doing the whipped dog look again. Orlando saw that for the money and the expensive haircut and the nice distressed-leather shoes, this guy was one button to press after another, and it was like recognizing a long-lost relative. Another member of the tribe.

Orlando said, "I told that crazy fuck, and I'll tell you, I don't know anything. I haven't seen Michael in like two years."

"But they were there, a block away. George Jr. and Michael."

Orlando shook his head. "I don't know anything about that, mister." He lifted his hands. "I'm sorry about what happened to your boy, but I got nothing for you." He dropped his hands to the table and pushed forward to stand up, but the guy put a hand on his, and the touch was like being burned, Parkman's pink hand hot as the top of a stove.

"Okay, wait."

Orlando sagged back into the chair. He said, "Look, the cops got somebody for this. It was on TV."

"Was it them? The papers said the one was, you know. Had an alibi. So did they really do it?"

Orlando shrugged. "I don't know. I told you. Look, this was my brother's kid got shot, you don't think I'd tell you if I knew? You don't think I'd tell my own brother?"

"Okay, all I'm saying is look at it, okay? The cops, they got a million things to do. I deal with the city all the time and it's just a bunch of bureaucrats. They get the wrong guys, they get the right guys, do they even give a shit?"

Orlando sat and looked across the table, and Parkman's eyes were suddenly rimmed with pink.

"All I'm saying is," but then the man shrugged and wiped at his eyes and sniffed. He lowered his head and fat tears dropped onto his slacks, darkening the khaki. Orlando waited, and then Parkman started talking, his head still down. "I was thinking, I don't know him. I don't know my own son. I want you to find out about him because I don't know anything about it. Was he on drugs? Was he just doing something stupid, because he was, I don't know, weird?" He lifted his head and looked hard at Orlando. Looked around him and said in a low voice, "You're a drug addict. Collins didn't lie about that."

"No, he didn't."

"You know these people. You know the people at that house and the people who shot at them. You can tell me if my son was buying drugs. Or using drugs. He hung out with all these weird kids, with makeup on and crap. I don't know. I tried to get him into sports, he wouldn't do it. You know what to look for and I don't know the first fucking thing about any of it."

Orlando shook his head, looked out at the street. He could smell rich food and it was making him queasy and he'd have to get moving soon. "Mister, I don't know what to do for you."

"I'll give you twenty thousand dollars." They looked at each other, and Parkman was looking defiant, his chin up, as if he'd been dared to do something stupid. He'd surprised himself, Orlando could see. It was plain on his face he hadn't meant to offer that much money. Then he shook his head, reconciling himself to what he'd promised.

"Twenty thousand dollars?"

"I need to know about my son. I need to know what happened."

"And if it's what it looks like? If the cops got it right and the kids were just standing there when those idiots from Green Lane rolled up?"

"But why there? Why were they standing there? Were they buying drugs? They were a long way from home in a shitty neighborhood." He touched Orlando again with his terrible burning hand.

Orlando pulled back his hand. "They were a long way from wherever the fuck you live, but they were ten blocks from where Michael grew up. And Roxborough isn't a shitty neighborhood. Yeah, there's dope there, but there's dope everywhere. You can score in this nice restaurant. Wherever you live, you can get high. I guarantee it. You think you got money, that makes you different? You live in a fucking dream world."

"Look, I'm sorry. I don't know about that. But this is a lot of money. For you. You can"—he lifted one shoulder—"I don't know. Do whatever you want with that much money."

"Kill myself, is what you mean."

"If that's what you want."

"I need some of it up front."

"No. I'm not stupid. Nothing now."

"How do I get my money, then?"

"You come to me. You tell me what you found out."

"Yeah?"

"If I believe you, you get paid. That's all. If you're lying, I'll know it."

"Look, you know, you hired a psycho, but there must be investigators or whatever, people you can get who aren't mental patients."

"What would they do? They'd come to you. Or people like you. They'd try to find people you already know, whose phone numbers you already know."

"What's your wife or whatever think of this plan? She on board with you hiring a junkie to get into your son's shit?"

"It's not up to her." The chin went up again, like a little kid holding his ground, but then the eyes shifted left and right, quick. "Anyway, she moved out. She's at her mother's."

The money was already working in Orlando's head, and something else, too. Something like the chance to do something for Michael. For his brother, Brendan. Or to show his brother something, maybe. He couldn't bring himself to buy it completely, to think it would be amends for the embarrassment he'd caused his brother, but it was something, maybe.

And did the money mean he was going to get high? That much money might be a way out, too. Rehab, or something. A place to go, to take Zoe, someplace down the shore or out in the country where he could get clean, get right. It was a possibility.

He looked at Parkman again, who was clearly exhausted. Staring into the middle distance. The guy might be a crazy, angry fuck, but he'd lost his kid and was desperate and alone, and Orlando knew that feeling. He let a long breath go.

"I'm going to need to get in your house."

"Why?"

"I need to see his bedroom. I need to talk to his friends."

Parkman's eyes widened—he hadn't thought this far—but he took a pen out of his pocket and scribbled on a napkin and pushed it across to Orlando. An address and a cell number. "Fine. Whatever you need."

"Gimme twenty dollars."

Parkman stared hard at him but pulled his wallet out and handed him two tens. "What's that for?"

Orlando stood up and tucked the bills in his pocket, knowing twenty dollars wasn't money to this guy. "That's my retainer." He pushed the chair in and stepped back.

"Where are you going?"

"To buy drugs. With my retainer."

.   .   .

Chris stood just inside the door at a strip joint on Second Street, waiting for his eyes to adjust to the dark at the entrance. The place smelled like perfume and cigarette smoke and beer, laced with the astringent smell of ammonia, as if somebody had been sloshing cleanser around every few hours. The music was loud and got louder when he moved down the narrow entry-way and into the main room, where the bouncer nodded at him and held out a hand. The guy made a face and said something Chris couldn't make out over the music, pointing discreetly at the bar lining the stage.

The ceiling was sprayed black, and the mirrored stage was set with blue Christmas lights that blinked out of sync with the music. There was a beat-down pool table and stains on the carpet you didn't want to look at too close. There were two dancers, a short blond girl hanging back and moving her hips slightly to the beat while shaking her head in disdain, and one with red hair at the edge of the stage with the look of a trapped animal. Gerry Dunn was standing in front of the red-haired girl, holding the thong away from her hip with two fingers and angling to look inside while his brother Frank howled with laughter and thumped his hands together in a fair imitation of a drunken seal. The bouncer raised his eyebrows at Chris and moved closer to shout in his ear.

"Help me out here, man? I can't have this shit in here." He was apologetic, with a little whine in his tone. Chris fronted him blow and dropped a lot of money in the place every night, which meant he was always welcome, even if his friends got out of hand once in a while and had to be walked politely out to the curb. He made a face, letting the bouncer know he was doing him a favor. Like it should be an honor Chris and his friends spent their money here when they could go anywhere.

The place was almost empty in the middle of the afternoon, a few guys clumped up at the other end of the bar at a safe distance from where the brothers were acting up. A couple of businessmen, another neighborhood guy, all of them studiously not watching the Dunn brothers as they manhandled the girls and poured drinks into themselves with the determination of men at work.

Once when they were young, Chris had come on his brother Shannon and Gerry Dunn with a dog cornered in one of the abandoned factories along Jasper Street. They had long metal poles they'd scavenged from the buildings and were banging them on the blackened concrete on either side of the animal, driving it between them so that eventually it was frozen, one quivering foot raised in the air as if in deliberation. It was a small dog with a tangled red coat, and it had a long black streak down its side. Probably something Gerry and Shannon did, marking it as theirs to mistreat.

Chris thought the look in its eyes was the look of the girl at the bar now. Like shame and fear and a basic confusion about the situation and her part in it, and seeing his two friends at the bar, their hands out as if containing the girl by some energy field they generated, Chris had some confusion himself. Not liking to see the girl victimized, not liking to have to step in and control his friends, but all of that mixed up with being on the high side of the display of power the scene represented. If the two businessmen at the other end of the bar had tried some shit like this they'd be out in the alley with their hands folded behind their backs, suffering a swift kick in the ass to tell them not to come back. But this was Gerry Dunn, and Gerry Dunn did what he wanted, and part of that was being in Chris Black's crew and fear was the lever under it all. Fear of what Chris Black might do, of what Gerry Dunn might be allowed to do, of all the money they spent and the dope they brought and the people who came around the club because Chris and his friends drank here, fear that all that money could be turned off like a hose.

He walked up behind Gerry Dunn and hit him hard on the shoulder, so that he turned fast, his hands up. Gerry smiled and hit him back, hard, screwing up his features like a little kid making a tough-guy face. The girl made her exit fast while the Dunns were distracted, and Chris called the bartender over and ordered more of the sweet, bright drinks they liked and threw money on the bar. He sat down with them and got into the flow of things. Another girl came out, this time with chalk white skin and black tattoos that were arcane symbols and letters like hieroglyphics written on her skin, and the music was Rob Zombie, "Pussy Liquor," music that droned and buzzed inside him, communicated less by his ears than through the soles of his boots.

This girl didn't care about Gerry Dunn; she was lost in her head, performing for somebody who wasn't in the room. The lights turned her pallid body red, then blue, then a brilliant white that was almost hard to look at. There was a wan smile on her face like she was listening to a joke; she hung just out of reach, untouchable, her eyelids hanging half over her eyes in a pantomime of drowsy lust so that the boys beat the wood of the bar and howled. She did "Fast Car," Wyclef Jean's version, and then "Fuck U Gon' Do Bout It" and "The Dope Show," and the way she was, the way she moved her hips twisted the meaning of the songs so that it was all about the boys watching and the thing they wanted from her that they couldn't have and anyway the wanting was better than the thing itself, even staring up at her, inches from it, aching, their pupils open so that Chris thought that to her they must look like a ring of reflective eyes, like animals circling her in the dark.

Danny sat up slowly, his neck stiff and a red pulse behind his eyes that made him sick. He was wearing only his suit pants and hadn't gotten under the covers. He looked left and thanked God that at least he was alone.

He remembered Rogan talking him into last call at the Shamrock, and he remembered shots of Jameson's. The good, eighteen-year-old stuff that went down like water. He remembered singing with John at the top of his lungs, banging on the bar. "Knockin' on Heaven's Door." "I Fought the Law."

He lurched to the bathroom and got sick, the pressure bulging his eyes as he emptied himself, then sat on the edge of the tub. He reached over and turned on the tap and drank from the faucet, lapping at the cold water, then rested his head on the cool white porcelain.

He forced himself up, dressed slowly, pausing after each item of clothing to pant like a dog, finally pulling on his tie and mak-

ing for the door at almost three o'clock. He drove north from
the river to Ridge and then followed it west until he came to
Jelan's street of low-rise apartments, parked, and counted doors
as he walked.

Jelan opened the door as he approached, and he was unpre-
pared for her, the fact of her, after conjuring her in his head the
way she was at Roxborough. She was no longer that agile child,
but she was still beautiful, and after he took in the lines at the
corners of her eyes, the worry etched in her face by her younger
brother, he had trouble keeping his mind on the task at hand.

"Danny," she said and pulled him into the narrow hallway of
the apartment. "Thank you." He saw that her mother was there,
a tall woman, a bright band in her hair. Proud in the way Jelan
was proud, her head erect, her eyes bright. He had to keep re-
minding himself to say Soap's right name. Darius. Soap was a
gangbanger, a would-be player. Darius was a wayward kid, basically good, loved by his sister, his mother, aunts from Kingston
and Saint Mary.

They told their story and as much as they knew of Darius's
life, though Danny could fill in more from his own experience.
He knew how this thing was in the air for kids with time and
not enough focus, and it was literally true that Soap—Darius—
was a good kid, and he had trouble banishing the thought from
his head as they talked that the kid was probably dead and
Danny should have seen it coming. There were countless kids
like Darius out there, and no one to care about them except their
families. Anxious mothers and absent fathers; that part of the
story as familiar as "once upon a time."

Jelan's apartment smelled like hair products, and her partner had a thick-waisted woman in a kitchen chair and was treating her head with some kind of brown foam. The two women, the one in the chair and the partner, a tiny woman with huge brown eyes and gold earrings like palm leaves, shook their heads and made affirmations of support while Jelan and her mother talked about Darius and his life. The lure of the street and his good-for-nothing friends. Danny made notes and tried not to look at Jelan too much and to remember why he was there.

She walked him to his car, wearing a purple smock and touching her head with the effort of making sure she had told him everything. He had to restrain the impulse to take her hand, but standing at the open door of the unmarked he touched her shoulder and said he'd find Darius, and she dipped her head.

"I told myself to think of him as lost when he took up with Darnell and Ivan. But I couldn't."

"I know. He's your brother." He thought of his own brother, Pete. Two years younger and a sniper in Iraq on his second tour. Sending Danny e-mails full of misspellings and impenetrable military jargon, digital photos of himself cradling a rifle and wearing blue wraparound shades. The memory triggering again in Danny's mind the constant shift of pride and fear, the disappointment that he hadn't gotten his brother to stay in school. Thinking more of Pete than Soap, he said, "How much can you protect them?"

She looked back up the street toward her apartment. "I always thought you were a good person, Danny. Even when we were kids."

It caught him off guard, and he nodded and shrugged to

keep himself from saying something stupid. About what he'd always thought of her. She smiled that knowing smile he hadn't seen since they were teenagers, and an electric current ran along his jaw.

"You liked me. Then."

He smiled, looked at his keys, his hands. When had he gotten this shy around women? Realized he hadn't been on a real date in almost a year, asked a woman out, gone to dinner. He met them in bars. Saw a nurse from the ER at Penn University Hospital a few times, but that was mostly swapping war stories in a bar near the university after work. Talking past each other. Hurried sex in her car, reaching under her whites to grab at her, both of them giddy from long shifts and lack of sleep. Filling a need, really, and it drifted down to nothing after a few weeks.

Now he let himself take Jelan's hand, slowly, letting something creep into it. Thought of different things to say, but then just nodded. When he stepped back and closed the door, she was looking at him intently, as if suddenly recognizing who he was.

Kathleen parked across from the hospital and walked through the cracked and canted lot, feeling the heat even as the sun began to lower in the sky. A group of neighborhood girls walked by her on their way to Ridge, dressed in shorts and sleeveless shirts, and it gave her a pang that Michael was missing these days, the start of summer. His older friends would be graduating in a few days, and Kathleen stopped to watch the girls go by, suddenly angry, wanting to go in and shake her son until he woke up, the way she'd done a thousand times, his long form stretched out, his pale legs exposed, the sheets wound around his torso. His face sweet in repose, mouth parted. When sleep was just rest, a few lost hours. Not a lost week, his face blank and empty and almost unrecognizable to her.

On the steps to the lobby she saw Jeannette Sullivan, watching the girls go by, her head tilted. She was wearing jeans and a top that looked too big, and she worked the tail of it in her hands. Kathleen stopped, and Jeannette turned and saw her and sat up straight as if caught at something. Kathleen noticed for the first time that Jeannette's eyes were gray tinged with blue and that there was an intensity in her, a self-possession that would have captured her son, who loved passion in other people, was drawn to it like fire.

"Jeannette. You're here early. How was school?"

The girl lifted one shoulder high. "I didn't go."

"Come on in and see Michael."

"No." She looked away up the street, her blond hair picked up in the wind. "See that girl, the one with the red shirt? She cheated on her boyfriend with a boy from Bala Cynwyd. I saw them down on Main Street. Just acting like, you know, whatever. And her boyfriend's sister saw them. So he dumped her." She looked down at her hands and tried to smooth the wrinkles she'd made in her shirt. "It's just so stupid, all these games. To make someone jealous or whatever. Just to mess with people. To make something happen, and you have no idea what you even want." Her voice skittered, broke.

Kathleen sat beside her on the hot concrete. She put her arm around Jeannette and the girl stopped moving and after a minute fat drops fell onto the backs of her long, freckled hands.

"We had a fight." Her voice was small, a whisper, and Kathleen had to lean her head in to hear over the sounds of the cars, the hot breeze. "Michael and me. Everyone is like patting me on the back because I visit Michael at the hospital and we're such a great couple and all of that. And no one even knows it was my fault." She pushed at her eyes with the back of one hand.

Kathleen waited. "Did you see Michael that night? Did you know what he was doing down there, Jeannette?"

"No. He told me Geo needed his help, but we were supposed to go to see that Jack Black movie. He wanted to tell me what they were going to do and I was just mad, okay? And I told him fine, whatever, all pissed. Go have fun with Geo. Like I care." Her shoulders were shaking and Kathleen put her hand on her head and her crying got worse, became little shrieking hiccups. "Please don't hate me. I didn't know what they were going to do. Buy drugs or whatever 'cause I made Michael upset."

"Geo is George Jr? They called him Geo?"

"Yeah, all of us did. Except Steve Chesna and those other retards, the ones who are always getting detention. They liked to mess with Geo."

"Geo. I didn't know that. Could those boys have had something to do with what happened?"

"Oh, no." Jeannette raised her head, horrified. "No, they were just dipshits who liked to make trouble because Geo was, you know." She shrugged. "He was different."

"Was George Jr. gay, Kathleen?"

"Geo? No. That's what Steve Chesna and his dipshitty friends thought. He was just, I don't know. He was just different. Smart. He read books that weren't assigned. He baked stuff for the bake sales and volunteered at a homeless shelter." Kathleen went into her purse and fished for a tissue and unthinkingly put it under Jeannette's nose. "He was seeing a girl. Marianne Kilbride. At least he was in the spring, then they, I don't know. They broke up or something."

"Did George use drugs?"

"I don't know. I don't think so. You can't always tell that about a person, can you? He just kind of went his own way."

They sat, and Jeannette leaned into Kathleen and she thought again about how it would have been to have a girl. After they'd had Michael she'd stayed home for a year and they'd struggled on Brendan's salary. Things got easier when she went back to work teaching ESL for the archdiocese, and they just never made the room in their lives for another baby. The time went by and the moment seemed to pass. She touched Jeannette's long hair and the girl's eyes filled with tears again.

"I just want to tell Michael I'm sorry. I just want him to wake up so I can tell him."

"Jeannette, listen to me. Whatever happened, I'm sure it had nothing to do with anything you did or said, okay?" Jeannette lifted her face again to look at Kathleen, who smiled at her, but Jeannette was looking over her shoulder, her head cocked, so Kathleen turned and saw one of the security guys in his blue blazer, holding the front door open and making a *come on* gesture with his arms. One of the ICU nurses was coming out the door, blinking in the sunlight, and the guard was pointing to where they sat on the steps. The woman turned to them, concerned, but when she saw Kathleen her face broke open into a smile, and Kathleen exhaled with a hard sigh, as if she'd been holding her breath for a week. He was awake.

CHAPTER

10

Angel Riordan sat in a bar on South Street. He hadn't noticed the name when he came in, but he ordered a beer and a shot and let his breathing ease, working his jaw and occasionally reaching into his coat to find the pistols he carried most of the time, touching the butt of each in turn. The gesture calmed him, the way working a rosary had comforted his aunt in Clonard in Belfast. She'd put him on a boat to New York when he was thirteen, thinking she'd make him safe from the violence that had taken his brothers and father.

He'd been taken in by his aunt's cousin in Philadelphia, Tom Devlin, who worked strong-arm for the roofers union. Tommy Devlin was tall and balding and silent, except when the rage took him and he'd grunt and chuff like some great animal about to put his horns into someone. Devlin put him to work burning nonunion rigs, and then beating the ones who didn't get the message, and then Angel was as lost as if he'd stayed home throwing rocks at British APCs in the Falls Road.

Now he sat and stared and realized a tall girl with a broad face and blond hair in braids was standing in front of him behind the bar. She was smiling, wearing a black T-shirt that read OVERWORKED AND UNDERFUCKED. She moved closer to him and extended her hands, slowly, toward his face. He sat up straight, holding himself still, and she put her hands on either side of his head and slowly took his sunglasses off. She put them down carefully on the bar by his elbow and nodded with her lips pursed, as if pleased at the effect.

"That's better. Whatcha doing there, Irish?"

He shifted in his chair, dropped his head, looked up and down the bar. Finally he said, "Trying to keep from putting a bullet in my boss."

"I hear that. Let's get a drink in you. That will help."

"It couldn't hurt, could it?"

She put a shot glass in front of him and got down a bottle. Jameson's, the twelve-year-old stuff, and he nodded thanks and pointed to her and she got herself a glass and ran the bottle across from one glass to the other without lifting it.

"Sure that's wasting good whiskey."

"I don't think we have to worry about them running out, do we?"

He nodded. "How'd you know I was Irish, just to look at me?"

"Please, I know the look. Like it's always about to rain. Like your mom just died and your dog got run over. Anyway I've been working in an Irish bar for six years, give me some credit, huh?"

He looked around him for the first time. It wasn't much, walls painted black or just gone black with grime. The little Irish flags, the Guinness signs. The copy of the declaration in the name of God and the dead generations.

"Fuck, I know," she said, as if he'd said something. "Like if it was so great back in Kerry, why did they come here to shovel shit in some slaughterhouse in Germantown, right?"

"Where are your people from?" He pushed the glass over to her and she refilled it. A big-shouldered guy in a green T-shirt came through a door in the back and jerked his thumb over his shoulder.

"Hannah, there's a bunch of shit that needs to go in the reefer."

She let her face go slack, rolled her eyes. "That's fucking Raul's job." She wound up and threw a wet bar towel down the length of the bar without looking.

"Then find fucking Raul. I have to go."

She shook her head, never taking her eyes from Angel, and mouthed, "What an asshole."

"Want me to shoot him?"

She smiled and her face changed, one eyebrow going up, the corner of her mouth lifted, and she was beautiful.

"Fuck," she said. "Definitely."

He stayed for two hours, drinking Jameson's and listening to her talk. She was Mennonite, from somewhere out near Lancaster. Her family had a place in Reading Terminal Market, a butcher shop. She'd been working there since she was nine and one day when she was sixteen she'd just taken what was in the till and walked out, figuring it was what she was owed for working the shop for seven years. All those years, she said, standing behind the counter watching the girls come through and looking at their clothes, their hair. The Mennonites kept plain, she said, with the little white prayer caps on the girls. Spoke some lost dialect of German to each other. One day she just scooped up all the money in the register and walked down to the Gallery and bought herself a pair of jeans and a leather jacket. She'd dumped her long dress, the cap, the long white pants she'd worn under her clothes, jammed it all in a trash can on Chestnut Street. Bought herself a thong and felt naked beneath the jeans. But liked the feeling, like for the first time a woman with something men would want. Slept on a hard bench in Thirtieth Street Station that night, listening to the trains.

She kept the boots, though, 'cause good boots are good boots, right? She kept calling him "Irish," and he didn't say her name until she walked away down the bar, and then he said it quietly to himself, like he was saving it somewhere for later. Hannah.

When it was dark, they gathered in a parking lot in East Falls. St. Bridget's was a black tower over their heads, and the trees over Midvale made Asa think of the jungle. Across the lot some kids stood around, smoking, tilting on skateboards, punching each other lightly on the arms and in the stomach. Asa smoked a cigarette and looked at his watch. Chris Black rolled up in his Navigator, got out, and lifted his hand in greeting as an old Firebird pulled in and idled. The Dunn brothers, both bulked up and traced with tattoos, got out and shook hands with Chris. Asa nodded, keeping his distance, and watched Chris open the back of his SUV. The brothers, Frank and Gerry, looked into the open hatch and smiled at each other. Gerry looked around, then reached in and lifted the barrel of one of the AKs and let it drop again, Asa thinking, *Yeah, brilliant. Like a little kid, having to touch the gun. And leave some more fingerprints, dumb-ass.*

Angel came last, pulling his car in next to Asa's Mercedes, muttering a few words to him the others couldn't hear, then gliding back out again. Chris watched him go, then went over to where Asa stood by the open door of his car.

"Is he coming?"

"It's our show. He's just going to be around, you know. In case we need help."

"We won't."

"Don't worry about what he's doing." He leaned in and looked up into Chris Black's eyes. "This thing, tonight? This is the deal. This is the thing. This guy, this African? This is us getting our hands on real money. This is on you. You want more, you want to be more, show me something tonight." His breath came harder, and the big kid wanted to step back because the man was working himself up. "There is nothing to worry about but getting this done right. Do you understand what's going on? Are you fucking paying attention? If you do this right, you get everything you ever wanted." Asa's eyes were big in his head, bright and wet. "We do this right, we get this going on regular, it's a pipeline. A pipeline that brings us money." Chris, a foot taller and fifty pounds heavier, shifted his feet and flinched when Asa lifted his hand to tap his muscled chest. "Get your head out of your ass and learn something."

.   .   .

Orlando sat on the edge of the bed in George Parkman's room and looked at Parkman Sr. until he let his head drop and walked away down the hall, every step ringing off the hardwood floors and old plaster walls. The house was a massive place on the edge of Chestnut Hill, fronted with dark stone and surrounded by walls, and to Orlando it had the look of an abandoned hill fort at the edge of some vanished empire. In his lap, Orlando had a picture of George Parkman Jr. standing with his mother next to a Christmas tree.

Orlando turned on the desk lamp, one of those high-tech-looking things with a long mechanical arm, and he grabbed it and swung its blue beam around the room, feeling like an alien intelligence scanning for clues, the light like one of those articulated metal limbs in *War of the Worlds*.

There were posters for bands like Rogue Wave and British Sea Power and Arcade Fire and for movies—*Paths of Glory, Classe Tous Risques, Rififi, Bob le Flambeur. Ronin* and *Le Samouraï. Ghost Dog* and *The Hidden Fortress. The Apartment* and *Irma la Douce*. Orlando couldn't get a fix on what the kid was going for, but he tried to let it all stick in his head. There was a big, slightly blurry photo of a bunch of people in aprons under a banner that read RIDGE AVENUE HOMELESS PROJECT. The kid was in the front row, beaming and waving a massive spoon next to a heavyset woman who held a ladle, her free arm crushing him to her colossal bosom. He knew the place, a shelter that catered to women and kids and was decorated with one of those staggering, operatic Philadelphia murals he loved: a family, homeless and desperate, and all around them angels with the fierce and resolute faces of children.

He folded himself into the chair at the desk, opening the drawers, each in turn, lifting out the pens and papers and running his hands up under the inside surfaces looking for whatever might be hidden or taped to the undersides. On the table there were photographs of kids trying not to smile too wide, trying not to laugh, looking at each other out of the corner of their eye. The kids were mostly the pale kids, some with white makeup and spiked hair, clunky boots, and leather straps around their arms. One picture, though, was of George Jr. standing between Michael and a pretty girl in a cheerleader's uniform, his arms around both of them. Someone had drawn arrows and names on the picture. A girl, from the handwriting. Michael and Jeannette and Geo, with an arrow pointing to George Jr. Next to that photo was another of a scowling bruiser with long hair holding up a diploma in one hand and jerking the Parkman kid's arm up with the other like George was a trophy fish. In the picture, Parkman Jr. looked helpless with laughter.

In one of the drawers he found another picture, a close-up of a fierce-looking girl with a fringe of hair above her eyes, the rest of her head shaved to red stubble, glowering with an intensity that Orlando recognized as love. She had her fist raised, and he had to turn the picture over to read what the girl had written on the back of her hand. A heart with GEO + M.K. in heavy black letters.

Orlando stretched, got up, and opened a folding door to the closet. He ran his hands across the coats, all with the antique look of thrift or army-navy stores, then put his face against the sleeves and breathed in. Smelled cigarette smoke on a couple of the jackets. There were hats piled on the top shelf. Berets, fedoras, a top hat. He lifted each, ran his hand through the linings. Got nothing from the clothes but the camphor tang of mothballs, the decaying smell of tobacco. In the pocket of an army officer's coat he found a keychain, a little replica of a green lightsaber. He stuck it in his pocket.

He left the closet open and went to an expensive-looking stereo system and flipped it on. Bright LEDs flashed, a motor whirred in the CD and Arcade Fire came out of the speakers, loud. "No Cars Go." He let it play, felt the antic bass in his legs and chest. There were hundreds of CDs in a rack by the stereo, and more piled on the floor. Another rack was full of DVDs. The French and Italian films from the posters. Books about the New Wave and postpunk music were stacked by the bed. Orlando recognized a textbook he'd read about media production when he'd been at Temple. Whatever allowance the kid was getting, this was where it was going. There was one of those ballistic cases for something big, a digital camera, maybe, though the bag was empty. A tripod and a stack of little digital tapes.

He pictured the kid, George, sitting at the desk with the music going. Geo, maybe, if you knew him. Getting himself amped up to do something. Listening to a song about a place you couldn't get to in a car or a plane. Maybe that meant a place you got to when you got high, but already Orlando didn't think that was this kid.

On top of the stereo was the yearbook from the school Michael and Parkman attended. Inside were pictures of boys and girls in uniforms and notes from dozens of kids, all addressed to Geo. Orlando found the page with the senior picture of the ferocious girl with the red hair, but there was nothing written there. He read the name, Marianne Kilbride. He flipped the pages, and stuck in the back of the book was a newsprint page torn from something, a newspaper or booklet. It had been folded up small, and Orlando carried it over to the desktop and unfolded it, smoothing it out to read it.

It was two columns of ads for escorts and massage parlors, each one with asterisks or arrows in a sloppy hand. Notes in the margin with question marks. "GFE? Roses? Greek?" The kid trying to parse the world of paid sex, maybe, but why? There were phone numbers next to the ads, or Web sites, and all but one had been crossed out. The ad was for a place called Continental, with a number that was probably a cell phone, a 267 exchange. Orlando folded it back up and stuck it in his pocket.

The song ended, and he became aware of Parkman Sr. standing in the doorway, rocking on his heels. He thought about what a guy like that saw when he looked in here. No trophies, no jackets with letters. No hockey sticks or baseballs. Nothing about conspicuous achievement or standing, just the trackless steppes where the brainy, awkward kids wandered, trying to make sense of the world. He realized, too, that nothing he could say was going to help Parkman understand his kid or comfort him. There was only one thing he could say, and he said it.

"He wasn't using."

George Parkman looked around the room as if seeing it for the first time. He hovered near the door, toed a copy of *Fear and Loathing in Las Vegas* open with his docksiders. "You're sure?"

"No, I'm not sure. But it doesn't look like it to me. I'll know more when I talk to his friends."

"Is that necessary?"

Orlando almost laughed. "Yeah, it's fucking necessary. Do you want to know what was up with your kid or not?"

When George Sr. walked away again, Orlando dumped a down-filled pillow onto the bed and stuffed a handful of CDs into its empty case. He opened a sweating window by the desk and looked out into the black night and dangled the pillowcase out the window.

After a minute he brought it back in and sat on the bed. He upended the pillowcase and fanned the CDs out where he could see them. The Chameleons. The Cure, an import the kid had probably spent thirty bucks on. Nick Cave. Morrissey.

He picked up the pillow and held it to his face, getting the faint tang of sweat mixed with the lingering artificial perfume of shampoo and deodorant. The smell would fade out in a few weeks or months, and there wouldn't be any sign the kid had ever been alive in this room. The parents would split up and sell this mausoleum, the mother would shut down or drink herself blind, the father would disappear to some other town, and in a couple of years even the people who loved the kid would forget his face. He began stuffing the CDs back into the pillow case.

Danny sat in the back of the RMP, listening to the radio traffic as they made their way down Grays Ferry Avenue. He remembered when it was new to him, being in the car, still trying to get comfortable with the belt on and the holster, all that bulk at his waist sitting at the wheel. He remembered when he was tuned in, cocking his ear to hear the calls, ready, no, *eager* to hear his unit number. He'd suppress a smile when he hit the lights, loved getting out of the car and having everyone look to him.

Everything about him changed the day he put the uniform on. The way he stood, his center of gravity different; the way he was with people and the way they looked at him. He had crossed some line and it changed who he was. He couldn't wait to get at it. Every day, then, and out at night half the night with the guys from the Third or the nurses from Jeff or Penn, telling each other stories, learning that ironic distance from the crap they saw, listening to the older guys and trying to impress each other with what they'd seen, what they'd been through.

In the lee of the expressway they passed oil tanks, or gas tanks; Danny didn't know. Pipes and smokestacks and small fires burning off the exhalations of the refineries. The car made a slow turn down Peltz, and the patrolman driving slowed and reversed at a dead end before looping back around to find Ellsworth. The place empty, dead acres of asphalt under showers of chemical light, ending in a little fringe of dusty trees at the edge of the Schuylkill.

Down Federal he could see kids running across the street, coming from shadow and disappearing again into the dark, silhouetted against the lights for a few moments as they ran flat out, and he wanted for a second to chase them down and see what it was about. Danny could see their teeth, white in the circle of light, their perfect faces split by wide smiles, throwing glances over their shoulders as they ran. Up to no good, a voice in his head told him. To be running like that, laughing like that.

No cares, no worries in that minute, running flat out. He tried to remember what it was like. He wasn't that old, should be able to remember when you could empty your head and just be moving fast and lost in the thing, but it was already gone. Now when he saw kids running, he could only think of chasing, or being chased.

The road stopped at empty train tracks. Danny could see the lights of the other cars, and out on the river the Marine Unit and the light going on that, too. He got out slowly, stretched, pulled out his notebook. Thanked the patrolmen who'd given him the ride down from the station. Took in the coroner's van, the news crews pulling up.

It took a long time to make the walk out across the tracks and onto the pier, and there were luminous clouds threaded with lightning piling up over the Grays Ferry neighborhoods. Cops and bystanders watched him come, a fat guy in red shorts and flip-flops holding a beer and sitting in the back of a white powerboat stained green at the waterline and named *Margin Call*. The wooden planks gave a little and made Danny feel unsteady, though he liked looking at the boats and the river at night. Thought he'd like to get a sailboat someday, just go from island to island somewhere where the water was that green color he'd seen in pictures. Was that real, that color from the pictures? Could he get away, take Jelan? He saw her sitting on the end of a dock in the white sunshine, wearing a bright bathing suit and one of those wraparound things women wore after they'd been swimming.

They were waiting for him at the end of the dock, arrayed motionless like it was one of those school nativity pageants and they were waiting for him to take his place. There were two cops from the Marine Unit wearing their ball caps; one of them he knew slightly. The guy from the medical examiner's office was down on his knees, but he was looking to Danny. The big lights on the patrol boat were on, and the body was stretched out on a black plastic bag that they'd use to carry it out.

The kid had been in the water almost a week, but he was dressed the same as when Danny'd last seen him. The Marine Unit guy was telling him the body had been caught in an anchor chain, given some weekend boater a hell of a scare, and Danny took in (small, quick glances) where the fish had been at the lips, the ragged hole in the side of the head. The horror-movie skin dissolving to slime. Danny let himself really look only at the shriveled, colorless hands.

Danny swore to himself, dropped to his haunches a few feet away from the body. The ME's guy asked if this was the one, and Danny said yes. This was the one. This was Soap, this was Darius. They'd talked for what, ten minutes? Twenty? Then Danny was off and running and Darius got a hole in his head and a trip in the river.

The guy from the ME's office was pointing at other holes in the body, through the shirt, and Danny was nodding, but he was thinking of what was next, of Jelan holding her mother in the ME's office, and that terrible refrigerated meat smell of the place, and the merciless green light, and the pictures they'd carry in their heads forever of this river-bottom skeleton that had been the boy they'd loved.

The clouds kept coming, drowning the stars. The wind picked

up, the air got cold, and it started to rain. One of the Marine Unit guys swore, and somebody else said, "Here it comes."

Angel stood in the dark, listening to the wind. He stood at the open trunk of his car on Fifteenth and looked up toward Broad along the shuttered fronts of businesses on Fairmount. After a minute standing motionless, he reached into his trunk and got out a short pry bar and a long black duffel bag. He closed the trunk and walked up Fairmount toward Ridge, his head down. On his right as he walked he came to a peeling wooden door in a steel frame and without looking around jammed the pry bar into the gap between the door and the jamb. He tensed his arms and popped the door open, quickly stepping inside and closing the door soundlessly behind him. It was almost black in the stairwell, the blood-colored light from the street coming through the crack along the door, and Angel pulled a small army surplus flashlight from his pocket and snapped it on.

He stood still again for a minute, listening to the cars go by, the sound of wind pouring like water through the cracks in the windows, the small animals burrowing in the walls. Finally he climbed the stairs, conscious of planting his feet on each step, as quiet as someone trying not to wake a sleeping neighbor. He paused at each landing and listened again, satisfying himself that the place was empty, and at the top of the stairs he got out the pry bar again and popped the lock on the metal fire door to the roof.

The roof was black asphalt, empty but for the abandoned nest of some homeless person; bunched and filthy blankets faded to the color of rain, plastic bags stuffed with cans and bottles. Angel walked to the front of the building overlooking Ridge and Broad and snapped off his light, looked across to the dun-colored brick front of the abandoned hotel. Heard music far away up Fairmount. A party or some unlicensed club. Men shouted and women laughed and the music was filtered by distance to a single drum pounding a steady tattoo. Angel liked the sound and nodded to it, moving low to where a massive signboard hid most of the top of the building. He made himself small in the shadow at the corner of the sign, then opened the duffel, exposing the long barrel of the AR-15 and the old Remington pump gun. He pulled a splintered crate to the low wall at the lip of the building and sat.

He waited, thought about having a drink, about getting high. About Hannah, picturing her with a small white cap pinned to her blond braids and standing at the edge of a field of green corn. Rows of tall stalks disappearing into the distance, contoured to low hills under a dark sky. The wind got louder, pushed at his hair and made him narrow his eyes. There was a light ticking noise from the asphalt around his feet, and it was raining.

Through a cracked window across the street he saw a small light flare for a second, go out. He smiled, thought about showing his own light to whoever was in there, the African or his man. *You're in there, and I'm out here, friend. Let's go.*

. . .

Orlando sat at Audie Murphy's kitchen table, watching Audie tie himself off while he hummed tunelessly, intent on the belt on his arm and watching his girlfriend Fran cooking the dope in a wide-mouthed spoon with a tiny holly leaf engraved in the handle. Orlando licked his lips, and Audie slid his eyes over him and Fran.

"Am I taking too long? I feel like I'm holding up the drive-through at fucking Burger King." Fran giggled and thumped Orlando's bicep and he laughed, too. Audie was short, compact, and muscular, a second-story man and a car thief, and Orlando watched him punch the needle into his arm through a tattoo of a smiling dragon he'd gotten in Korea, where he'd been in the army.

After Audie hit it, Fran took the needle and did herself, then pushed the spoon across the table with a languid, boneless arm and motioned extravagantly for Orlando to help himself. She reached behind her to turn up the CD player, Cities doing "Cons, Thieves, and Murderers." On the table, the CDs from George Parkman's room were splayed out like a collapsed deck of playing cards.

There was lightning outside the window and the room dropped into blackness for a minute and then the light buzzed and blinked back on and Audie made an approving moan. Fran nodded and got up unsteadily, her thin hips waving as if she were caught in a windstorm, and she made it to the wall and snapped off the lights and they listened to the wind and watched out the kitchen window as tongues of lightning dropped from the clouds.

They sat there a long time saying nothing, Fran letting her head drop to Audie's lap while he stroked her hair, Orlando watching the lightning and applauding in his head for every white, twitching filament of light that seemed to reach down for the tops of the houses. He missed Zoe, home sleeping so she could work a day shift. The song ended and there was nothing for a while. Orlando wanted that song the Irish guy had played, the one about the wolves. He let his head drop and he might have been out for a while.

Later Franny poured whiskey and Orlando picked up the conversation from earlier, when he'd come in with a bottle of wine from Chile that he knew Franny liked, and they'd all sat at the table and Audie had brought down a box of Franken Berry cereal and dumped out an ounce of Mexican heroin the color of wet beach sand.

"So you know those guys from Green Lane, do you think they did what the cops said?"

Audie shrugged and nodded and there was a long pause. Audie getting ready to talk, taking his time. "I don't know. Darnell is stupid, that's for sure. And him and Trey, they love guns." He lowered his head and talked out of the side of his mouth. "I did that, you know, business with them and all they wanted was guns, guns, guns. I think they were the only dope dealers I know who spent more on guns than dope."

"But?"

He made a face. "But I don't think Darnell has the heart for any move like that. Ivan is the brains, Ivan has the connections. Darnell's all show. All mouth. You know Pook, right? No? Pook's a good kid, smart. He runs with Green Lane cause Ivan and Darnell are his cousins, but he's smarter than those guys. Me and him were out at Camp Hill together. He went with me when I went down to do that thing at the shore. He said Darnell was letting it all go with Ivan locked up."

Orlando nodded, trying to think what that meant, if it meant something. How did you sort out why anybody did anything? If Darnell was too stupid and lazy to even do what the cops accused him of, hit the Dominican house, then who did? And why? And did it matter? He wanted to ask more questions but didn't know what to ask. He wondered if he could figure this out, wondered if trying to know, trying to help, would be just one more aimless junkie misadventure.

When he got up to leave, Audie walked him out, Franny sleeping openmouthed on the couch and clutching a stuffed dog. At the curb, Audie grabbed his arm.

"Listen, man. I know you want to know what happened to your brother's kid. I get it."

"Yeah, I'm just, you know." His heart sped up a little; he was trying to read Audie's face. Where was this going?

Audie leaned in and lowered his voice the way he did when he was talking about business. "I'm just saying, you know? Watch who the fuck you say shit to, okay? I know you, man, I know you don't mean to get into anything. But somebody else might not, right?"

Orlando nodded and turned away, but he began to see it differently. What he was doing, where it might go. Somebody out there had turned a gun on two kids. Whoever did it might be locked up now, and they might not. If they weren't locked up, then they were out on the street, and not far away. It wasn't six degrees out here, separating the guilty from the innocent, the living from the dead. It was two degrees. The city was a box between the rivers, a couple of miles up and down. Chances were he really did already know the shooters. And that they knew him.

CHAPTER
11

Michael was awake for a while, and then had to close his eyes again. Kathleen had been giving him ice chips when Brendan came in, still in his uniform, and kissed Michael's clammy forehead and let himself go, finally, the way she had. Balling the thin hospital blanket in his hands and shaking, butting his head against his son's shoulder and sobbing for a full minute before getting himself under control, lifting his head again and wiping at his eyes, touching Michael's face and asking questions that ran into each other. Are you okay, what were you doing, what do you remember, are you hungry, thirsty? Kathleen had started crying again to see Brendan so upset, and Michael caught Jeannette's eyes and lifted his eyebrows, embarrassed, like *What are you going to do? Parents.*

The doctors and nurses came in and out; there were a thousand calls to make to let everyone know he was okay. Jeannette texting and calling and tearing up each time in the retelling. Brendan and Kathleen feeling wrung out, the long week catching up with them, and both of them falling asleep themselves, Brendan in the ancient vinyl-covered chair, Kathleen tucked into herself on the other bed. She kept waking herself up, looking at Michael, checking compulsively, as she knew she'd keep doing after this was long over.

He was in and out, not saying much, asking about his car. Not understanding at first why he was at the hospital. Not remembering much of the day he'd been shot. He wanted to answer, to account for what had happened, but he'd get little bits and then shrug. At midnight he woke up again and started talking. He remembered getting out of the car at school. Seeing Jeannette between second and third period. There was more, though, he knew it. There was something else. Something about Geo and looking for a girl.

Gerry Dunn had been arrested more than anybody else Chris Black knew. He was huge through the shoulders and wore a black beater with a gray hoodie and steel-toed boots. He had the thickened brows of a street fighter and tattoos that were lines pointing to his scars and legends explaining their origins. There was a pink runnel on his neck and a tattoo of an arrow with the words 3/24/2004 PAT M. HIT ME WITH A POKER HE IS WITH THE OTHER PUNKS IN HELL. On his arm was a stellate patch of brown skin with the label 3/17/2003 FRANK CRASHED HIS LINCOLN INTO A DAIRY QUEEN I BURNED MY ARM HERE HE IS A DOUCHEBAG WHO CAN'T HOLD HIS LIQUOR. Gerry got into fights whenever he was drunk, and he went to bed drunk every night, but Chris knew he was afraid of nothing and could be relied on to stand his ground no matter what came at him. He had been shot, stabbed, and beaten, including the loss of two toes to an axe wielded by his own father, though Gerry would only tell that story when he was drunk and teary and Chris could never dope out whether it had been an accident or for cause.

In the car now, Gerry kept looking over at Chris until he said, "What?"

Gerry put his hands up. "I'm just saying. I see how the man treats you. You must get something off it, I guess."

"I'm making money."

"And you have to eat shit from that little freak, huh? It comes with the territory."

"Fuck you. You know how much more I made with Asa than all that time we did strong-arm in Fishtown?"

"Okay."

"Yeah, I'm making money, so back the fuck off. This, right here? This is me doing you a favor 'cause we go back. This is me throwing you a bone. What do you got to show for all that fucking around, getting in bar fights in every joint on Frankford Avenue? What do you got for two years in the can, Gerry?"

"Nothing. I got nothing. But nobody talks to me like I'm a fucking idiot. That's what I got to show." He looked out the window while he said this, like a little kid with a fuck-you attitude being dragged along on an errand by his mother. Chris shook his head.

Gerry talked to the closed window. "How much is in the briefcase?"

"Shut your mouth."

"I'm not saying shit."

"Shit is all you ever say. Why did I call you?"

"That's right, why did you call me? You called me 'cause you needed me here to pull your head out of your ass. You knew. You knew exactly what I'd say. You knew I'd take one look at this here setup and tell you exactly what you needed to hear. The man's got you turned around. Doing his errands, taking his risks. Where's the man going to be when we're down on Broad Street with the shine? Do you even fucking know? Asa Carmody. Who the fuck is he? Nobody knows him. You say that name on Frankford Avenue, you get blank looks. Gerry Dunn, they know. Chris Black, they know. Shannon Black, God rest, they knew."

"That's what he wants, shit-for-brains. The man is invisible. He moves without getting his fucking hands on things. Without his fingerprints showing up. He's got a guy who runs his corners in North Philly, and another guy who runs the corners in West Philly. Guys from Frankford and Christ-knows-what-all. He's got guys I've never even met. He's the puppet master."

Gerry finally turned back and leaned toward Chris. "Yeah? What's that make you, then?"

Before they went into the old hotel, he called Asa. Gerry shook his head, and Chris gave him hard eyes.

"You ready?"

"Yeah, Asa. I know what to do."

"What the fuck's wrong with you?"

"Nothing."

"This is easy. You walk in, show the man his money, he shows you what he brung, you walk out. This is a test. It goes good, we get the whole thing."

"I know. I'm not stupid."

"You're giving me a bad feeling. What's up with you?"

"Nothing. How many times I did these things for you, you don't have to tell me every fucking thing."

There was a long silence on the other end of the line. "I have to be there? You got your head right on this?"

"No, it's okay, you don't have to come down."

"Anything goes wrong, come right back out to the street where you are right now. Angel's got the street in front, you understand?"

"Angel."

"Yeah, he's covering the street. You come right back out here, let him take care of it. Why do I have the feeling you're not listening to me?"

"I'm listening. We got trouble, Angel is out here to cover us."

"That's right."

Angel took out his cell and laid it on the asphalt, fit an earpiece, and leaned back on the crate, the barrel of the AR-15 resting on the metal lip of the low wall at the edge of the roof. He watched a long, old car pull up in front of the hotel and idle there. The doors opened slowly, and there were a lot of pauses and discussion as Chris Black and Gerry Dunn got out on the curbside, then Frank pulled slowly away to circle back around at Brown Street. The glass in the hotel windows was frosted with dust and grime; the street was quiet except for sirens far away.

Chris had a briefcase under one arm, and he stood talking to Gerry for a minute in the rain, his shoulders hunched, before Gerry punched him lightly on the arm and turned to the front door, his hand on something at his waist. They squared themselves to the door like gunfighters and went in, Gerry stopping to slowly push the old barricade aside where it had been loosened to let them in.

Then the street was empty and quiet for a while. The music changed at the party up the street, the drumming faster, louder, and there was a cry, maybe the sound of one dancer encouraging another. Frank's car reappeared on Fairmount, coming back west toward Broad, and he edged it to the curb and idled, killing the lights. Angel took his hands off the rifle one at a time and wiped them on his shirt under his jacket. He waited, staring at the empty face of the old hotel.

He thought he heard a pop, then one of the windows to the right of the door blew out and suddenly the place was full of light. There were two more shots, then the steady clacking of an automatic weapon and bits of the door sprayed the street. Angel put the front sight of the AR-15 on the window where he'd seen the small flare of light and fired three shots, starring the glass.

The front door opened and Chris came out fast, his empty pistol locked open and two cases under his arm. Gerry Dunn was right behind him, limping, his left arm hanging and dark with blood. Angel walked the AR-15 over the windows, shooting blind, and when he'd emptied it he picked up the duffel and banged through the door to the stairs, jamming the long gun into the bag and pulling the pump gun out as he dropped fast down the dark stairway.

At the bottom of the stairs he dropped the duffel and ran across the street, where Frank Dunn had run from the corner and was unloading his AK into the front door of the hotel while Chris passed him going the other way. Chris jumped into the car and ground the gears, his face white and sweat standing out on his face and darkening his shirt. Angel ran up the three stairs to the door and kicked it off its hinges, putting the Remington out in front of him and stepping into the glare of two portable halogen work lights set up on the stairs across the lobby.

Angel crab-walked sideways from the door, keeping the shotgun up, but there was no more shooting. The walls were pink, mottled with brown water stains and decorated with old panel moldings and medallions outlined in black dust. The floor was littered with expended shells, long rifle casings standing in a bright puddle at the base of the stairs and squat, dull shells from the pistols Chris and Gerry carried scattered around near the front door. In the center of the floor was the African, sitting upright in a pink chair, his eyes open, still trying to talk. Angel crossed the room fast to stand flat against the wall.

He reloaded the shotgun and lifted it to shoot out the light standing on the floor near an elevator door. The single blast echoed in the long room and the light heeled back, spraying glass across the far wall and leaving one lone bulb working, throwing long shadows in the room so that each shell casing left a long tail on the floor and the shadow of the African in his chair suddenly loomed on the wall by the front door. Blood ran in vivid streaks down the short legs, as if the chair itself were bleeding out.

Angel dropped low and sighed, then pushed himself out in front of the stairs, raising the gun to his shoulder and firing three times fast, working the short pump as he took the stairs two at a time to reach the landing and kick over the blind the African's man had made. The stacked doors collapsed onto the sagging mattress; the walls were pocked with holes from the pistols and now from the buckshot in Angel's Remington. There were more bright shells from a rifle and Jesus, belts of ammunition for a machine gun. Long trails in the white dust leading back down the hall, but there was no blood, no body. The man with the rifle was gone.

Angel walked back out through the lobby to the street, where he found himself alone in the rain. He went around the corner to Fairmount, where Frank Dunn's old Firebird idled at the curb, leaking blue smoke. The streetlights were ringed with white circles of fine drops. Frank got out from behind the wheel, holding a hand up as Angel rounded the edge of the building.

"We got to go." His voice was strangled with the effort to keep himself in check. "Gerry's shot and we got to go." He stepped away from the open door to point back into the car and then there was a loud rattling that became a roar of rapid-fire pops from the blackness down the block toward Thirteenth. Bullets cracked and sang, punching through windshields and parked cars. Frank Dunn grabbed at his throat and went down, spraying the open car door with his blood. Angel dropped behind a rust-colored Escort a few feet away and listened to the wet coughing noises Frank made as blood poured out of him into the street. From inside the car Gerry screamed and thrashed, trying to get to his brother in the street while Chris struggled with him.

Angel shook his head and made a motion with his arm as if pushing something away. "That's what he wants," he said under his breath, but Gerry was winning the fight with Chris, pulling his own huge upper body out onto the street to clutch his brother's legs. There was more firing, the cracking noise of the rifle echoing down the street. The big 7.62 rounds Angel had seen in the hotel that didn't stop when they hit cars or walls. The bullets missed Gerry but punched through the open door, splintering the glass and knocking the door handle off to clink down onto the pavement a few feet from where Angel crouched. A thin rivulet of blood moved past his shoes carrying bits of paper, a cigarette filter with a band of gold.

Angel stood up and fired the shotgun down the black street, seeing only rows of parked cars lining the north side of Fairmount where the man must be hiding. He ducked back down again and more shots splattered against telephone poles and the old brick hotel. There was a pause and then two more shots, one kicking up water and chips of asphalt from the wet street and one smacking Gerry Dunn in the band of white belly exposed as he leaned out of the car to grab at his brother.

Angel shook his head and stood up then, running into the dark between the streetlights and firing down the line of cars. The heavy steel shot rang dissonant chords off the car bodies, bits of plastic and bright cubes of glass spraying the wet asphalt. He kept moving, pumping the gun fast and putting the sight on each car in turn, trying to drive the man out into the street.

There was a lull when he dropped behind a green Acura and re-loaded, and then he heard laughing and the man yelling something in French.

He popped up again, the gun at his cheek, in time to see him, the African's man, running flat out with a rifle in his hands, rounding the corner on Thirteenth Street. He was tall, wearing a red shirt, and had long plaits of dark hair and limped slightly as he ran, appearing under a streetlight at the corner and then moving fast out of the circle of light. The machine gun, a big FN with a handle on the top, Angel thinking, *Jesus, that must weigh a ton.* Angel ran the last yards to the intersection and turned, his breath coming hard. He could hear the sound of the tall man running, the rhythmic slap of his feet on the wet pavement fading into the tapping sounds of the rain.

After a minute he jogged back up toward Broad. People had begun to come out of their houses on Thirteenth, cell phones stuck in their ears. He got up to where Frank's car had been and found it gone. Frank and Gerry lay on the street, their blood running in long lines toward the gutter and diffusing in the rainwater. Frank's eyes were open, his face slack and white. Gerry lay on his stomach, one arm thrown across his brother's chest and his right ear to the blacktop as if listening for some noise from under the ground.

Brendan drove north along Memphis Street, counting houses from the little park, and there it was. The house he'd been raised in, the house his half brother had been born in. He tried to picture them all together, his crazy mother, his damaged brother, his straight-arrow father, trying to think of when they'd been a family and not getting a single image of them in the same room at the same time.

The place was empty, it looked like. Plywood covered one of the downstairs windows, the front speckled with holes as if some war had been fought out on the street. Some kind of notice stuck to the door. Foreclosure, seizure for back taxes, something.

Staying out of the house and away from her, that was the thing. He'd come home from school to find her holding court in a room full of rummies from some bar she'd been in all day. Having a party, she'd called it. Hanging with the mushmouthed drunks, talking about how she was going to Florida, about all the people who fucked with her who were going to get theirs.

The day he'd packed and left. His mother gone somewhere, his father moving fast, looking at his watch. Taking out the little plaid suitcase, grabbing his trophy from Little League and jamming it into a box from Beer City. His father trying to hurry Brendan along and it making him nervous, afraid of what she might do if she came back.

There wasn't anything of him in that house, he thought. His father had taken him to live in South Philly, and when he'd grown up and gone onto the force he'd moved into Manayunk with Kathleen. He couldn't even call up the inside of the place he'd grown up, even sitting on the street outside, but got little snapshots. He remembered hiding from his mother in an upstairs closet. He remembered spying on her in the kitchen while she drank and muttered to herself. He remembered taking his little brother down to the corner store to buy ice cream, and watching the kids who sat on the stoops and smoked, who watched the two of them go by and called to them, laughed and looked at each other, passing some signal, their mouths open with their terrible, feral smiles.

Had he made some promise to Orlando? To go back and get him, to rescue him from their mother, the strange, bitter drunk she'd become? He'd been a kid himself when his father had taken him away. He'd have taken his little brother with him if he could have. It wasn't his fault. What happened to Orlando. Where he ended up, what became of him. Where he landed when he fell.

Angel stood in Hannah's small living room in the middle of the night. His shirt was off and he'd pulled his jeans over his skinny hips. He looked back in through the open bedroom door to where she slept, her yellow hair splayed out over the pillow. She screwed up her features and muttered something in German. Her half of an argument playing out in her dreams, he figured. A mother or father and some argument she could never win, no matter how she laid it out in her head every night.

When he first came over he used to write postcards to his mother, long dead by then. He'd been a strange and a lonely kid, and he'd swiped a handful of postcards from a store down on Market near the river for no reason other than the owner's back was turned and there they were. At night he'd lie on the floor by the oblong of light coming under the door to his room, forming each letter with painful slowness. He'd start each one

Dear Ma, and he'd write a line or two about school, as if he were still going, or how kind the Devlins were to him, though he was terrified of them both and would stay away for days at a time. He'd leave the cards at St. Peter's in Fishtown, stuck between some votive candles in their red glass holders.

One winter night when he was seventeen Tommy Devlin had driven him up to Frankford and pointed out a garage where a roofing rig stood half out of the bay, the thing black with tar, and handed him a rolled-up newspaper and a heavy lighter. He'd wedged the paper under the tank and lit it and the thing went up, burning with a stingy blue flame and black, stinking smoke. Angel had watched it go up from the street, his thin raincoat gathered around him like a cape, and was standing there still when a guy came out and went for the hose. The guy was big across the shoulders, with curly black hair. He was wearing a purple robe flapping open to show thermal underwear and ripped work pants, and his feet were stuck in unlaced boots with lolling yellow tongues. The tap was frozen solid and the guy swore and kicked at it and one of the boots came off.

He finally took in Angel standing there, shaking in the cold. The guy screamed something at him and grabbed him by the arm, going up and down on the one boot. Angel dropped to his knees, pulling the guy off balance so that he flapped his free hand in the air and swore. Angel grabbed a piece of cinder block that had been used as a chuck for the rig tires and brought it hard up into the man's temple and the guy went down, blood springing from his head like a tap opened in the street. The man moaned as the rig slowly drifted into the road, burning tar dripping behind as it rolled. Tom Devlin honked then, one long blast from the horn, and Angel dropped the block in the street and walked away without looking back.

He went home that spring, back to wander Belfast like a ghost. His aunt's house had been torn down to make way for a market and his friends were all scattered. He saw two little kids in Clonard in the shadow of the ragged wall they called the peace line, playing with a junked bike turned over, spinning the wheels. He asked where everybody was and they'd said they'd buggered off, and laughed a secret laugh to each other and told him he should bugger off, too.

He got a tattoo in Wellington Place, a wolf biting a sword and the words NEITHER COLLAR NOR CROWN. He had a picture he'd given to the girl at the shop, his father at eighteen sitting on a parked car, the same beetle brows, the same full lips, wearing a white shirt with one sleeve rolled up and the tattoo fresh and bloody on his arm. He'd pointed it out to the girl and apologized for the small size of the picture, but she'd said it was a design she'd seen before on some of the old-timers around the Falls and Shankill and she'd sketched it for him in fast strokes on thin white paper.

He'd gotten it in the same place as his father, his lower right bicep, and standing in Hannah's narrow living room he held it up to a small mirror on the wall near the front window. It was black in the weak yellow light from the street. On the left arm was a design he'd gone back and gotten the next day, before leaving again for Philadelphia. A cross with a flaming heart wrapped in razor wire. Below that were the words BY KNIFE, BY GUN and twelve tick marks in small neat groups. The last small mark was still fresh, surrounded by a penumbra of red.

. . .

Orlando got off the bus on Lancaster Avenue, pulling at a suit jacket Zoe had picked out for him from the Goodwill on Front Street. It was too big, but it made him look like he had shoulders, and he ducked to catch himself in the sideview mirror as the bus pulled away, turning one way and then the other, admiring the effect. Zoe followed and stood by him, pursing her lips. She was dressed in a white blouse and a dark skirt and had makeup on and pale lipstick that softened her features. He felt something, a flush of heat in his chest that he knew was guilt at seeing her looking like a young girl again. Which she was, or had been, before she'd met him.

She turned to him, opening a small makeup case, and rubbed her finger on a pad and then smoothed a pale line onto his brow to cover the bruises there. He caught her hand and kissed her fingers, and she smiled and shook her head. They walked up a long drive from the street, past a wrought-iron fence and wide fields of grass that were a wet, hypnotic green. Kids stood in clumps and couples, sweaters tied at their waists, book bags swinging. Ahead were redbrick buildings and old trees hanging over slate walks.

Orlando got quiet, so Zoe tapped the arm of a boy wearing a blazer and tie and asked him some questions. He pointed to where some kids stood around a girl with bright red hair sitting on the steps to one of the buildings. Her hair was growing out, but Orlando recognized her from the picture in George Jr.'s room. Marianne Kilbride. She wore a white shirt and a tie, red sneakers that set off her hair. When she looked up to talk to another girl, Orlando could see thick mascara around her pale green eyes.

"Marianne?"

She looked up, her eyes guarded, and lifted her book bag into her lap as if trying to hide behind it. She looked from Orlando to Zoe, took in his scuffed boots and her cheap bag, and dropped her gaze to her own hands plucking at the strap of her bag.

"Are you reporters?" She lifted the bag higher on her lap and looked around her as if for help.

"No." Orlando took in the jagged black lines she'd inked on her forearms when her sleeves rode up.

"There have been a bunch of fucking reporters. They ask you all these questions and they don't even listen to goddamn answers and then they put all this shit in the paper that you never said." She looked at him fiercely, suddenly the girl in the picture come to life.

"I'm Michael Donovan's uncle." He told her his name and put out his hand, and she shook it.

"You're the one, then? I heard they were on their way to see you or something? Did you see them? That night?" She lifted her small hands, looking from him to Zoe.

"No, Marianne." He kept his voice low, conscious that other people were watching them talk. He saw a kid with a fauxhawk of moussed hair walk fast toward a parking lot at the side of the building.

Marianne Kilbride dropped her head. "Like it matters now. What happened to Geo. Like anybody can do anything."

Zoe sat on the bottom step and tried to catch her eye. "We're trying to figure out what happened, Marianne."

"I heard Michael was awake or whatever. What did he say?"

Orlando knelt down next to Zoe. "He's still in pretty rough shape. He doesn't remember much yet. He might not ever get it all back." Somewhere a bell rang, and kids began to drift into the buildings. "Marianne, the cops think Geo was going to score in that house. Do you think he was getting high?"

She looked up and her eyes went wide, and Orlando became conscious of a shadow falling across his shoulder as a big hand grabbed his sleeve and jerked him to his feet. It took Orlando a minute to place the face—the big kid from the picture, holding George Jr.'s arm up and wearing a cap and gown. Now the kid had Orlando bent backward over the iron railing of the fence and was pushing him hard, squeezing the breath out of his lungs.

The kid's hair was shorter than in the picture and he had on a blue button-down shirt with the name KEN over the breast pocket. His eyes were huge and black and his breath hissed in his nose, which Orlando could see had been broken and reset. A brawler, Orlando thought. He tried to get a purchase on the kid's enormous hand as it bore down on his chest, but he couldn't draw a breath and was starting to get panicked. He could feel the stitches at his shoulder cutting through his skin.

"Ken!" Marianne Kilbride snapped her fingers at him, like trying to wake a sleeper. Orlando looked over at her and saw her face change, a little thrill of fear in her eyes. There was a bright flash over the kid's shoulder and Zoe laid her straight razor against his throat. She had to reach up, tweaking his Adam's apple with the blunt edge of the blade.

"Calm down, go-tard. Ease the fuck up."

"Jesus, Ken, will you settle down?" Marianne Kilbride moved

closer and put her small hand on the kid's huge bicep, and he seemed to register her for the first time and let up on Orlando's chest and blink as if coming awake. More slowly, Marianne put her hand under Zoe's and lifted it away from Ken's neck. There was a pause, and Orlando rubbed at his chest and flexed his back, feeling a knot where it had been bent back over the railing. Ken touched his neck and looked at his fingers.

"Jesus, everybody's so touchy." The little red-haired girl shook her head, looking at each of them in turn. She pointed at the big kid. "Ken, man. What the fuck?"

He threw up his hands. "I was up the street at the Dunkin' Donuts and Ryan called me and told me they were here. Didn't you just say you wished I was there when the reporters came around? Didn't you just say that like yesterday?"

"Man, I didn't mean so you could break somebody's back. And they're not even fucking reporters. Next time, ask a question before you start playing Twister with people you don't even know who they are." She pointed at the kid with the moussed hair, hanging back at the edge of some bushes. "And you, Ryan. Keep your fucking nose out of my business. I look like somebody who needs help from you? Yeah, you better run."

The kid disappeared around the side of a building, and Marianne reached over and took the straight razor from Zoe's hands. She opened it, held it up to look down its shank. "You got that right out. I wish I'd been there with one of these when they fucked with Geo. I'd have cut their heads off." She gripped the thing tight, her knuckles going white beneath her freckled skin, and Zoe took it off her, gently, and put it back in her purse.

The young girl deflated somehow, got smaller, and her eyes

went dull. Her head sank between her shoulders. "I'd have fucked them up. No question," she said, but there was no force in it and she sat back down and dropped her head to stare at her shoes. "They wouldn't have dared."

Ken looked from Marianne to Zoe and then Orlando, and he raised his eyebrows and pointed to Orlando's chest. He looked down and caught the sight of blood titrating into the weave of his shirt.

Zoe swore and dug some tissues out her purse, but Orlando just shrugged. Ken looked embarrassed, lowering his eyes like a giant, chastened dog. Marianne sighed and stood up, swatting his solid shoulder with one small hand.

"Jesus, Ken. You have to excuse my cousin. He's supposed to be taking medication for whacking the shit out of everyone who pisses him off."

"Christ, man, I'm sorry. I just get, you know. Everybody's been over here fucking with us and I just get, like, fuck it. You know?"

"It's okay, man, no harm done. Stitches giving out."

Zoe unbuttoned his shirt and stuck the wad of Kleenex over the spreading red slick of blood.

Marianne said, "Yuck. Man, sorry my cousin broke your boyfriend." Ken walked away and stood by himself, looking up at the high windows of the buildings around them.

Marianne looked up at Zoe and Orlando as he buttoned his shirt up. "He's all fucked up about Geo. He almost didn't graduate. They were going to kick him out. Geo tutored him and got him straightened out." She smiled. "Geo turned him on to Bukowski. Ken didn't know, you know, anything about poetry, and then to find out there were actual poems about drinking and fucking? You see what he's like. I used to find him in the day-room, moving his finger along, under the words. *Love Is a Dog from Hell*. Sounding it out, you know, moving his lips? Ken read 'Girls Coming Home' out loud. At an assembly. I thought the nuns were going to shit." She was flipping back and forth, Orlando could see. Smiling with her eyes full of tears. He knew how that was, when something was so big you couldn't hold it in your head.

CHAPTER

12

Danny walked along Fairmount Street in the sunshine. Evidence techs moved up the street ahead of him, dropping little cones where expended shells lay on the drying asphalt, catching the rays of light slanting in from the east. There were pieces of glittering plastic and glass littering the street where they'd been shot off of parked cars. Two uniforms stood talking to a tall homicide dick, Frank Keduc, who was making notes while one of the cops pointed away toward Broad Street. It was starting to get hot, and mist was burning off the empty lot behind the old hotel.

Danny had gotten the call around nine that morning. Homicide and the evidence techs had already been on the scene for hours, talking to people from the houses on Thirteenth, tracing the long trajectories of automatic rifle fire. As he walked, he passed a drying pond of red ringed with yellow. There was a long black tail of powdery rubber running around the mark, and Danny figured it for a car that had pulled out fast from the curb, veering a little to miss whoever was lying in the red puddle. He could see shotgun shells lined up along the curb where they had rolled. One stood up on its brass end on the trunk of an Acura with a shattered windshield.

Danny shook Frank Keduc's hand and turned back up the street. "Who won?"

"Who knows? It's Alien versus Predator. Did you see the size of these shell casings?" He flipped back through his book. "Looks like it started back up at Broad, inside the building, and they decided to bring it out here onto the street. You know, you spend all that money buying automatic weapons, you want to see if they work."

Danny shook his head. "Wild West."

Keduc used his pen to draw lines in the air, pointing up toward Broad and down Fairmount to where they stood. "Shotgun shells from a twelve-gauge, I'm guessing that's the home team. Which means it was the visitors who brought the machine gun." He pointed to a pile of brass, long casings that had rolled into bright lines in the gutter.

"Jesus."

"Yeah. We've got three folks on their way to the morgue. Amazing nobody else was hit, when you think about it. Talk about dumb luck. The people on Thirteenth Street started calling 911 when the shots from the twelve-gauge started breaking windows."

"Who got killed?"

Keduc looked at his notes again, tapping the page with his pen. "One's a Somali national, a new flag for my map, and two guys who look local to me." He handed Danny a digital camera, pushing a button with his thumb to bring up pictures on the display. Danny had to turn out of the sun to get an angle on the picture. Two dead men in the street, their features washed white by the flash. Keduc clicked the button and the men got closer and the red around their heads got more vivid. The one facing up had half-closed eyes and his throat was open in a ragged line as if dogs had been at it. Danny didn't recognize him. The next pictures were taken from the side, and Danny could see the profile of the second man. His eyes were closed, his features distorted as if in pain. Keduc made a face. "Right through the lower abdomen. That must have hurt."

"I know this one." Danny took the camera and turned it on its side, bringing the face on the display upright. "Yeah, this is— What the fuck is his name?"

"Going by the tats, the clothes, the chains, I'm betting they're in the system."

Danny had just seen this guy, he was sure. He could see him moving, hunching his big shoulders, but it was like seeing a cutout against a black background. He couldn't place him. He closed his eyes, tapped his head. It would come to him.

Ken walked with Zoe and Orlando back to the gate. As they walked, Orlando looked back at the stone steps where Marianne sat, lost in her own thoughts, her splayed feet and the bright red sneakers making her look young again for a few moments. He could see the kid, Ryan, with the ridiculous hair, watching them and keeping pace as they walked out, hanging back in the trees and trying not to be seen.

Orlando didn't know what to ask, so he said, "What was he like? Geo."

Ken shrugged, lifted one hand. "He was a good kid. Smart."

"Did he, you know, use? Get high?"

"Nah." Ken shook his head fast. "He wasn't the type." *Not,* Orlando could see in his eyes, *not like you clearly are.* "A lot of the kids here, they're rich, their parents don't give a shit, don't know where they are or the kind of shit they get up to. So the kids get high, fuck around." He looked up, thinking how to say it. "I mean, Geo's dad is a total asshole, but somehow it didn't rub off on the kid." He stopped and looked at them. "I mean, how fucked up is this?" He looked left and right, making sure they were alone, then dropped his voice and leaned in toward Orlando. "He thought his own kid was gay. And that guy? To that guy, his kid being a fag was like the fucking sun blowing up. No, that ain't even it. People just *thinking* his kid might be a fag, that's all it took."

"Did he say something, Geo? Something about the father?" Orlando pictured the man, hovering in the doorway while he sat at the Parkman kid's desk. His pinched, disgusted look.

"Nah, Geo never said anything. But something happened. There was a picture in the school newspaper. Geo was in this band, with some of the kids here? Anyway they took a picture of all of them dressed up, I don't know, and Geo had on like . . ." He made a circle around his eyes. "Eyeliner. Don't ask me. You had to know the kid. Nobody thought twice about it."

"Except the father."

"Fuck, yeah. He hit the roof. Marianne said the father went fucking nuts. Called the school, threatened to yank Geo. That kid, Ryan, the one hiding over in the trees thinks we can't see him? He works in the office, it's his co-op, the little bullshit job the students get here. He's got a crush on my cousin, in case you haven't figured that out. Anyway, he told her about the father calling, all the bullshit."

"Geo was embarrassed."

Ken lifted a shoulder. "He never talked about it." He lifted his meaty hands and ticked off his fingers. "But I do know one, he disappeared for like three days, and two, when he finally comes back to school he breaks up with Marianne. Like the same fucking day he comes back." He dropped his hands and started walking again, and they walked along after. "After that, he's not the same kid."

"When was this? How long ago?"

"A month? Two? I don't know. We figured the old man told the kid he was yanking him out at the end of the semester. People were saying it, anyway. That's the usual thing around here. The kid fucks up one too many times, the parents take the kid out of day school here and ship him off to some boarding school in Jersey or Connecticut or some fucking place."

"So the last two months, he knows he's not coming back." Thinking, maybe the old Geo wouldn't use drugs, but the new one? How much bad news would it take for a seventeen-year-old kid to get fucked up enough to do something stupid? A sensitive kid who knew his own father couldn't stand the sight of him?

Zoe looked at Orlando, both of them knowing how quick it could go wrong, how strong the current was that carried you away, and if you wanted it, courted it, it didn't take much time at all. You didn't have to be a stone junkie to end up on the wrong set of steps with a couple of bucks in your hand. Smart kids, kids who were unhappy or curious or reckless or just lost. Zoe kept his gaze, both of them thinking about which of those things had been true about them.

At the gate they shook hands and Ken apologized again. Orlando told him he understood and to forget it. They turned back to face the school across the wide lawn.

"You know, Marianne's here on financial aid, right? She's smart, she'll do good. My old man owns a Dodge dealership. He dumped me here so he wouldn't have to look at me, I think. Marianne's his niece, he never lifted a fucking finger to help her or her mom. When I got the diploma he acted surprised. Almost disappointed, like it didn't compute. 'Cause I was such a fuckup." Ken looked at them. "Parents, right? I can't, you know, I can't figure it all out." He wiped a big hand across his eyes. "That stupid kid, Geo. My cousin Marianne told you what he did for me, right? We should've done more, you know? I should've. Looked out for him. Found out what was going on with the kid and been there."

Chris Black sat in his car on Delancey in Society Hill watching his cell phone. He was wired, gamey, had barely been out of Frank's car since he had driven away from Fairmount Avenue the night before and left Frank and Gerry to die in the rain. The phone buzzed and jumped on the seat beside him, and he knew it was Asa calling for the tenth time. He kept himself from looking at the two briefcases on the backseat where he had thrown them. One full of money and the other full of drugs.

He was going to have to make a decision, and soon. He'd driven around for hours after Fairmount, first barreling west in a panic till he hit the park, then dropping south to pick up the Vine Street Expressway and moving fast back across town to cross the Ben Franklin and only feeling safer as he moved deeper into Jersey. The first time the phone rang he was in Marlton, sitting in the parking lot of Olga's, the big diner at the circle. Watching teenagers and cops come and go. He'd picked up the cell and looked at it, working the different lies he'd have to tell in his head and afraid they'd sound tinny and unconvincing coming out of his mouth. Asa would want to know why the African was dead, and where Chris was with the heavy briefcase full of money and the even heavier briefcase full of heroin. He'd thrown the phone down and pulled out of the lot, heading east down 70 away from the lights, wanting to find some dark and deserted place in the woods where he'd feel safe.

He wasn't running away with the money and dope. Not exactly. He just wanted to think, wished there was someone he trusted to talk to about this. He'd thought he'd trusted Gerry Dunn, but it was Gerry who nagged at him until he pulled his pistol in the hotel lobby. Feeling that dislocated feeling of things going wrong, of making the wrong move, feeling sweaty and out of control, the gun shaking in his hand. It was hot and close in the old hotel. It stank like mold and there was an inch of dust on everything and the trails of small footprints in the dirt on the rotted old flooring. The African had been sitting in the pink chair looking pissed, starting to say something when Gerry just backhanded him and lunged for the case. The African was talking fast but Chris couldn't understand, slowly getting that it wasn't English. It was something else, some other language the guy was speaking, but it was clear he was telling them to fuck off, lifting the case into his lap with a shake of his head as if denying a little kid the thing he wanted, and Gerry had pulled the big silver .45 from under his jersey and shot the African in the chest. The guy drew up, pulling on the case, and the next shot went through it, expelling a little huff of white powder.

Gerry said, "See?" and picked up the case, one of those expensive-looking black cases with ridges. The African opened his mouth again, but no sounds came out and Chris could see blood on his teeth. A little trail of powder leaked from the hole in the case as Gerry lifted it, and he smiled and stuck a finger in the hole.

Then there was a soft crackling sound, an electrical circuit being made, and the lobby filled with a harsh blue light and when he'd thrown his arm up to shade his eyes the automatic rifle opened up on them from the stairs. Christ, it was loud, louder than Gerry's cheap pistol going off right next to him, a series of echoing pops that he felt in his chest as much as heard. The first one breaking Gerry's arm so that he howled and dropped the case, bent over to run for the door as if in a storm, and Chris

right after. Not even realizing until he hit the cooler air of the
street that he had picked up the second case before he'd run.
Somehow, without even knowing he'd done it, he'd stuffed his
gun in his belt and grabbed the drugs and gotten out of there.
Sweat streaming out of his hair. Gerry yelling for his brother
and cradling his bloody arm while bullets knocked pieces of the
old hotel into the street around them.

Later, driving around Jersey in the middle of the night,
pieces of it would come back, terrible fragments, like the sound
of a rifle bullet punching through Gerry's stomach and the sew-
ery smell of his opened gut when the blood poured out of him.
Did he see that? He had an image of Gerry's eyes as he died, but
he knew he'd been pushing his friend's heavy body out into the
rain in a panic.

Chris smoked a joint in the parking lot of a diner in Vincen-
town and fell asleep for an hour, then drove back into Philly
and cruised Fishtown and Port Richmond all night, unable to
go home or call anyone he knew. He got coffee at the Wawa on
Richmond Street around dawn, having to slide out the passenger side of the car because of the ruined door on the driver's side
with the hardware shot off. He drifted south to Society Hill
and parked on Delancey.

The road on Delancey was like brick—there was a name for
the brick, something old-fashioned, but he couldn't think of it.
There were trees in planters and expensive-looking houses with
brick fronts and black shutters like in olden times. He felt like
he was a million miles from what he knew, though he was about
a mile from where he'd grown up. The phone began to buzz

again, and he rubbed his eyes and picked it up. It was warm, and he felt it move in his hands like something alive. He had to start dealing with the situation. He could tell Asa he'd hidden, dropped out of sight until he knew what was going on. He could say Gerry'd gone crazy or that the African had made a grab for the cash. Whatever he was going to say, he had to say it now. There was a line and he'd be crossing it soon. Whatever he intended, he'd have to face up to it and either get back in touch with Asa or admit to himself he was stealing the money and the drugs.

He hadn't even opened the cases. Usually Asa told him what to do and where to go, Gerry was right about that, but now maybe he'd take the money and run. Asa had dreams of big things, but they were his dreams. Where would he go with the money? What would he buy?

A door opened in a house and a woman came out with a puppy on a leash. She was tall, in her late teens, maybe, wearing a green fleece and expensive-looking boots with tall heels. The puppy was white, some kind of retriever or something. Her eyes flicked over the beat-up Pontiac as she turned, scolding the dog, who nipped at her heels so that she laughed and danced a few steps and then took off jogging down the street, her boots making a clopping noise on the bricks.

He would like to talk to her but didn't know how. He could talk to girls on Frankford Avenue, dancers and neighborhood girls from the places he got drunk and did lines off the bar with his friends. He'd get pictures of himself with girls on a beach, but he'd never been out of Philadelphia except down the shore. The last time was a year ago, with a girl whose name he couldn't remember when they went to see Shakira at the Taj. Asa had gotten him the tickets. She'd been appreciative, but distant, and blown him in the high-rise parking lot afterward and then gone quiet, retreating into herself so that by the time they got home he'd been glad to see her go.

The phone buzzed, buzzed, and he opened it and started talking.

Zoe knew the thing was not to stop. The thing was to stay up, coasting off the dope as long as they could, not let it slip away. Because what followed was a long drop into nothing. So they'd smoke weed, if that was around, or take pills, if they were around, and when that was gone they drank. Zoe thought of it as formulas, as math; how much it took, how much that cost, all of it to hold off the end, when the world turned back into gritty ash and everything smelled bad and people just seemed small and worthless and music was just sounds and didn't take you anywhere or show you anything.

Tonight the moon was up and it was hot. They had scored from the boyfriend of a girl Zoe knew from rehab, and they were still at that point where being out in the street was like walking on the moon, with all the shadows long and crisp on the street and Zoe conscious of her legs moving, the long strides that carried her impossible distances as if gravity itself were tweaked back a little as they made their way up the long hill from the river.

She wore a black dress and boots and it was a long walk,

passing the little cramped houses and churches tucked into the side of the hills overlooking the Schuylkill. There were kids on the street playing with sparklers and they watched them run the blocks, their hands leaving yellow-white trails as they screamed and sang. Zoe touched Orlando's hair and he smiled at her, though she knew he was thinking about the things the kids said about the boy who was killed.

His head was hot to the touch, something they joked about. His brain going a hundred miles an hour all the time, she said. The way he watched everything, read compulsively, turned over stones to see the white and eyeless things beneath. The day they'd met he'd started talking to her in the bookstore in Port Richmond and they walked all night in the snow and he talked, his thoughts bouncing from one thing to the next in a way that left her dizzy, straining to keep up. He walked her through bookstores and record stores and libraries, shoving things in her pockets, pointing out things she needed to see, videos she needed to watch, songs she needed to hear.

They moved up through the neighborhoods, hearing music from the open houses and the bars. He finally stopped, looking up at a boarded-up house and then up and down the block, and she realized it was the house where the shooting had happened. She watched him back up, looking up and down the block, finally coming to rest and pointing toward the block where he and Zoe lived. It was a nice neighborhood. There were kids' toys in some of the little yards. The dark house with the bullet holes and yellow tape seemed like an aberration.

"What were they doing here?" He looked up and down the block.

"Kids wander, Orlando. They go where they're not supposed to go. They might have been just taking a walk and gotten turned around. Maybe they were looking for a store." She pointed down the hill toward the quiet neighborhoods close to the river where his nephew lived.

He held up a finger as if telling her to wait, then started going through his pockets. After a minute he fished out a folded piece of newsprint and walked toward the streetlight, bending the paper one way and another and furrowing his brow.

He motioned her over and started digging through her purse, finding the cheap cell phone her parents had given her the last time she'd seen them. Which brought back the whole scene, her mother crying and her father alternately spitting curses at her and begging her to come home. Telling her they'd pay for rehab, all was forgiven. Which was bullshit. Old bullshit, and it made her tired to hear it. She knew them, and it was more about how people saw them and their disgrace of a daughter. Even the pleading and the cursing, it was a role her old man put on, like a show for some audience in his head.

Orlando turned on the phone, waited for the signal, and dialed a number from the piece of paper. While it rang she took the paper off him and looked at it, then raised her eyebrows at him. A list of sex ads, one number circled. He gave her a thumbs-up. "Hey, I saw your ad and wanted to, you know, come over?" There was a rattle of firecrackers from up the block, and he stuck his finger in his ear and hunched his shoulders. "Well, when?" She put her hand on his shoulder, and he waggled his eyebrows at her. "Okay, where should I come?" He listened for a minute, then straightened up. "What? Where did you say? Number what?" He started looking around them, swiveling his head fast, then jogged to the corner and turned down Pechin.

She heard him talking as she ran to catch up, then saw him look at the phone and hang up, standing in front of a house with black shutters and a small porch. On the door was a tile plaque with the number spelled out in script. Her mother had the same thing on the house out in Berwyn. The number was different, of course, and this one was *Forty-two*. Her dad hated it because he said it looked common.

They stood in the living room of number 42, Zoe and Orlando and the girl, who said her name was Mia. The room smelled of perfume, and the furniture was cheap and covered with slip-covers and sheets in purple and red. On an end table was an old porcelain lamp with a cupid base and a jacquard silk shade that colored the room a purplish red. The girl was dressed in a black cocktail dress like she was going to a party. It reminded Zoe of an outfit she'd had once, except that this one had a little black rose at the base of her throat, sculpted out of the same silky material as the dress.

They talked for a few minutes, the girl friendly, like she was glad for the company, and then the back door opened and another girl came in, taller, a few years older, wearing a red dress and working a scrunchie in her hair until she saw them and stopped short. She was carrying a plastic sack with big bottles of cheap gin and vodka that Zoe could see through the bag. She set the bag she held down on the floor, and her eyes went around the room and then settled on Mia, who told her who they were.

"They came to ask about the kids."

The tall woman dropped her head, wary. Zoe saw they could almost be sisters. Mia introduced her as Tisa, and the woman looked at her with a disapproving roll of her head. "What kids?"

"Remember, the boys who came by? That night?"

"No, I don't remember, and neither do you." She looked harder at them. "I'm sorry, who the fuck are you?"

"My name's Orlando. I live up the block. Mia said your cousin is Santi, right? I know Santi from PICC." PICC was the prison in Northeast Philly where Orlando had done thirty days.

"You know my cousin? That supposed to do what? Make us friends?"

"Look, wait, okay? I'm not running a game, nothing like that. My nephew and his friend were shot. Right up the street, a couple houses away."

"You got trouble, I'm sorry. But that's got nothing to do with me."

"The boy with my nephew, the boy who died, he had the ad for this place in his house. And Mia said they were here."

"She said that?" Tisa turned and looked hard at Mia, who pouted, her lower lip stuck out like a little kid would do. "Well, she should know better than to say one fucking word about this. But she don't. 'Cause she's the kind can't get her head on straight." Tisa glared, dug in her purse for a cigarette, and lit one in a fury of quick motion, snapping the lighter like the hammer of a pistol. She pointed the lit cigarette at her friend. "You got to wake up, girl. Everyone is not your friend. This is a business. These boys don't come around here 'cause they in love with you. Honest to Christ." She covered her face with her hand.

Zoe stood up, crossed the room, and slowly took the pack from where it was crushed in Tisa's hand. "Look, we don't want to get you jammed up. We're not the cops, we're not talking to cops. We just want to know what happened to the kids. You tell us something, we're gone and we don't come back." She put a cigarette in her mouth, then guided Tisa's hand to its end, and after a beat Tisa flicked the lighter and lit it for her.

"Talk or not, you don't come back. You think we run this place by ourselves?"

Orlando spoke quietly, trying to seem harmless. "Mia already told us the kids were here that night. Why were they here? Were they looking to party?"

Mia started up, "No, I told you they were looking for that girl," but Tisa made a noise with her lips and stood over her so that she stopped.

"Go upstairs." She turned to them while Mia rolled her eyes and scooted off the couch to disappear into the back of the house. "Look, you got to go. We got work to do."

They got up slowly and moved to the door. Tisa laid a hand on Orlando's arm. "Look, you know? I'm sorry what happened, but that girl thinks everybody is her friend. You know what we do, what happens here. We can't be helping everybody's got trouble. Somebody looks over our shoulder, you know? I don't own this place. I got a kid, and her?" She pointed with her cigarette into the back of the house and shrugged her shoulders. "She loses this job, what's she going to do? She got a record already and a boyfriend who takes it out on her when things go wrong, you know? You from the neighborhood? You know Santi, you been locked up, then you know better. You know what goes and what doesn't." She looked back and forth from Orlando to Zoe.

He said, "I know, I know you're just trying to take care of everybody. I know it all falls to you. Yeah, I been in jail, I fucked up a lot, and that's why I know Santi. I'm just trying to figure this thing out so this guy can know why his kid ended up dead down the street. If there's anything you can tell us, I promise this is the last time you'll see us." She shook her head and closed the door softly.

They walked back out to the street, and Orlando took out the newsprint ad again and just held it, looking back and forth between the end of the block where the kids had been shot and the end of the block where Zoe lived in the kicked-in little apartment with its ocher walls and sagging beds.

Zoe said, "What're you thinking, Sherlock?" He turned to her but didn't speak, his eyes caught by something moving in the dark by number 42. She turned to look, putting one hand in her purse, and Mia appeared, brushing at her hair, which had been caught in the branches of one of those little weed trees that grows up where no one pays attention. They heard her curse to herself; then she took a few steps to the curb, smiling shyly and looking back over her shoulder.

She spoke softly, touching the little black flower at her throat, fingering one long earring. "She would help, she's not bad. Tisa looks out for me, but she thinks she's got the weight of the world, you know?"

They stepped closer so the girl wouldn't have to raise her voice. "Sienna. Those kids came by, looking for her. She used to work here. She don't now. She's pregnant and all fucked up and the guy who owns the place told Tisa to get rid of her."

Sienna. Orlando tried to remember when he'd seen her on the street. She had looked bad. Her hair stringy, grime caked in the corners of her eyes and the lines along her mouth as if she were made up for a play, to look like an old woman.

"How did she get messed up? Did she use?"

Mia lifted a shoulder. "This job is hard, people don't know. They think it's a party. You got to pretend all the time, men touch you whether you want to or not and you got to make them think you want to. She wasn't cut out for it." She smiled. "Tisa thinks I'm an idiot, but that's just how I do it. Act like a dip or whatever. Plus, you know, if you're nice, people, usually, they're nice back. But there was something wrong with that girl. She did get high, like a lot. A lot. But she's also a little, like, unglued or something, you know?"

"You know where she went?"

Mia extended her arms, taking in the neighborhood. "Who knows? She came by that night, all fucked up, told Tisa she had a date. But she came and went before I had a chance to talk to her. Wish I could help more." She looked over her shoulder, then turned and began to move back into the dark.

Orlando whispered thanks, and she turned and winked at him, and then looked out of the corner of her eye at Zoe and smiled.

Danny sat in a diner on Second Street, his computer open and the table crowded with printouts and files. He picked up a stack of sheets and paged through them. Here were Gerry Dunn and his brother, Frank; Chris Black and his dead brother, Shannon. He had a diagram drawn on the back of a copy of a tax bill for a house on Lehigh Avenue. Arrows went from name to name, property to property, stars and asterisks and question marks, all surrounding a hole in the center that was Asa Carmody.

Danny had thought of Asa as a character, a sport—something his dad used to say—but he hadn't seen everything, hadn't looked closely, and it made him feel sick. Had he been no better than all those sisters and mothers and cousins in court, the ones that cried and fainted in the hearings, come to find out their brother or husband was a drug dealer, a rapist, a killer?

Was it because they grew up together? Maybe because he remembered Asa as a little kid with a sunken chest, seen him hit on girls, and listened to him spin out bullshit teenage stories of the money he was going to have, the places he was going to go. The stories they told each other at night when Asa slept at his house, all those nights after his father skipped out and his mother took a downward slide into drinking and sketchy characters from the bars.

Now he had to see it all, carry away handfuls of dirt like he was unearthing some great fossilized heap of bones and eyeless skulls. The waitress came and asked him something and he stared through her, blank, his eyes unfocused, and after a minute she walked away. Periodically the phone buzzed, moving in an agitated circle on the table. His supervisor, Lieutenant Barclay, and John Rogan both looking for him. He had other cases and should have been working them. A drive-by in West Oak Lane. A guy in his fifties shot dead washing his car on Fairmount Avenue. He was going to be in serious trouble soon if he didn't start spending time on these things, but he was stuck somewhere in his own thoughts. He'd pick up the phone and picture a conversation, trying to explain himself to the lieutenant. How could he work on anything else until he knew what had happened? Not just what happened to Soap, but how everything had happened to put him and Soap across that table from each other on the same night the boy ended up dead in the river. This wasn't just about murder, it was about something else. Who Asa Carmody was, maybe who Danny himself was.

What was it Asa had said that night when they'd met Soap? That once Soap was there he wasn't in it anymore. Asa had stayed in it, though, sat there coaching Soap on what to say. Making things come out the way he needed them to, maybe. Soap, Darius, looking like he'd rather be anywhere else.

Twice he'd called Jelan and hung up before she'd answered.

Drove past her house, saw cars coming and going. Looked at the photographs and reports on Darius Williams. Made himself look. Taking it in. Trying to turn it into something he could use, that sick and helpless feeling. To see the truth of things. To make things right.

CHAPTER

13

Brendan came out of the hospital to find his brother standing in the parking lot, smoking a cigarette. His back was turned, working the lighter, and when he turned to face Brendan, Orlando wondered how he must look. Bad, he knew. Worse, even, than when they'd seen each other last. Orlando's face thinner, paler, with hollows under his eyes. Brendan stopped, sighed to himself. Orlando could see the effort it took for his brother to talk to him.

"Bren, how are you? How's Michael?"

"Good, he's looking good. Home tomorrow." He shrugged, jiggled his keys. "Everything okay?"

Orlando smiled, trying to look nonchalant. "Yeah, good. Listen, did he say anything yet? About what happened?"

"He doesn't remember much of the day. He gets little bits and pieces. He says he remembers him and George were looking for someone. He's not clear, you know, whether he can't remember why or if little George never told him."

"Looking for someone."

"A girl, he says."

"Sienna."

Brendan dropped his keys. "What?"

"The girl, her name was Sienna."

"How do you know that?" His voice was quiet, but he moved closer to his brother, kicking his keys under the car.

"Your keys, Bren." Orlando bent to look, and Brendan caught his arm.

"Fuck the keys, Kevin. How do you know the girl's name? Why do you know that?" There it was again, his middle name. Orlando thought, *He doesn't even see me as a real person. Zoe was right.*

"Why can't you call me by my right name, Bren?"

"Why can't you answer a simple question? Is this some kind of game to you? This is my son."

"You think I don't know that? You think I don't want to help?"

"What do you mean, help? If you know something, we'll call the detectives. Otherwise, stay the hell out of it."

"You think I can't do this?"

"Do what? I don't even know what the fuck we're talking about."

"That guy, that crazy fuck who shot me. He thought I knew something. I just thought, you know. Maybe I do. Maybe at least I can get to the people who know."

"Jesus Christ."

"Do you think the cops got it right? Do you think Darnell and those morons from Green Lane shot the kids while they were trying to buy drugs?"

"No, but I think they were looking for this girl and were in the wrong place at the wrong time. What are you trying to do?"

"I'm trying to find her."

"Find her? Why?"

"I don't know. Hear what she has to say, I guess. I'm not sure. It's something about Parkman Jr. and the girl and his father. I don't . . ." He trailed off with a helpless gesture, lifting his arms and dropping them. "I know what you think of me. Kathleen, Michael, I can't think what they see when they look at me. And what the fuck good am I if I can't do something for Michael? For my own family." He ran his hands through his hair, all yellow spikes and tangles, not entirely clean, Brendan thought, and saw him again as a little boy, standing on the stoop with a bruise on his face, his eyes red.

"Kevin, don't do this."

"See? That's not even my right name, Brendan. You can't even say my name." He shook his head then turned and walked off.

Orlando walked up Kensington in the rain, looking up at the underside of the El and the streams of water pouring off the tracks. It was the kind of hammering rain that wouldn't last, steaming when it hit the hot asphalt, and people hurried off the street into open doorways, the bar at the corner, the check-cashing place, some of them holding newspapers over their heads. A guy with broad shoulders pulled a red hood over his head and hunched in a doorway, watching the street. Two young kids took their turns handing him something that he palmed without making eye contact. One wore a sweatshirt with an airbrushed image of Daffy Duck smoking weed, and the other had a yellow T-shirt with something printed on it in Gothic letters like an elaborate tattoo.

One of the kids crossed back over to the corner nearest Orlando, and he stuck his hand in his pocket and felt the tens folded there. When he got close enough to the kid that he could see his yellow T-shirt read CREEPING DEATH, he took his cash out of his pocket and held it close to his thigh. The kid made eye contact with him, held his hand out, and had taken the money when he stopped, close to the front of the check-cashing place, and pulled a cell phone out of a long pocket on his thigh and looked at it. He looked at Orlando for a beat, then stepped closer and handed him back the money.

Orlando looked at him and then down at the cash in his hand, and the kid backed away, holding his hands at his shoulders and flashing the palms up. His eyes went over his shoulder and Orlando turned to look across the street at the big guy with the red hood pulled up. The guy shook his head slowly. Once, twice, three times, his face expressionless.

The kid turned down the corners of his mouth and stuck his hands under his sweatshirt. "Sorry, little brother. What can you do?"

Orlando stuck the money back in his pocket but didn't move, looking at the kid and then back across the street. The guy across the street stood up slowly and put his hand on his hip. Up Kensington the doors opened on a maroon Olds with a custom paint job, and two tall guys got out and stood on the street. Both of them had on wraparound shades and jackets, one with oversized dreads pulled back with a bandanna, and the other wearing a hoodie that shadowed his face. They stood by the car as if awaiting a bell.

The kid who had refused his money shook his head. "Get along, now. Live to fight another day."

It took three hours to get to the prison where Derrick Leon was locked up. Danny had been out before, going along with a detective who was trying to get a confession on an old case from a convicted child murderer who was set for execution in a few days. The inmate, a former schoolteacher from Scranton named Baumgardner, was a shaking mess, sweating through his prison clothes, talking nonstop, smoking. Danny went with an older guy, Matt Gialdo, who had worked the case years before, and Danny mostly watched while Gialdo tried to establish enough of a rapport with Baumgardner to find out whether his case, a young Hispanic girl found in a cardboard box in Fairmount Park, was one he had done. It went nowhere. The guy was trying to work some scheme to get a few more days before his execution and strung them along for an hour, trying to get them to talk to the state's attorney to buy him some time and half-promising to confess to three more murders that might or might not include the little girl in the park.

Gialdo had worked hard for an hour and a half, listening to the crazy old bastard rant, alternately blaming the murders on a kid he'd abused from his neighborhood and then hinting there were more bodies. On the way back, Gialdo had stopped at a tavern on Route 30 and had two quick Scotches and then walked off to a corner of the gravel parking lot and sobbed with frustration. Danny had driven home while the older detective snored in the passenger seat, but thinking the whole time of the image of him facing off into the trees, the tail of his rumpled coat shaking while he made terrible, strangled sounds into his fist.

The Leon case had made Danny. Derrick Leon started out in the drug business at thirteen, selling his brother's asthma medication cut into powder. He kept getting locked up and kept coming back out with more friends and a bigger crew that he put to work selling dope down on Fifteenth Street. He picked up his street name, Supremo, from the food market at Fifteenth and Wingohocking, the corner where he sat every day watching his crews sell Wet, what they called grass soaked in formaldehyde. But the more money he made, the more paranoid Leon got. He stabbed two of his own lieutenants because he thought they had designs on his corners, then used a hammer to kill a crackhead named Zumi who tried to pass off a xeroxed ten-dollar bill to one of Leon's runners. Derrick Leon was seen walking away with the bloody hammer. When a young cop pulled him over on Oregon Avenue in South Philly, Leon shot the cop in the face, then went home and killed his own pregnant girlfriend and his mother and disappeared.

The runner who got stuck with the phony ten was named DeAngelo Barnes. Leon had been hiding for two days when Asa put Barnes with Danny, and four hours later Danny walked out of the garage on Thompson with Derrick Leon in cuffs, and Danny got a promotion and a shot at the Violent Crimes Task Force. Danny could remember how scared Barnes was of Leon, the kid sitting hunched on a stool in a diner on Germantown Avenue, trying to be invisible, while Asa coaxed him into telling his story to Danny so Danny could get Derrick Leon off the street and nobody else would get his brains beat out with a hammer in the middle of Seventeenth Street.

The prison administration building reminded Danny of a suburban vision of a fortress, a brown stone castle as imagined by somebody who normally designed office buildings and tract housing, maybe, and had the look of a large post office with turrets. Danny parked across the street and checked in. He was wearing jeans and a sport coat and checked his gun with the duty sergeant. There were forms to fill out and a few people to talk to. At the last second there was some question of whether he'd get in; some misfire in the bureaucratic mechanism had kept his name off the list of approved visitors. In the end, a pear-shaped woman in civilian dress gave him a short lecture on chain of command in the prison before he was allowed past the sally port and into a waiting room where he sat for thirty minutes and read a copy of *Correctional News*.

He'd expected to have to get all the way out to SCI Greene in Waynesburg, where Pennsylvania kept its death row and most of its condemned prisoners, but Derrick Leon had been involved in an escape attempt and smuggling dope and had been transferred to Camp Hill, where he was held in segregation. When they brought him in, shackled and with leg irons, Danny saw the difference between three years inside and out. Leon's skin had gone ashy and gray, and he'd gained weight, gotten jowly and slack-eyed from the medication they used to control the most violent inmates. Danny had forgotten Leon's scar, a pale line that ran from his right eye in an arc along his cheek. It looked like a frozen tear, suspended in its fall.

He moved slowly, wiping his mouth with his manacled hands before speaking, but his eyes glowed when he saw Danny, and he smiled and shook his head. "Detective Martinez. You come all the way out here to exonerate me of these charges?"

"Hello, Derrick." He smiled in spite of himself. "How you making it out here? Staying out of trouble?"

"I shouldn't complain, but I do. I do." He looked around him at the guards. "These country-ass rednecks out here all get nervous around a strong black man still has his power. Still has his mind."

Danny could see Leon was, in fact, barely in control. His hands shook, and his eyes couldn't seem to settle on anything in the room. He'd look at Danny and then away, back over his shoulder.

"You still in touch with anyone from the neighborhood, Derrick?"

Leon lifted his chin and lowered his eyelids, affecting the bearing of the street king he'd been years before. "I hear things. People know who I am."

Danny knew it wasn't unusual for bigger criminals, names, to still retain some authority on the street. It was an issue for the prisons, guys who were locked up but still moved drugs around or had people killed or messed with on the street.

"You still plugged in out there, Derrick? Still moving and shaking even from all the way out here?"

Leon let his smile fade away to a twitch at the corner of his mouth. He let his head hang. "Nah, not really. I can make things happen inside here, but on the street I'm a ghost, tell the truth. I got a cousin came up a couple times, but everybody from my corners all locked up or dead now. Your boy seen to that."

"My boy?"

Derrick Leon stared, seeing things that weren't in the room. "You know they moved up my execution? Ain't that a bitch? Nothing better to do than to run a man to the death house."

"Well, you surprised?" Derrick had killed four people in twenty-four hours, the crackhead Zumi, another one of them the young cop, and Derrick's own mother and pregnant seventeen-year-old girlfriend. He had probably killed—or had ordered killed—at least six other people before that. It was tough, Danny thought, to know how much of drug-trade killing was the blood-less calculus of power and how much was just brutal paranoia and poor impulse control.

"Nah, that's what I'm saying, they got to bury me." He smacked at his chest and the chains swung and rattled. "They can't have somebody around willing to stand up."

"Derrick, you think you're here because what, you speak truth to power?"

Leon made a gesture, throwing it all away, and the chains on his wrists clanked and sang. "We know why I'm here, don't we, Detective? I mean, come on, give it up. I'm a dead man. There's no games to play with me."

Danny shifted in his chair, felt the absence of his gun, a weightlessness at his right hip where he usually carried the hol-ster clipped to his belt. "I drove a long way, Derrick. Say what's on your mind."

"You go right now to my corners, what will you see? You'll see runners and dopers. Not a damn thing different 'cause I'm locked up."

"People buy dope, Derrick. We supposed to close our eyes to that?"

"You see what you want to see. Who put you onto me?"

"You know I can't say that."

"Yeah, I'll tell you who. Asa Carmody."

Danny shifted in his seat, tried to give nothing away.

"He brought you somebody. Like he was just helping you out. All innocent." Derrick Leon was almost laughing, his eyes suddenly much clearer than when he'd first shambled in. "Yeah, I see it in your poker face. He brought you, I'm going to guess it was DeAngelo Barnes."

Danny gave a little headshake, but he felt something like a cramp in his neck and along his jaw. Leon leaned closer, his hands on the table between them.

"Yeah, don't even lie, it just make you look stupid. Now, Asa Carmody hand you DeAngelo Barnes and you say thank you, Asa, you're a good citizen, and you catch me asleep, huh? And what happened next? You don't even know." Leon smiled, rocking a little, the chains swaying. "How you ever make detective, anyway? I go up on death row, and DeAngelo Barnes is gone, and all my corners still open, all day, every day, and everybody still working, still slinging dope on Fifteenth Street, only now the money goes east instead of west. Never even missed a beat. I made them corners. I built them. There should be a plaque with a picture of Derrick Leon. A movie about me, like with Denzel."

The guards stood up behind Leon and he turned to look at them, then back at Danny. There were fast changes in his face, flickers of humor, of fear. Danny tried to imagine what it was like, how he'd be, sitting year after year on death row.

"Yeah, I'm going to burn. They can't wait, not a minute. Nobody ever cared this much about me before." He stood up and held his cuffed hands out to Danny. "But I learned my lesson. See, if I had fed my enemies to you, instead of taking care of things straight up, I'd be walking around free like Asa Carmody, huh?"

By the time it got dark Orlando was home, walking the narrow rooms and licking his lips. He'd been four places he knew to score and found himself shut out everywhere, stuck at a distance, pacing with the baggers and glueheads working their thin, scabby arms and haranguing customers and bystanders for spare change until they got run off by the jugglers.

At Fifty-second Street, he got too close to a big runner called Evil Eye, a twitchy, angry, low-level dealer with a giant gold Ra pendant, who kicked his legs out from under him and booted him in the ass down the sidewalk while everyone on the corner laughed. He pulled himself up on skinned palms and kept moving, his cheeks burning, and they shouted insults at him until he was out of range down Market Street.

He'd heard of guys turned off at some corners, usually baseheads who tried to run games and beat the dealers out of money, or people suspected of snitching, who seemed untrustworthy or wrong, or who were just a pain in the ass to everybody. Pestering the paying customers for handouts, or just too crazy to have around.

Orlando, though, had been to places he thought were run by different crews, so he knew whatever word was out against him was general, and there was nothing he could do, no one to appeal to. It was a nervous business that ran on rumor and vendetta and lying so intricate it became a kind of mythology. Back at Zoe's, he paced and wondered when she was going to get home, moving between the front windows and the stairs like a dog on patrol. By the time she came in, walking slowly, head down, the way she always was after work, he was tapping his raw hands against his thighs in a jerky bebop and his nose was running.

She stopped on the top step of the stairs to see him there, leaning toward her, his eyes wild. "What's going on?"

"You're late. We got things to do."

"That asshole Julian, the manager?"

He held up a hand. "We got to go, Zoe. We got things to do. I'm stuck here, going nuts while you screw around."

"Will you listen to me a minute?"

"What?"

"Jesus, what's up with you? What happened to your hands?" She retreated a step, and he clamped his arms to his sides in a manic simulation of stillness, his eyes moving in his head like a metronome.

"I got shut down. Nobody will call me back. The word's out on me or something."

"Where? We'll call somebody."

"Everywhere. Are you fucking listening to me? Who are you going to call? We got to get somebody to front for us. These fuckers are telling each other something about me. Do you have money?" He pointed to her purse, which she pulled against her chest protectively.

"That's what I was trying to say. Listen, I got fired. That fucking Julian—"

"Today? Today you get fired? What the fuck?"

"Well, what the hell are you going to do about it? Give me shit? That's helpful. You can't even hold down a job, Orlando."

"I'm working. I'm working for that Parkman guy. I'm working every day." He stuck one hand in his pocket to cover the shaking and stabbed out with the other toward the street. "I'm making things happen. I'm drawing lines. You don't get it."

"Oh, bullshit. That's a fucking dream and you know it. That guy's never giving you a dime." She stamped up the final step and leaned in toward him, her face terrible. "No, but that's okay, I'll just go get another fucking shitty job doing some fucking useless thing so you can float around the city all day and pretend you're a philosopher, or a detective, or whatever the fuck it is you think you are."

"I'm trying to make things right. Don't you get that? I thought you understood."

"This? All this bullshit? This is about your brother. You're trying to get your brother to treat you like a human being instead of a fucking junkie cartoon. Which he'd fucking do anyway if he wasn't such an asshole."

His hand jerked at the end of his sleeve and he slapped her. She dropped her purse and clapped her hand over her face. Everything fell out of the purse and rolled and clattered on the stairs, lipsticks and change, an eight-ball lighter. The razor opened, flashed and spun on the landing. He stuck his fingers in his mouth and bit down until he tasted blood. She dropped her eyes, bowed down slowly and retrieved her purse, moved without straightening down the stairs sweeping everything back in, and then stood up on the landing, turning from him and walking back out through the door.

The cell reception on the turnpike was bad, fading in and out while Martinez left messages. He called the Captain and left messages, tried John a half-dozen times before reaching him, coming out of court. He talked about Derrick Leon, about Soap Williams, about DeAngelo Barnes. The call ended with a frantic chirp as the signal was lost, and then Danny called back, his voice high.

"It was the same shit, John. I didn't even put it together until I was in that room with Leon."

"You don't know that, Danny. Have you looked at the file on Barnes? Do you even remember?"

"I remember Asa Carmody sitting across the fucking table from me. Just like with Soap Williams. Feeding me bullshit with a teaspoon."

"It wasn't bullshit. Derrick Leon was a bad guy, and so is Darnell Burns. You need to calm down and think."

"We have to take a look at all of this again. I don't think Darnell did this."

"No one is going to want to hear that. Not the DA, not the Captain."

"John."

"Not the families of those kids that got shot."

"You know I'm right."

"I don't know shit. And neither do you."

"I got played. You were the one asked *me* if I knew why Asa was feeding me information. Well, you were right."

"Just because the guy's got an agenda doesn't mean the case is no good. You know that's what they'll say. Criminals flip on each other. And we help them do it. Christ, Danny, it's what we do every damn day. Derrick Leon was a cop killer." Through the phone Danny could hear John moving, his voice getting low, like he was afraid someone else would overhear. "If you start opening up old shit? Get defense lawyers opening up old cases? Man, that's a place nobody wants to go."

"Are you going to back me on this, John? I need to know where you are."

"I think all that boy-wonder shit messed with your head. You don't have the years in yet, and you think it was all too easy for you, and maybe you're right. But these are good cases against bad guys. We sent Derrick Leon to death row and the fucker belongs there. I'll tell you something else, Danny. My name's on those cases, too."

"I just, I don't know." There was a long pause. "I want to talk to the Captain about this."

"Are you sure you have enough to do that?"

"I just want to talk to the man."

"Yeah? Then ask yourself this, kid. Does he want to talk to you?"

. . .

Orlando was standing at a pay phone in Chinatown, one of the last ones in the city, it seemed like. For a while he had tried to get a stolen pay card to work, but it was bullshit. He had finally taken a pipe to a Coke machine outside a muffler place and run away with a couple of bucks in quarters.

"Bob, man, how's it going?"

There was a long pause. "Are you kidding?"

"No, man, don't—"

"I wish I knew who this was, on the phone, but I don't."

"Bob, wait."

"If I knew who this was, I'd tell him to get his head out of his ass and stop pestering people before he gets a tire iron wrapped around his nuts."

"Jesus, don't say—"

"But who this is I have no fucking idea, so I got nothing to say."

The phone went dead. He stood back with the receiver in his hand for a minute before smacking it down hard on the cradle. He turned and was rocking on his heels, trying not to freak out any of the nice Chinese ladies on their way to work, when he saw Parkman Sr. come out of a place down the block between a restaurant with an aquarium in the window and a place full of that Hello Kitty stuff that was like crack for preteen girls.

Orlando moved fast, catching him as he stood in the street with his keys, looking up at the coiled eels moving languidly at the bottom of a murky tank.

"Mr. Parkman."

He looked up startled, as if caught at something. He took a

few steps farther down the block, then turned and grabbed Orlando's jacket.

"What the fuck is wrong with you?"

"Whoa. Hands off." Orlando smacked at the hand and Parkman released him, but poked him hard in the chest.

"What the fuck did you take from my son's room?"

"Nothing. What are you talking about?"

"Come on, come on. I'm not a mark, junkie. Just give back the stuff you took and I won't call the cops."

"Look, I don't know what the fuck you're talking about. Why the fuck would I take anything when you're going to pay me?"

"Yeah, I'm not paying you shit now, am I? That camera alone is worth almost four thousand bucks."

"Camera?"

"Please, you can't even lie right." He turned and started walking again, shaking his head. "I would think that would be the one thing you're good at."

"Mr. Parkman, just wait, just wait, okay? I'm telling you this is important."

Parkman stopped but didn't turn. Orlando caught up and talked to his side, just as happy not to be in the man's eyes. "I didn't take a camera, okay? If the camera is missing, it was taken before I got there. Or it's just somewhere else, at your son's school or something."

"Without the case? Please." He didn't turn but kept looking down the block. It was like a movie where two spies are talking, hoping not to be seen in conversation. "Look, this was a mistake. I just wanted to figure out what the truth was, but I don't think you know the difference."

"Wait, when did you notice it was missing?"

"Just stay away from me and stay away from my home. And my son's friends."

"His friends? Did someone say something?"

The older man kept walking, dropping his head and holding his hands up. Orlando turned and drifted back toward Race. He turned to see the restaurant where Parkman had been eating, but it wasn't a restaurant. The restaurant's entrance was a few steps from the street in a little alcove. The door he'd come out of was red and flush with the wall, and next to it was a small, cracked window with neon ideograms and a small sign in English that read MASSAGE.

CHAPTER

14

The lights in the parking lot came on silently, glowing a faint green and then brightening, though Danny thought the light they gave off added a kind of yellow haze so that nothing in the lot was any clearer for the electricity expended. Across Lincoln Drive the woods were almost black in the oncoming night. It was late, and there were gaps in the traffic, and in the long silences he could hear things moving. Leaves rattling, a stick breaking with a pop that echoed off the closed face of the building. What could be out there in those woods? What animals were big enough to make that much noise so close to the city? He was sitting on the hood of his car staring hard into the pockets of black shadow in the trees when the Captain came out and stood, his keys in his hand and his briefcase under his arm. He took his hat off when he saw Danny sitting there, showing his thinning gray hair in tight curls, a rivulet of sweat disappearing into his collar from behind his right ear.

"Danny, what's up?"

"You didn't return my call, so I thought I'd sit out here awhile."

"It's been a bitch of a day. Want to go get a drink?"

"I just want to make sure we're doing everything right."

"So do I, Danny. We all do. But that's not always possible."

"I don't know. I just don't think I feel good about—"

The Captain shook his head, putting his hat back on. "I know what you think. I talked to John Rogan."

"So you took John's call."

"He's your friend. I'd like to think I am, too."

Danny stood up, swaying a little. "I don't think Darnell Burns shot those kids."

"If that's true, his lawyer will make the case at trial. That's what he gets paid to do. That's how all this works." He laid a hand on his neck and suddenly looked ten years older, the hairs on the back of his hand tipped with white. "We don't have to say what we think. What we suppose. We have a gun that did the shooting in the living room of one suspect, marked up with the prints of another suspect. We have confessions—"

"The confessions are bullshit."

"We have confessions from the suspects. Statements they signed. Of course they wish they hadn't signed them. That doesn't mean they aren't true."

"Asa Carmody. He set this all up somehow." Danny sat back on the car hood, looking distracted. "I can't . . ." He looked into his hands. "I can't get it all straight, but I know none of this is how it looks."

"Are you all right, Danny?"

"There's a kid going in the ground tomorrow, a kid I talked to. The brother of a friend of mine. I was this close to him. Like we are now. Across the table. I keep trying to remember the look in his eye. I can't prove anything."

"Then that's the case you should be working, right? You think this Carmody is the man pulling the strings, make that case.

But I think you should go home now. I think you should get a drink and let it all go and come at it fresh tomorrow."

"You know how it is? I keep seeing him in my mind's eye, you know? The kid. Trying to remember exactly what he said. How he said it. Wondering if he was trying to signal me or something."

"Go home, Danny."

"I can't look at her. I can't face the family."

The captain closed the gap between them, put his hand on Danny's arm. "Let it go, son. You start waiting for certainty, you'll never leave the house. These people you're worried about? Darnell and his friends? These are not good people. They've all been locked up a dozen times. Whatever you're trying to protect them from they already chose for themselves. Over and over. We ask questions, we listen to the answers. Sometimes the answers aren't what we want."

Asa looked out at American Street from the office window of an old garage he'd bought from a cousin who'd moved to Tucson. The place was empty but for a few tables, a broken-back couch, a mattress on the floor in front of him, the ancient blue steel desk he sat at now. He watched the trolley go by, looking small and antique, wondering how the hell it could make sense for the city to run the damn things.

He liked American Street up here, north of Diamond on a block of garages and closed shops. It was wide, the neighborhoods running flat and empty north and south, and he could see for blocks. Anybody who wasn't about his business would stick out. On the desk a police scanner chattered, the sound muted.

Through the open office door he could see the two cases lying in a square of sunlight—the silver case with his money and the black case with the bullet hole through the middle. Asa stuck his thumb in his book, a slim, greenish thing with a broken spine he'd picked up from a table on South Street ten years before. *The Science of Getting Rich*. There were flags of red tape protruding from some of the pages, places where Asa had underlined passages, and he was trying to memorize the whole thing in little chunks.

He looked at the street and murmured to himself. "All force begins to be exerted in that direction, all things begin to move toward you." He opened the book again, glanced at the page, and closed it. "Desire is a manifestation of power. All the promises are unto them that believe, and them only." He laid the book down and drummed his fingers, then picked up a bulky, rust-browned screwdriver from the desk.

He crossed to the case with the dope, sticking the screwdriver under the hasp and prying it off the case with a dry crack so that pieces of black plastic catapulted into the dark corners of the garage. Inside were flat, dusty bricks wrapped in brown plastic. Asa imagined, as he always did when he saw bundled dope, some little clearing in a sandy place. Dirty dun-colored buildings teeming with women in white cotton, kneading a wet slurry with small brown hands in an oppressive heat. Men slouching in doorways, automatic rifles hanging on long straps. The men in sandals, the women barefoot. Radios going, hissing out some tinny rendition of old Europop. The men smoking and looking bored, trying to maintain that casually brutal distance that gunmen all work to project. The women chatting to each other; it's just work in the heat. Nearby men weigh money, the way they do in the bulk dope trade—stacks of bundled currency cycled through grimy old scales while a long man with a milky eye makes notations on a clipboard. The women talk about their children, boyfriends, they push at their lank hair with the backs of their tiny hands in unconsciously erotic gestures, and in Asa's mind they're a confusion of vaguely Asian and nonspecific Latin women in their twenties wearing white cotton undershirts, so that the natural eroticism of the women is all mixed up in his head with the vaguely arousing vision of money stacked in bundles, so much massed that it's lost its reality as currency and become something that generates a kind of energetic heat, like an atomic pile. Somewhere nearby is a man, sitting in the shade in a wicker throne, wearing sunglasses and a brilliant guayabera shirt. A dog sits at his feet, tongue going in the heat, and the men all know better than to make eye contact with the man in the guayabera, and the women pause from the work to arch their backs and lower their long black lashes.

He closed the case again, getting the sour smell of dirt and the faintly vinegary smell of the dope itself. There was music coming from the street, and he straightened, walked up the stairs to look out the small, streaked windows over the garage doors in time to see Chris pull his Navigator into the driveway in front of the old bays. He saw him turn the key but let the music play out a little. "The Beast" by Tech N9ne, Chris trying to get an edge off the music. To be hard, about business, whatever that meant to a kid like Chris. Probably some gilt-edged dream from a Dre video of wearing silk and drinking Cristal from the bottle. He moved his head for a minute, then finally shut it down and got out, pulling his T-shirt down in the back over the pistol and reassuring himself it was there. Asa smiled.

He stood at the top of the open stairway to the old parts loft and let Chris come in slowly and look around before announcing himself by banging the rail so that the tall kid jumped a little and backed up.

"Man, boss. Scared the shit out of me just then." Chris shook his head.

"How many times I told you not to call me that?"

"Okay." He dropped his head, and Asa wondered again about how easy it was to break Chris Black. His brother Shannon had been unbreakable, was always ready with "fuck you," or to go at anybody, anytime. He'd crack bones in his hands beating their heads in. The downside was he was insane. Could only get the outline of an idea, not take a job on as his own. You told him to collect, he came back with money every time, but he smacked people around, touched other people's women, showed the cops his ass and took whatever he wanted wherever he was.

Shannon didn't listen, couldn't learn anything. He'd fuck with people, think he was being clever and coy and tell everyone his business without realizing he'd done it. He'd been locked up a dozen times, had that jailhouse radar for being disrespected that did not serve when the job called for more than smacking somebody and taking their money. It wasn't worth cleaning up after him after a while, and when he turned up dead it was no surprise. Everybody he'd ever met, Asa knew, wanted Shannon Black dead, at least a little.

His little brother Chris didn't have the heart. He'd make slight moves in that direction, but it wasn't his nature and there wasn't anything you could do about that. Once again, Asa'd have to work with the materials at hand. It was what the great men did, all the ones he taught himself about and tried to emulate. He'd read a book about survival, all about how when the shit comes down the ones that make it are the ones who keep thinking, keep adapting, and Asa liked that because he knew he was one of those types. Since he was a little kid, he'd been the one who made it, kept thinking, kept figuring it out. Made the most of his opportunities. He'd always done it. He'd do it now.

Ken McBride worked at a quick-lube place on Lancaster Avenue, down the street from the school. Orlando used the last of his quarters getting out there on the bus. He walked in, aware suddenly of how he might not look too bad on a pay phone in Chinatown, but out on the Main Line he stood out like a sore junkie thumb. He straightened his collar before walking in and asking for Ken. Maybe he got a lot of guys coming around that looked like Orlando, 'cause the girl behind the counter didn't seem to notice him. She yelled into the back, and the kid came out, smiling when he saw who it was.

"Orlando, right? You all right, man?"

"Yeah, yeah, just been a little, um. Under the weather."

"Got it." Shit, he probably did.

He asked if he remembered seeing Geo with a camera and Ken said sure.

"He was always filming stuff. His band. The kids at school. Marianne."

"Do you know if he gave it to anyone? Or sold it or something?"

"I don't know, man. I didn't see him that much in the last couple months. Gimme a minute, okay?" He disappeared into the back for a minute, then went outside through one of the bays, already talking on a cell phone. Orlando walked out and stood in the sun, spooked a little by the trees and grass and knife-edge flower beds at the curb.

"You know, this is like the nicest garage I've ever seen." He saw a woman in a suit talking on an iPhone. Started adding up things in his head; what he could get for her bag, her phone. The chain around Ken's neck, the little TV on the counter inside. It was the calculus he did all day. He couldn't shut it off.

Ken hung up, his eyes narrowed at something he'd heard on the phone. "Main Line, man. You got to keep it nice out here."

"What's up?"

"I talked to Marianne, she said that little rat Ryan has a really nice camera that looks a lot like the one Geo had. I called the little fucker."

"Thanks."

"What's with the camera? You think he filmed something?"

"I don't know. I think maybe he sold it."

"For dope."

"I don't know, but it's just weird."

The phone rang again, and Ken put it to his ear.

Asa sat down on the stairs above Chris, looking down. "When are you going to tell me what happened on Broad Street?"

"It was fucked up. The guy opened up on us. I guess he wanted the money without giving up the product." Chris had run this line in his head a hundred times before coming to see Asa and sold it to himself with conviction, but here he was now in the king's court and it sounded thin, even to him.

"But you . . . persevered, huh?" Asa said, reaching for the two-bit word. One of those things he did to keep Chris off balance. Showing off from those fucking books he was always carrying around. "Kept your head and came out with the money and the man's things, yeah?"

Chris was wide-eyed, expecting anything but praise. "That's right."

"You were lucky to get out."

"They shot Gerry. And Frank."

"Uh-huh. The OK Corral. I heard about it. You get away clean?"

"Yeah. I think so. I don't think, I mean, it was Frank's car, and I dumped that in Jersey." Actually, he'd left the car about a block from his mother's house in Fishtown. 'Cause how the fuck was he going to get back from Jersey, and Asa would never know, so fuck him.

"Open the cases, let's see."

Chris crossed to where the cases lay on the floor and opened each one, fumbling with the hasps while Asa watched from the stairs. When he opened the case with the money he paused for a minute, finally taking in what he'd been driving around with all that time. He flipped a bill with one finger, as if testing its reality.

Asa shifted on the stairs. "A lot of money, yeah?"

Chris looked up at Asa, squinting in the glare from the front windows. "I brought it back. And I got the dope."

Asa stepped slowly down the stairs. "So the African made a move? Tried to grab the cash?"

"Yeah, I thought we were going to get jacked. We had to shoot our way out."

"Right. The African guy shot at you?"

"No, somebody else. We couldn't see him. Angel came in and looked for him, I guess, but the guy got away from him." Chris screwed up his face, a little gesture of exasperation at Angel Riordan's incompetence. Asa smiled and looked sidelong at him so that Chris could see his ploy was getting him nowhere. "It was pretty crazy, I guess. The guy was blasting away, so, you know, Angel had to back off. I had to get Gerry to the car, get him out of there. He was bleeding all over the place."

"So where did you take Gerry?"

"Right, well, then Gerry wouldn't get in the car. Because of his brother. So I didn't want to hang around until the cops showed up and threw a net over everybody. Took your money, right?"

Asa came down to kneel in front of Chris at the cases. He picked up a bundle of cash, rifled it, turned to the dope case and stuck his finger through the bullet hole Gerry had put in it. "So, you walk in, the African's there, sitting there with the dope, and you come in and some guy just opens up on you from wherever?"

Chris moved his head this way and that, like he was trying to work out how to see his story in a way that didn't look ridiculous. He stood over Asa, who barely looked at him, and thought about the gun tucked in the back of his pants. As far as he knew, the little redheaded freak never carried one.

Asa closed the cases one at a time, then sat back, staring off into space for a minute. Something about watching him snap the cases closed put the thought into his head that he was being shut out of something, some door was closing to him. Chris actually put his hand behind him, touching the cold butt of the pistol, a little SIG SAUER he'd bought off a kid in a bar.

The door opened and Angel Riordan came in. He let the door close, looked behind him out into the street, and moved to stand in the shadow with his back to the wall.

Carmody smiled again, that weird smile he got when there was no joke Chris Black could see. "Angel." He cocked his head a little. "Chris was just telling me why somebody brings six kilos of heroin to a hotel when all they plan to do is beat you out of your money."

Angel looked off, not interested in any of it. Chris watched him carefully, like you'd watch an animal with its cage open, waiting to see what way he moved.

Angel lifted a corner of his mouth. "Ah, bullshit."

"Hey, he wasn't in there. He doesn't know how it went."

Asa stood up and turned to him, reaching up to pat his

puffed-out chest. "Chris. Forget it. I asked you to do something that was too hard. It's my fault, not yours. I should have known better."

Chris backed up, freaked by the proximity to Asa. "I never let you down."

Asa shook his head, "Don't run away with yourself. You fucked this up, and every thing I've asked you to do, yeah?" He grinned again, that weird thing he did where his lower jaw dropped open like he was going to take a bite out of something. Jesus. He leaned in even closer, and Chris backed up involuntarily. "It's what you do, now I think of it. You fuck up. You hang around, waiting to be told what to do. And the one time you think for yourself, what happened?"

"The guy made a move."

"What happened?" Asa put one soft white hand out, and Chris backed up again, aware of the empty garage behind him, all that black space.

"I told you."

"Stop that bullshit." Asa shook his head fast, his hands twitching a little.

Chris shifted his eyes back and forth between the top of Asa's red head and Angel, who at least stood still at his post against the wall. Sweat began to form on his back, like a line pointing to where the little gun was wedged. In another second he'd reach behind him and end this shit. "I don't know what you want."

"I want you to stop thinking you can lie to me. Ever."

The fucking guy was pushing him around the floor like a little kid on a playground. How did this happen? The little fuck didn't even have a gun. He looked at Angel again, who was off in his own world. Why did Chris keep letting this happen? He dropped his head, his face burning.

"You spent ten minutes alone with that retard Gerry Dunn and you got in front of the African and you started acting up, right?"

"I don't—"

"You let that idiot into your fucking head and you thought you'd make some stupid fucking move and it got away from you." Asa was talking fast, quiet, and it was somehow scarier than if he'd been screaming. "You reached over and grabbed the dope. Or he did. That idiot, Gerry Dunn. That idiot. The African was just sitting there, just sitting there, and it got into your head because you're weak and stupid and can't keep your fucking eye on the ball." He tapped the side of his own head, hard, the end of his finger bending back with the force of it. Chris was breathing fast, almost whimpering. Asa pointed the finger at Chris, moving it closer to his chest, and he had the idea that if the finger touched him, he would die.

"I'm going to give you one thing to do. You're going to do it. If you want to keep coming back here, keep getting paid, you're going to do it."

"What can I do?"

"You know already."

"I don't."

"I sent you to do something and you didn't do it. On Roxborough Avenue."

"No, that went right. We hit that place hard."

"I'm not talking about the place. That's not the problem."

"What was wrong?"

Asa grabbed a handful of Chris Black's shirt, twisting it in his fingers so that Chris had to bend closer. He turned to avoid getting his face close to Asa, who talked quietly and fiercely into his ear. "That girl. That fucking girl. You shot everybody on Roxborough Avenue except the girl."

CHAPTER 15

Ken drove Orlando down to a record store in a strip shopping center. He looked over at Orlando a few times on the road down, Orlando wondering what he saw.

"You have to hit it more than once a day now?"

Orlando kept his eyes on the street. "You think you know something?"

"It wasn't just Bukowski poems and good thoughts got me through school."

"Yeah?"

"Rehab. Twice before it took. Pills and alcohol."

"You got any pamphlets?"

"Okay, I'm not going to twist anybody's arm. That's one thing definitely doesn't work."

"Yeah? What works?"

"Fuck, I don't know. Really, man, I don't get in anyone else's shit about it."

They pulled up to where a bunch of kids were clustered in a corner of the lot, sitting on the hoods of their cars. A Corvette, an S10, two BMWs, one a convertible. The dozen or so kids were wearing expensive clothes and wore jewelry that went with the cars. Ken and Orlando got out and stood by the car until Ken noticed Ryan, who looked startled and jumped off the hood of the S10 to move toward one of the BMWs with his keys out.

Ken caught him fumbling with his keys and stood him up against the side of the car, Orlando ducking his head so if something stupid happened, maybe nobody would have gotten a fix on his face. Ken held Ryan easily against the door, using his free hand to push the kid's fauxhawk down.

"Ryan, that's one fucked-up haircut, man."

"Really? I only got it 'cause your mom likes it."

The kids around them gave off a low moan followed by laughter, and Ryan looked over his shoulder at them, his tongue out. Ken grabbed his throat with a hand like a catcher's mitt. His voice was low.

"Ryan, man? You are so not that guy."

"Yeah. Sorry." He dropped his head.

Orlando kept his back to the crowd and moved closer to Ken and Ryan. Ken let go of Ryan's neck and straightened the collar on his knit shirt. "You have George Jr.'s camera."

"What camera? I have one like his. It's not his."

"Jesus, do you suck at lying. Pick one lie, dipshit. That's how it works. Did you steal Geo's camera?"

"No. Fuck. That retard."

"Watch it."

"Shit, I knew it. I knew I was going to get in trouble for this. He fucking sold it to me. I didn't steal it. I told him his father was going to fucking freak."

"It's not about his father. This guy—" He swatted Orlando

on the arm. "Geo owed this guy money. And this is a guy you don't want to owe money to."

Orlando looked at Ryan through heavy-lidded eyes, and the kid shifted and made a pained face. "Man."

"Yeah."

Orlando held up a hand, the thug granting dispensation. "Just tell me what you gave him for it."

"Five hundred bucks."

Ken shook his head. "Ryan."

"Okay, seven fifty. Jesus."

"What did he need it for?"

"A girl, he said."

"What do you mean, a girl?"

"He told me this girl was in trouble. I don't know. I was looking at the camera."

"Did he say her name?"

Ryan shrugged his shoulders, and Orlando wanted to grab his throat, too. Something must have shown in his face that made the kid throw up his hands. "I don't know! It was some girl he met at the homeless shelter or something. I said it sounded like throwing away money. Unless she was hot or something. Man."

They walked back to Ken's car, stopping to look back at the kid, who was fumbling with his keys and trying to open his door. Ken said, "Geo is gone, and that little prick . . ." He lifted one shoulder and let his eyes go wide with the injustice of it. Orlando felt his stomach seize up and had to bend over at the car and spit. Ken waited patiently.

Orlando stood up straight, his eyes red. He let his mouth hang open, breathing hard. "Okay, what did work?"

"What?"

"In rehab. The second time, it took. You said."

Ken looked away. "I told you, man, I don't know. I just know, the first time it was work, it was a lot harder. The second time, I don't know. I was ready, I guess. Like I was really there, paying attention."

"Okay."

"Why? You think you're ready?"

Orlando bared his teeth, his eyes red and bruised, his hands low on his abdomen like he'd been punched there. "No."

He had Ken drop him off at the library on Ridge and looked through the newspapers. He found articles about the shooting, pictures of George Jr. and from outside the viewing, quotes from Marianne Kilbride that didn't sound like her and from staff at the homeless shelter in North Philly where Geo had volunteered. He took some of the pages and stuffed them in his jacket, then walked up the aisles for a minute, stopping to pull out *The Day of the Locust* and some old Ray Bradbury stories he loved.

He had a library card. He'd spent a lot of time hanging in the libraries when he was between places to live, and after he'd hooked up with Zoe he got a card using her address. It was late and the place was closing, so he took the books and walked down to the apartment, hoping she'd be there, but there was no sign of her. Her clothes were still there, and he sat for a long time with a piece of paper and the little fine-line pen Zoe used to write poetry trying to think what to say, and in the end he just wrote that he loved her and stuck the note in the frame of the Frida Kahlo print near the door.

He walked back up to the place where Sienna had worked and knocked on the door and braced himself. Mia answered, her eyes big, pointing over her shoulder inside and stepping out to pull the door closed behind her.

"What you doing? You coming back alone without that little Cuban girl?"

He reached into his jacket. "I'm a little short on cash right now, you know? But I wanted to ask you one more question."

"Oh, cops and robbers again. Like Monk on TV." She hunched her shoulders and made a conspiratorial face, playing amateur detective. "You sure you don't want to come in and have a party? You can even bring that girl." She was high. He could see it in her heavy lids and the way she propped herself up in the door, and then he smelled it, the peppery smell of cheap weed coming out of her hair and her clothes and warring with her perfume. He thought about asking her if he could get high with her. It was on his lips to say it, but then he didn't.

"Thanks."

"Everybody says they're broke, but you be surprised how many people find the money if they really, really want to."

He showed her the pictures in the paper, conscious of his shaking hands as he pointed things out. She made a sad face and touched the school picture of George Jr. "That poor boy. So young like that. Did you figure out what was going on? That night he was here?"

"I'm trying to. But how about this guy? Did he come here? To see Sienna."

"I don't know about saying. We got confidentiality, hon. Just like a priest, you know?" She giggled and touched his arm.

"You know why I'm here, right? I'm not a cop, I'm not looking to get anyone in trouble. I want to understand how this mess happened."

There was a noise in the house, voices.

"I got to go." She gave an apologetic smile. He smiled, too, and touched her arm lightly, but lifted the paper again so she could see it. She shook her head at him in mock exasperation, but then she touched the picture and nodded. She opened the door as if to check, then closed it again and dropped her voice. "Okay, yeah, he was here. Bunch of times and always for that same girl. Sienna. Some guys like the little crazy ones, I guess."

He thanked her, and she shook her head again. "You come back with that sweet little chula sometimes, okay?"

He walked back out to the street. It was getting dark, and he took the articles and stood under a streetlight and looked at the picture again, the one Mia had touched with her manicured finger. George Parkman Sr. He looked back at the house and wished he'd let himself bum a joint off Mia. Why hadn't he? Did he really think he was a detective, a man on a mission? With Parkman tweaked at him there was no way he was getting paid now. He should forget about it and concentrate on his own life.

. . .

Orlando wandered all night. He left home with a tire iron on a loop of rope inside his jacket and sixteen dollars he'd taken from where it was taped under the desk where Zoe wrote her poetry. He walked by the corners he knew and ones he didn't, and it was the same everywhere so that he stopped even trying, sick as he was, and just wandered south. He rode the 21 bus out to West Philly and stood shaking on Fifty-second Street, watching the runners move between the cars and the buildings. A cop car went by, giving a short whoop on its siren so that all the traffic froze for a minute, the customers and runners, but the car kept moving and everyone unfroze again like in a children's game and went back to business.

Orlando stood in front of a shoe store near Ranstead, watching the corner. He was far from home and hadn't tried scoring out this far west before. He started walking back north to catch the eye of a runner, but two kids appeared from between some parked cars. One kid was small and narrow and the other big, wide across the shoulders, so that the two of them together were like a cartoon and Orlando almost laughed. The small kid, dark, with a narrow, intelligent face, leaned into him and the big one, lighter skinned, with wide-set, frightened eyes, hung back, almost shy.

The smaller one said, "Lend me some money, white boy."

"Man, look at me, I'm broke." Orlando pulled his jacket around him, letting his fingers touch the bent iron under his arm.

"Nah, you got at least ten dollars, I predict."

"Nope, I got nothing."

The kid shook his head sagely. "No, you need at least ten dollars to score dope. You're not down here one in the morning to buy shoes. Terrance, show him."

The big kid looked up and down the block, then lifted his jersey to show the dull gray butt of a pistol.

Orlando sighed. "Man, you take that money, you're killing me. I'm sick."

"Yeah, that's a sad story." He snapped his fingers in front of Orlando. "Come on, I'm not standing here all night. Come on."

Orlando twitched a little, rubbing the back of his neck. Up the block he saw a runner with a loose black T-shirt etched with white hexagons and connecting lines, the chemical formula for heroin. "You seem like a couple of good kids—"

The tall one clapped a hand on his shoulder, hard, jarring the narrow bones around Orlando's throat. The short one said, "Yeah, we're not, though. I'm through with you. Give up that money or I'm going to start beating on you and I mean right now."

Orlando finally went into his jeans and slid the thin, almost weightless bills out, and the small kid took them fast and started walking away while Orlando still stood there with his hand out. After a beat, the big kid followed, hitching at his pants.

He circled the drug corners like a hungry dog, thinking, thinking and coming up empty. His nerves were raw, his stomach periodically cramping so that he had to stop and breathe through his mouth. He could feel circles of sweat under his arms and kept running his fingers through the pools of moisture in the hollows under his eyes. Near Hazel Avenue he saw a rotted wooden door leading into an alley next to a little corner shop with barred windows and a weak, greenish light from the dying bulb left on after closing. He drifted right as he walked south, letting himself come to rest flat against the door and watching the street, motionless but for his head, looking first down the block at the dark street and then up, to see two men coming out of a tavern under a streetlight, swaying and calling to each other as if lost in a gale.

As they wandered away up Fifty-second Street he turned, reaching under his jacket to pull the iron from the loop of belt under his arm. He stuck it quickly under the piece of lath that was serving as a door handle and worked the pry bar back and forth, the old nails groaning a little and then slowly pulling free. He drove the bar deeper beneath the latch and popped the piece of wood off the door, and it clattered in the street with a noise that seemed to echo up the block.

He stuck his boot over the piece of wood on the sidewalk and stood motionless, not even looking around him while he counted slowly to ten. Then he pulled the bar away from the wall and stuck it under his jacket again and forced the door open slowly on its rusted hinges. The door gave slowly and then stuck, and he squeezed through the small gap, scraping his chest on the rusted latch.

He was in a narrow alley between two buildings. It was almost pitch black, inches deep in dented, rusted cans and broken glass. Halfway down the alley he had to scrape past a tree that had grown up over the years, displacing the wooden siding on the south side of the alley. He almost got stuck but levered himself up on the opposite wall and shimmied through the gap.

There was a window on his right, covered by a loose metal grate. He lifted the tire iron and put it between the grate and the brick but was too low to get an angle on it, so he backed up, stepping up onto a brick ledge and putting one foot onto the wall behind him. It was awkward but gave him a purchase on the metal and a view through the window.

He could see into the back of the store, a little room walled by cases of canned goods and detergents. An Asian girl, Korean maybe, about eight or nine, was sitting at a table surrounded by books. She was writing something, chatting to herself. There was a radio going on the table, and she sang along in a high, broken voice and rocking in time to the music, pointing into the dark corners of the room with her pen as if cuing an unseen audience. He recognized the tune, the one where the girl sings about her baby taking the morning train. After a minute a woman came in and put a small plate of something next to the girl, and the girl grabbed her hand to make her dance. The woman pulled back and gave the kid a stream of complaint that Orlando couldn't make out, pointing to the books and turning to snap the radio off.

The girl dropped her head and picked up her pen. Orlando's legs started to cramp, but he kept himself propped upright though he couldn't say why. He took the pry bar off the brick and held it. When the woman, who looked too old to be her mother, disappeared again, the girl got a book from under the stack and started reading it. It was a comic book, something with a lithe woman in flight on the front, wearing green and black, and the girl moved her finger along the frames, then closed it and looked at the cover. She turned and tried to position her body like the woman in the picture, fists up, legs cocked. She jumped up onto the chair, made flying noises, whooshing and zooming noises, spinning on the chair.

He watched, his nose streaming, his stomach turning. He was truly dopesick now, and he put out a hand and saw it vibrate, a wild, theatrical shaking that rattled the fine bones in his knuckles. This was the start of something terrible, he knew, inexorable, a revolt in the provinces of his body that would spread generally until it ran away from him and he'd twist and writhe and wish he was dead. This was a moment, like standing in cold water up to his knees and watching a wave coming, building power and force as it came down on him. It wasn't bad yet, but it was going to be, and he clutched the cool iron bar to his chest and watched the little girl on the chair as she spun and danced, her eyes closed, moving through clear air and clouds.

He came out of a Baptist church on Pine Street with his arms full. He was making too much noise, he knew. The door stood open and he was moving back and forth between the church and the long silver van parked at the curb with FIRST THESSALO-NIANS BAPTIST painted below the windows. He dropped a small amplifier next to the speakers he'd already loaded and pushed the sliding door shut, climbing from the passenger side across the long front seat to the driver's seat. He sat for a second, breathing hard, then lifted the iron and awkwardly banged at the steering column to open it.

The van was nice, well appointed, and the engine was quiet as he moved along Pine Street getting the feel of the big thing. He drove south by a darkened school, zigzagging to put some distance between the van and the church. A cop car went by in the other direction, lights going, and he ducked his head and turned the van down the next street he came to. His arms jerked, making it hard to keep the van to tight circles on the turns, and his nerves were like plucked wires under his skin, radiating waves of pain as if he were being pricked everywhere, along his arms and legs, his spine. He was sweating, the fear of getting caught and the increasing need for dope merging so that he pulled hard to the curb, gripped by a wave of nausea. Orlando looked up and found himself in front of the hospital where he'd been born. The name was different, but he knew it used to be called Misericordia. He tried to remember what it meant, the name. He couldn't now, but wouldn't it be something about misery? Wouldn't it just? He almost laughed.

Orlando stashed the van and called Audie, who sounded glad to hear from him, even in the middle of the night. He'd said sure, he'd come down and take a look at the van and the stuff and get him a few bucks for it, and why didn't they meet at noon down where the shit was stashed? Orlando said okay, a little disappointed, and wandered up to a squat on Arizona to crash with Arthur the vet and two hopper friends of his. The train hoppers were wiry little fuckers who talked to each other in an impenetrable code, and one of them showed Orlando a chain with a big padlock on it that he swung around his head, he said, whenever he felt threatened. He bobbed his head with the effort of spinning the heavy chain.

"Don't take it the wrong way. I'm just claiming my space, you know? You got to claim your space everywheres you go. Otherwise they get up on you and that's how it all starts."

Arthur rolled his eyes at the display and told Orlando they were basically harmless if you stayed out of their way. He showed Orlando a room on the second floor with a space cleared for him to lie down and gave him a couple of pills from a stash he'd been hoarding, painkillers he'd scored from the VA hospital before he'd left the last time.

When the pills began to work Orlando lay on some old quilted pads from a freight truck and closed his eyes. He couldn't sleep, but he ran through the last days in his head and tried to sort out what it meant. He would try to hold it all laid out in front of him but he would lose it just when it all started to line up, and there was a buzzing in his ears and bright lines and flashes in his eyes as if he were seeing his own electricity, the power that ran him.

Geo and Michael had gone looking for a girl, a prostitute who had been a favorite of Parkman Sr. They tracked her down a block from the house where she'd gone to bum money from Mia and Tisa, and then while they were all standing there they were shot at and Geo was killed. The cops said it was just drug war stuff, Green Lane guys shooting up the Tres Nortes, and that just made it bad luck. They were trying to help a girl who was pregnant and strung out. Messed up even before she saw the boys shot down on the street. Orlando had seen her a few days later down by Mexican Bob's, and she was completely broken then. Talking to herself, wandering in a daze.

So had it just been a kid who felt bad for a woman he thought his father had victimized? If that was true, how did he know who she was? Geo had the sex ads in his room, so he was definitely looking for a girl he knew was a prostitute. He worked at the homeless shelter, so maybe that's how he knew she was messed up and pregnant, but how did he know who she was in the first place? The girl had said she had a date. Was that just bullshit because she was crazy or high? Or did someone make a date with her? A date to stand in front of a dope house and get shot at?

However it had played out, the kid had died trying to do a good thing, right? He had found out his father was screwing this girl, and when she showed up at the homeless shelter pregnant and messed up and broke, he'd tried to find her and help her. He sold his camera to Ryan to raise money to give the girl, and got shot for his trouble. Then when Orlando had asked around about it, talked to a few people about what happened that night, he was cut off at all his corners. So somebody knew he was involved and didn't like it.

It made him feel connected to the kid, like carrying the little keychain he'd taken from the kid's room. He wished now he'd kept the CDs he'd stolen instead of giving them to Audie and Franny for letting him get high with them. He touched his pocket and felt the hard outline of the little keychain with its lightsaber charm. The kid who watched movies about men with a code. Samurai and warriors and lonely dreamers who followed their own lights. It was worth doing, trying to know this. Trying to understand what happened to a kid like this. Even if it cost him something. Even if no one else wanted to know.

It was about noon when Orlando got off the El at Girard, assaulted by the noise of the trains, the smell of piss on the landings going down. There was a fine, misty rain coating everything and fog that had eaten the expressway and all the buildings past the end of the block, so that there was that feeling of being inside even out on the street and the traffic noises seemed to come from everywhere.

He'd parked the van in an alley off Hope Street and gotten a promise of dope and a little money from Audie, who said he'd have to meet him there and look it over before he came across. He wished he'd been able to score some more pills from Arthur, who was gone when Orlando had woken up after a couple hours of thin sleep, his limbs falsely reporting pricks and stings as if he were lying on broken glass. He wanted to go back up to Roxborough and talk to Zoe, straighten things out and explain, apologize, but he needed to be himself to do that.

At the bottom of the stairs from the El station there was a PennDOT crew with the street torn up, one of those giant orange Ingersoll welding rigs putting out a painfully loud hum, a couple of neighborhood people watching a guy with a mask in the street hunched over a pit throwing a yellow-white glare, as if he were doing some kind of magic there. Orlando walked up toward Hope and stood in front of the little stand just under the tracks, counted change in his pocket, watched a woman buying lottery tickets and wanted one, just for the sensation of scratching the fine, ashy layer off the card and the little tremor of anticipation in the gesture.

He looked up and down for cops, but saw nothing. A guy in work clothes ducked into Club Ozz, a strip joint that billed itself as the land of make-believe for gentlemen. A bunch of PennDOT workers stood around in orange vests, but he didn't read them as cops. Across the street, a woman unlocked the door at the tattoo place next to a shuttered clothes shop.

He retreated down the alley a few steps to watch for Audie. It was cold in the mist and rain, and he shook a little and zipped his jacket up. After a few minutes he saw Audie get out of a beat-up old Honda and stand waiting for the traffic to clear. Orlando hadn't noticed the car pull up, and there was somebody else still in the car that he couldn't make out behind the wet glass.

Audie caught his eye and nodded, crossing in the middle of the block to where he stood. He looked serious; he kept his head low in the light mist and kept moving past Orlando down the alley, his hands in his pockets.

"How's it going, man?"

Orlando moved to keep up with him. "Oh, you know. Anxious. I'm a little behind, you know?"

"I hear that. Where is it?"

Orlando pointed to where the van was pulled half up on a

rotting curb between two derelict buildings, down where Hope looked like a wide alley. Weeds cascaded over a broken fence and pooled around the tires of the van like it had been there for years. Audie kept moving, going quickly down the alley without looking back. He moved around behind the van and pulled at the door, motioning Orlando over.

"So what is all this shit?" He stuck his head in, and Orlando got a strange vibe, Audie's voice too loud, his eyes all over the place except on Orlando's face and acting busy with his head buried in the van.

"It's an amplifier, some speakers and cables and shit, from a church up on Pine. Everything okay there? Did you bring me anything?" Two pigeons wandered in the trash by the curb, and he thought how it seemed like the streets used to be full of birds and that you hardly saw them anymore.

Audie said, "Yeah, sure. Just seeing what's what." He finally turned then, facing Orlando. Audie flicking his eyes over him and then up the alley the way they had come. Scratching at the bright tattoos on his arms, the dragons and kimonoed girls. The pigeons went up, lifting with a rattling noise, and Orlando took a step back and pivoted to look behind him. There was a guy moving down the street toward him, a guy with black hair and a ratty black raincoat whose face he knew but couldn't place. He was out of it, not thinking right, and when he finally remembered he'd gotten high with the guy in the dope house and that he'd played the music Orlando liked so much, he smiled and pointed.

The guy wasn't smiling back at him. He was going into his coat, concentrating on him with an intensity that finally set off an alarm, but all Orlando could do was back up, hitting the wall with his elbows, looking fast at Audie, who was watching everything with a sick and fascinated look, one hand on the open van door.

He was too tired and beat down to run, Orlando thought, too out of it, stretched too thin over too many days, and the guy, the Irish guy, was closing the distance with his hand in his coat, his face sad, his mouth turned down. The gun came out then, a small black pistol pointed at Orlando, and his chest moved up and down, an exhalation that was a sigh of resignation. *Why would anybody shoot me?* He thought this, forgetting everything that had happened and falling back on his own image of himself as a wandering eye that took in everything without comment or explanation. Forgetting that he had asked a lot of people about murder, and that his quest had gotten him shut down on every corner he had ever scored drugs. Forgetting it all and thinking himself harmless in the last moment.

There was a squeal of brakes from Girard and a little red car stopped hard and they all turned to look, frozen. The car had blacked-out windows and there was music coming from inside it that got clearer as the passenger's side window went down. The music was loud, hard drums and a foreign language, and Orlando cocked his head to hear it. Audie actually said, "Is that French?" Then the big automatic rifle in the window opened up, a sawing roar bounced around the hard brick surfaces of the alley, followed closely by the ringing of the bullets as they punched through the metal skin of the van, making a line of holes, a wild track running left to right and up, finally smashing the rear window before catching Audie in the side so that he made a noise, a hard plosive exhalation, and blood sprayed out of him over the weeds and the fence and the brick wall before he fell.

The Irish guy swung, somehow not hit that Orlando could see, and he walked toward the car, Christ, how was that possible? Who walks toward a rifle, the yellow sparks and gray smoke going like in a movie? But the black-haired guy squared to the car like it was nothing and had the pistol up in front of him and was pulling the trigger again and again, an arc of shells coming over his right shoulder and his shots breaking the rear window of the little red car and making small black holes in the door.

Orlando should have been running, but he stood against the wall and watched it happen. Audie lying on the ground, his legs jerking, his eyes open but unfocused, his hands plucking the air, blood on his face and coming out of his mouth. The Irish guy dropping the big pistol he'd been firing and going under his coat again. A kid, a skinny, tall kid with long braids getting out of the car, loosing a cascade of spent shells off the seat that chimed musically in the street. The kid unsteady, hurt maybe, leaning against the car door as he wrestled with a long belt of bullets that was draped around his neck. He was laying the belt into the gun and screaming something in French, hitting the bolt with his opened hand, when the black-haired Irish guy got another pistol free from the folds of his coat and fired twice fast, the bullets snapping through the kid so that he dropped his head, somehow still holding on to the rifle.

The car drifted forward a few feet, and Orlando could see the guy in the driver's seat slump forward, his head hitting the steering wheel and setting off a long, loud blast of the horn. The Irish guy stood still, the pistol pointing straight out at the kid with the rifle, whose own head was down as if he were thinking hard or just acknowledging the damage the Irishman's gun had done. The kid stood weaving, the rifle in one hand, the barrel pointing down and out.

They all stood there for a minute, the car horn going, the shot-up guy in the braids trying to lift the barrel of the gun, and then Orlando took a step back, and then another, and then he was running flat out, past Audie and south down Hope Street into the fog. Past the beat-down empty factories with their grilled windows, across the old concrete-bottomed lots dotted with rain and through the rusted, gaping chain-link fences. He ran south and then west, losing himself in the flat, empty spaces before throwing himself down behind a hedge on American Street and staying there, prone and still, his heart going in his chest.

The whole thing had looked simple to Angel. The way it should go. One junkie pointing out another on the street so Angel could shoot him. Asa Carmody wanted to tell him about it, about why it had to be done. This guy, Orlando, a junkie from around the neighborhood, was asking questions of mutual friends about their business, but Angel wasn't interested. Angel kept shaking his head, holding his hand out for the burglar's number, telling Asa not to confuse it with details about who said what. He would ride with the older junkie, the burglar from

Fishtown, down to Girard to see the younger junkie, who was some kind of half-assed thief, and Angel would shoot the young guy and solve Asa's problem.

So Angel had seen it all in his head, the way he always did, but it didn't play out the way he'd seen it. There was no way to see what was coming today. The African's man throwing down on him with the giant machine gun from the other night. Somehow missing him from how many feet away? Though it was hard, he knew, making a big, belt-fed gun like that do what you wanted while you were hunched over in a little car. It was dumb luck, for sure, but then also on him not to panic, to stand his ground and empty his guns until the kid went down, those magnificent braids spread all around him in the mud on Hope Street. The man's mouth open in something like a smile, and blood in his teeth. Angel would remember that.

It was a good trick, the African picking him up somewhere and following him here. Part of him admired the man for doing that and was sorry the man was dying in the street, small bubbles opening in the blood on his chest. Ruining his shirt, a bright print with tall black girls and African colors. Angel got the smell of rain and weed and gunpowder.

Asa had set it all up, called Angel and told him what to do, got the thief with the dragon tattoos on his arms to cash in on his friend, the junkie Angel was supposed to kill. It was tough the little thief got shot up, but he had turned on his friend, and Angel thought, *There you go*. Fuck him for informing. Himself, he'd always been lucky, never even nicked by a bullet, but of course it wasn't just luck. It was something he'd learned, and so early it was like he'd always known it. To keep going, stand your ground and fight it out and not run. To keep your head. It was a talent, or just the way he was, but it served him. He liked how the big African kid fucked with him, called him out in French, and he wished he knew the language to know what it was the guy was saying. Now they were his last words. Imagining wild, flamboyant insults that maligned his family, his manhood, the generations that spawned him—but who knew? He felt bad again, seeing the guy lying there with the rifle in his open, useless hands. His eyes blinked once, twice, then opened finally in the rain, and Angel wished he knew his name.

Angel had lowered his head to get a view of the driver, dead, slumped across the wheel, laying on the horn with his forehead. Bad enough to have a gunfight on the edge of fucking Girard Avenue in the middle of the day; now the horn was going so that everybody for two blocks was looking their way, and he'd have to move. He shook his head to see the two cars ruined, the dead man lying stretched out in the street. Next to the van was the other one, Audie, the rat, the one who'd put them onto the little junkie he'd come here to end. Audie was lying on his side, drawn up, his face gray. Spitting blood onto the side of the shot-up silver van. Trying to talk around the blood.

Angel stood over him. "You're Murphy?"

Audie moved his mouth, but only blood came out.

Angel shook his head. "You're Irish, you should know better. It's what comes to the informer." He spat.

At the end of the block he thought he saw the junkie pivot and turn west, just a flash of the leather jacket, but that could wait for another day. Would have to, now. He could hear sirens going, even over the racket of the horn. Took one last look back and had to shake his head again, smile at the man who tracked him down and opened up on him. Not give a shit where or when, just roll down the window and blast away like an old-time gangster and fuck it all. He found a hole in the fence and stepped through.

Zoe knocked on the door of a house on Shurs Lane, and the guy who ran the house let her in. They didn't like the place, she and Orlando, though she couldn't exactly say why. It was partially the people who ran it, the tall Puerto Rican kid, Benigno, who had kind of a superior attitude, or the spacey Asian girl with the half-smile. It was run-down, but all the places they knew were run-down. There was a lot of trust in going in to a place to score, or hang out and get high, and whether the people or the place seemed cool was a complex and a shifting thing.

She sat for a while and talked to a girl she recognized from the neighborhood, somebody she'd met at Fluid, a club down on Fourth Street. She was there waiting on her boyfriend and lounged on a sprung couch draped with an Indian print, and they talked about people they knew, bars they liked, the vintage place down on Third where the girl had gotten her dress, a bright blue chiffon with a beaded neck that Zoe coveted.

It took a while, longer than it should have, and the Asian girl just ignored them with her strange smile, and the Puerto Rican kid pled a slowdown and asked could they wait, which was fine with Zoe, there being nowhere to go since things were all fucked up with Orlando. Her body was tired, but her mind was alert, up half the night at Mary's, talking the thing with Orlando out and drinking coffee. They were straight, Mary and Marty, which was cool for them, but she had come away wanting to get high. The baby was beautiful and well-behaved, but something about the quiet, the order of the house, got under her skin and made her edgy in a way she couldn't bring into focus.

The girl in the blue dress had a flask of something sweet in her purse, and she shared it with Zoe, who took a bigger hit off it than was probably polite. She wiped her mouth with the back of her hand and called for dope, dope, and the girl laughed and took it up, calling, "We want to get high." They went back and forth with the flask, getting to be best friends, Zoe feeling the drinks fast, laughing too loud and too easily. The girl's boyfriend came back from wherever and she left with him, waving and making extravagant promises now about how they would get together, go somewhere, and hang out.

The Asian girl came out and put something in her hands, and Zoe touched her cheek, now everybody's friend, but the smile didn't change. The tall kid, Benigno, with the bushy Afro, hung back in the doorway, talking on the cell, and she had the crazy idea it was about her, and that made her laugh, too. She wanted to do the dope there, but the guy came out and said they were done for the day and she should take the dope and go. In fact he was pulling the girl into the back, waving Zoe off, turning off lights like it was a fucking bar at closing time.

She almost ran home, crossing the few blocks to the house and half hoping Orlando would be there, though she didn't know how she'd be when she saw him. She'd been angry and tired and he'd been frantic. Still, he'd raised his hand to her, something he'd never done, that she hadn't thought was in him, and that opened a lot of bad doors in her head, thinking about her father standing over her, breathing hard, his eyes red and heavy fists hanging. When she'd first met Orlando she'd slept with the razor on the nightstand, close by, and would wake up to check it was there. He knew that, knew all of it, and should have never. Not ever.

So now she sat with the little glassine bag on the scarred table in the kitchenette, looking at it, feeling antsy, wanting to wait and not wanting to. Wanting to talk to Orlando and not wanting to, wanting to mark his thin white skin with her small hands, pull his hair, feel his hands on her, feel him move inside her. All of it, and where was he? Did it mean anything, that he was cut off, or was it just paranoia or him acting up at a corner and taking it for conspiracy, as if Orlando Donovan were at the center of things in the world?

She laid out the dope, then got out the spoon and the little velvet ribbon he used to tie himself off and a clean needle from the exchange down on Girard. She opened her Japanese puzzle box and took out her iPod from its secret drawer, put on her headphones, and dialed up an Algerian CD Orlando had found at Beautiful World down on Passyunk. Her heart went faster, timed to the echoing drums and bursts of distorted guitar. The words were in a language she didn't know, but they made her think of seduction, of nameless longing. The word "abandon," the word "bereft." She lit a red candle and opened a bottle of wine and waited. Looked at the dope, went to the window and watched the street. Watched the flame gutter, listened to it hiss.

CHAPTER

16

Danny had been going through old files, talking to older homicide guys he knew and Drug Enforcement agents, connecting dots in a chart in his head. He talked to Frank Keduc about the dead Somali and two beat cops from Kensington about the Dunn brothers. After three hours in cold cases, he called Matt Gialdo, and the retired detective had Danny come out to his house, a neat little three-story house in Mt. Airy.

It was raining when he pulled up, but Gialdo was in the open door of the garage. Danny remembered him as a fastidious guy. All the homicide guys he knew were dudes, dressed sharp, *were* sharp, but even in that company Gialdo stood out. His family was from Trinidad, which threw everybody who thought he'd be Italian when they heard the name. He had a way of changing the feel of a room, the temperature, just by focusing on a suspect. Danny had watched him close, had seen him get confessions, it seemed, just by listening intently, nodding his head when he heard the truth. It was something he did with his eyes, some wordless transaction between him and the people he talked to that eliminated bullshit as an option.

There was a tarp spread out on the floor and motor parts

neatly arrayed under a work light. Matt pointed to a little sports car under another tarp.

"MG. I bought it ten years ago, but now I have the time to spend on it." It was the kind of meticulous job Danny could picture Matt doing. "It keeps me from driving Dessie crazy." Matt walked past the tarp and started running his hands along a row of cardboard file boxes. He lifted one and set it aside, then pulled one along the floor and spun it to face Danny.

"DeAngelo Barnes."

Danny knelt down. "Do you remember it?"

Matt Gialdo looked away. "Summer of 2002. They found him in the river near the boathouses. Two coeds from Princeton down to practice rowing. Crew, I guess they call it, when it's kids from Princeton. He was shot once, up close." He tapped the side of his head. "His mother called me every day for six months. After I heard about DeAngelo giving up Derrick Leon, I spent a lot of time looking at how Leon could have had it done, but I couldn't see how. Leon had already killed all his friends out of paranoia, so who was left that would care enough to kill DeAngelo because he had given up Leon? I think everybody I talked to was glad Leon was off the street." He looked at the box. "I talked to him. To Leon. And he gave me that smile, that crazy smile? So I knew he knew something, but he never said. He was so crazy he wasn't making a lot of sense anyway."

Neither of them touched the boxes. The recall was standard, Danny knew, for homicide guys. They'd be able to tell you chapter and verse on unsolveds from ten, fifteen years before. He knew he was already doing it, just in his time. You take things out

271

once in a while, dust them off, look at them from different angles. After a while they stay in your head.

Danny was thinking of his kid from the river. Soap Williams. "Anything, you know, stand out?"

Matt touched his stomach, his chest. "He had these holes. Holes, not gunshot. From some kind of long knife. A bayonet, the coroner thought."

Danny went into his pocket and pulled out his notebook. He had a sketch he'd made of Soap's body, a crude rendering of a featureless body. Alongside the head was an arrow pointing slightly up, the angle of the shot that had killed him. On the torso were three spots he'd inked in, and the notation *long knife, military?*

He thanked Matt Gialdo and loaded the case into the backseat of his car, squinting through the light rain. "I'll copy a few things out and get them back to you."

The older detective shook his head. "It doesn't matter. Mrs. Barnes died a year ago. His sister moved, somewhere out west, but I don't hear from her. I don't think anybody much remembers DeAngelo but me."

The rain stopped, and the sun poked holes in the clouds. It got hot, and just as fast, unbearably humid. Orlando walked south and west, stopping to look back, zigzagging at the corners and alleys. Still not sure whether it had all happened the way he remembered. Audie acting so weird, and the Irish guy, who definitely had a gun because he'd shot that tall black kid with it. If the kid hadn't pulled up and unloaded, Orlando knew he'd be dead back in that alley. He'd gotten a pretty good look at the shooter with the rifle and didn't have a clue who he was, or why he'd want to help Orlando, so it must have just been something between the Irish guy and the shooter with that enormous goddamn machine gun. A nice-looking guy, he'd have said, with neat features and wild braids and wearing a bright print shirt.

At a little park in Northern Liberties he tried to jump a chain between two posts and went over hard. He got up fast and moved away from the street, limping. He couldn't remember the name of the park, which was just a couple of green blocks with a little playground and some trees. He and Zoe had watched a movie there the summer before. A crazy Western with Gregory Peck, all lurid, dense colors and people so in love they had to shoot each other to escape it. He limped to the center of the park and dropped to his knees between two small trees. Two women were setting up lawn chairs a few feet away, wearing sunglasses and tank tops. One of them cradled a baby wrapped in a yellow blanket.

He pulled himself into a sitting position, tried to seem harmless or normal while he planned what to do, where to go. The women looked at each other, and the woman with the baby went into a complicated-looking backpack studded with pockets and got out a bottle while he tried to avoid their eyes. He drew up one knee stained with dirt and grass, his eyes going to the edges of the park. He couldn't stop looking at the baby's fragile head out of the corner of his eye, the weight of it in its mother's slender hands.

Something was jabbing him through his pants, and he reached

in and pulled out the little lightsaber keychain he'd taken from Geo's room. He held it in his hand, putting his fingers against his chest and feeling the air and blood moving through him. So it had been Audie who warned him about talking to the wrong people, and Audie himself turned out to be the wrong people. But did Audie give him up to the Irish killer for money? Or did he get in trouble, too? And acting to protect himself and Fran, he'd given up Orlando?

He looked at the keychain in his palm. It all had to do with the kid, and asking questions. That's why he'd been shut down, and why people were trying to kill him now. The Irish guy had talked to him when they'd been high back at the house in East Falls, about the people dead in the river. It wasn't some kind of dope dream; the guy had put people in the river, and that's where Orlando would have gone. Dead, into the van, with a bullet in his head, and then into the river somewhere, down with the river silt to wash away, his bones to become ash sifted by the current.

What else had the guy said, back in the dope house? Nothing he could remember. He remembered the tall, angry Puerto Rican kid with the bushy 'fro, and the other guy, Asa, the red-haired guy who told the kid to let him in. The kid not liking it, but doing it. If he could overrule the angry kid, outrank him, then he owned the place and the kid just ran it. He'd been there before, Orlando, with Zoe, and they didn't like the place, didn't like the angry kid, but he'd never seen Asa there before.

He watched some people carrying gardening tools to a little community plot, squinting skeptically at the new sun. Moving through the little furrows and bending to the green shoots in the orderly rows. He got to his feet, slowly, feeling his skeleton through his skin, feeling like he didn't belong there. Thought about how he'd look to the people coming down in their rubber boots with their kids to plant cauliflowers and squash. He had that feeling he'd had before, of wanting to explain himself, but why, and who would want to hear it?

He started jogging, feeling like bones wrapped in the thin sheet of his skin, every footfall an electric shock that ran through him, a little wave of pain communicated through his slight frame from his feet to his head. He was sick, he was hunted, and for what? Zoe was right, it was all for his brother, wasn't it, really? Nobody was paying him and nobody cared. It was a show he was putting on, to get something from Brendan. To be treated with respect, to be worthy of respect and love? Is this what it took? And was it worth it? For the first time he let himself worry about Zoe. Let himself wonder if she was safe. If it was smart for him to even go to her. He was already moving, though; he'd have to find her, talk to her, tell her to get away. With no one he could trust to carry the message, he'd have to tell her to her face.

He ran north, cut right to find an open road. He came out at a little island in the street at Second and Girard, a shard of concrete pointing south and clotted with green bushes. He puked, bent double, his hand on the cool stone base of a statue of a tall man on a horse. The figure held a lance that towered over Second Street, and his horse was canted back as if about to rear, but the man, helmetless, looked serene, almost happy, ready to move alone against whatever was arrayed against him in the blocks south of Girard Avenue.

Orlando dropped to his knees, then pulled his shirttail out

of his pants and bent to wipe his face clean with shaking hands. He stepped out of the bushes and sat hard on the curb, noticing a kid was sitting in the shadow of the statue, selling water bottles from a cooler full of melting ice. The kid looked at him for a minute, his expression mournful, and then he held a bottle out to Orlando, who waited a beat before taking it.

"I can't pay you. I got nothing."

The kid shrugged. He had one of those kid faces that was already a thousand years old. A line of constant worry above his brows and eyes so full of disappointment it looked like there was room for nothing else. Then the boy let a smile break through, and it was like watching a swimmer break the surface of a dark lake. "Everybody's got something."

Orlando stuck his hand in his pocket and came up with the keychain. He looked at it for a minute, then held it out on his palm, and the kid looked at it, too. He lifted one eyebrow, then went into his own pocket and came out with the same lightsaber keychain, his in royal purple.

The kid looked down the block, then knocked his hand against Orlando's in salute and put the chain away. Orlando nodded and stood up and started walking away.

The kid called to him. "How we doing?"

"Same as always."

"That bad?"

The kid sat back down, and Orlando held up the bottle, walking west toward Zoe and the apartment, picking up speed as he went. He needed to see her face and hear her voice. He saw a trolley moving west, and he started to run.

. . .

Brendan's cell phone rang, a number he didn't know, but when Orlando started talking he tagged Luis on the shoulder and they went across Roxborough fast, lights and sirens, and called an ambulance. It came over the radio a second later, a woman lying in the street a block off Green Lane. The guys who picked it up first requested an additional unit to deal with the crowd, and they pulled up to see a few kids from the neighborhood clustered at the curb, and two old Polish ladies Brendan had seen around before who were shouting at the kids to stay back. Luis called in while Brendan got out and looked for the girl and his half brother.

She was young, with long black hair. Pretty, before whatever had gotten to her. He realized he'd seen her before, in the hospital room where they'd taken Orlando when he'd been shot. She was lying on her side, cradled in his half brother's arms, her body absolutely slack in the boneless way of people who are unconscious. Her face was slick with sweat and there was a froth on her parted lips. His brother was sobbing, lowering his head to hers, a trail of spit from his mouth, and he was saying something Brendan couldn't understand. He put one hand on his brother's arm, gently, so that he would let Brendan get close enough to hear the faint whistle of her breath and see up close her skin leached of blood. He gave Luis the high sign, and his partner hit the mike on his shoulder and put a rush on the ambulance while the first two guys on scene pushed the kids and old ladies back into a rough loop, half on the curb and half in the street.

Brendan turned, shifted his body slightly to see her face in profile, and remembered her from the hospital room. He swore under his breath and put his hand to her throat to find a slight, rapid pulse there, like a faint code transmitted by her failing heart. He looked around at the crowd and the buildings nearby, saw the open door, and ran up the stairs till he reached the third landing and looked into the tiny apartment, the carpet thin as dust, the kitchen table with its veneer peeled up in one corner. Took in the open glassine bag on the table, kept moving through the apartment, banging open the bedroom door, pulling the shower curtain off its gaping rings. Swearing at his grieving brother, at the poor, dying girl in the street, at his son, at his own failed luck at being tied by blood to all this self-destruction and bad judgment and pain. As he came back down he could hear the ambulance coming closer, the shriek and whine of the siren hitting the hard surfaces of the narrow streets.

He got back to the street out of breath, just in time to see Orlando struggling with Luis and one of the guys from the other RMP as the ambulance guys got to work. Mouth open, his face contorted and terrible, he was trying to get to Zoe, and Brendan caught his arms and pulled him close, taking in the bruises and scrapes on the kid's face, the rank smell of him, the water streaming from his eyes and nose. He was still talking but the words seemed random and it was impossible to make any sense of it and Brendan didn't think it mattered. Orlando windmilled his arms over Brendan's shoulders, pushing, screaming, finally dropping to the ground to beat at his own face with his hands. The old ladies crossed themselves, and the kids looked at each other, eyes wide.

Brendan put one hand on Orlando's shoulder, hard, as if anchoring him to the curb. He saw the white soles of Zoe's feet, her shoes neatly peeled off as she fell, as if she'd kicked them off and let herself settle flat into the asphalt between two parked cars like a child playing dead. Luis brought a blanket from the car and covered her legs, and Brendan let Orlando put one hand out to touch the edge of it, work it in his fingers while they waited for the ambulance to move her. He talked to the crew and told his brother her pulse was still there, she was still alive, but his brother looked up at him with such concentrated misery in his eyes he doubted himself and wanted them to check again. The ambulance guys fetched some bags and an orange composite board, and Brendan moved his brother back to stand upright.

Orlando grabbed his sleeve so hard he could feel the nails bite his skin. "Get the dope."

"Let's just get her to the hospital—"

"I'm going with her. Get the dope. Grab the bag and bring it to me."

"It's evidence now."

"Then put it in a plastic bag or something. I don't give a shit. I need it." They both turned to watch the medics roll Zoe onto the board, her face slack, and they heard Luis grab one of the EMTs by the sleeve and whisper, "She's family."

Orlando followed them as they carried Zoe, who looked even smaller on the gurney, a sick child, her half-closed eyes sunk in dark, bruiselike circles. He called to his brother, his eyes red with blood. "Get it and bring it to me, I'm not fucking kidding." He climbed in after the crew and stood on the bumper. "Brendan, it's about Michael, too. Get the bag. Do it now."

The sun went down, and Chris Black drove through Kensington and Frankford, then back to the river and south again, looking for the girl. Asa said she'd lived on Richmond Street a while back, but now she was just a homeless junkie and how tough could it be to find her? He cruised in nearly aimless circles for three hours and decided it was pretty fucking hard. He tried to talk to two kids sitting at the curb in front of a squat on Tulip Street, and one of them started talking about Jesus and spinning a chain over his head with a big fucking lock on the end, so Chris pulled away fast and kept moving.

There were a lot of homeless people wandering the Parkway in the blocks in front of the art museum. More than he remembered, and it was tough to figure out much about them. Every one looking the same in colorless bundled clothing despite the heat, their coats and their hair and their skin all gone a kind of reddish brown, like old brick. Lugging bags and bundles, pushing carts heaped with shit no one sane would want.

He found a shelter down on Thirteenth, but it was for men only. He parked near City Hall and walked the parks, seeing everything but young girls who might be the one Asa wanted. He couldn't ask around, couldn't show anyone her picture, so he walked circles in the humid dark, trying to eyeball every homeless woman under sixty. All this to kill her. It was insane and getting crazier by the minute. Wherever this girl was, she was gone, and what did it matter? What did she know? Who would listen to her anyway?

He got back in his car and drifted past Franklin Square, his heart not in it, then turned north and drove past the Electric Factory on Seventh, passing long lines of kids waiting to get into a concert. It was nice to see them after looking at the decrepit and destitute for hours. The girls in short dresses and heels, drifting in clouds of perfume and talking on cell phones. Half present and half gone in dreams, the way the pretty ones were. A couple of the young ones checked him out, or checked out the SUV anyway.

He took the picture out again and turned on the overhead light and held it up to see it and get her fresh in his mind. She was pretty, with impossibly big eyes, and a kind of sly smile where you could clearly see she was going to be trouble. He'd known a few girls like that, the ones who seemed to like fun without any limits, who would let you do whatever you wanted to them, who always wanted to go out, drink and get high, and they were cool for a while and then they weren't. They tipped over, from that hunger to be entertained, from being afraid to be still for two minutes, into a manic and then an angry hyperactivity, or just got sad and quiet and disappeared into themselves in a way that made you feel guilty for even buying them a drink.

He noticed for the first time the ragged edge of the picture where it was torn. A man's arm came out of the lost part of the photo and went around the girl's neck and she held it bent over her shoulder with a closeness more proprietary than affectionate. He saw the man's pale hand, the edge of the brown vest at the torn border. It was Asa. He wasn't too surprised, he realized. He'd never seen the little creepy fuck with a girl, but he figured the guy had one stashed somewhere, and it didn't surprise him that at some point anyone who had any real knowledge of the guy and his life would end up dead. Dating that guy seemed to Chris like going for a run in the dark woods with some kind of animal with steely claws and a mouth full of teeth.

He was sitting in his car, making himself laugh by picturing Asa buying flowers and making a mixtape, when he saw her. She was standing at the edge of the crowd on Seventh, watching the lined-up kids, talking or maybe singing to herself. She was dirty, thinner than in the picture, her face drawn and lined with a sooty gray, as if she'd washed her face with ash. She was rubbing her hands together and mouthing something, watching the kids from a distance at the edge of a bright circle of light from a streetlamp.

The other people at the corner averted their eyes as they went past, like she was the ghost of good times past and to see her was to invite bad luck. She was wearing a heavy jacket that made her shapeless above the waist and her hair jutted in stiff bristles. He saw a gap in the cars at the corner and pulled to the curb, craning his neck to keep her in sight as he maneuvered the big Navigator.

He jumped out, his keys in his hand, moving slowly from behind her, wondering what to say to her to get her to come with him to the car. Grabbing her seemed like a bad move. There were too many people around for him to muscle her, all the kids appearing out of the dark toward the end of the line for the show, and she was probably out of her mind. He kept his head down, aware of the people passing, the lights ahead, of trying to seem cool, of his own bulked-up shoulders and height. In clubs and most of the time in the street his size worked for him, but now sweat bloomed on his cheeks and under his arms, and he stopped at the corner, a few feet behind her, holding on to the iron fence.

He was just a couple of feet behind her, and he could begin to make out what she was saying. Her head swiveled as the kids went by, and it looked like she was searching faces, looking for someone. He noticed a big paper bag between her feet, and once in a while she'd reach down and touch the bag, like she was making sure it was still there.

There was music from the passing cars, and the kids called to each other as they moved down the street, but he began to hear snatches of what she was saying, her voice small and quiet, but rushed, like she was afraid she wouldn't get it all out. He had to hear it a few times to get it all, and at first he thought it was a song, the way she let her voice waver up and down as she said the words.

"Saint Michael the Archangel, defend us in battle. Be our defense against the wickedness and snares of the Devil. May God rebuke him, we humbly pray." She touched her head, quick, one dirty finger to the center of her forehead. "And do thou. O Prince of the Heavenly Host. By the power of God."

He let himself move closer, his head cocked to hear the words, and he saw her small hands rub together again. He hadn't been in church in years, not to stay and listen. He'd take his mother down to meet her friends at Holy Name, give her money to drop in the basket, but to stay and listen? It was a prayer, though, he knew, and she had some kind of crazed ritual going. Touching her head, the way she rubbed her hands together, over and over. A little kid, frightened of things in the dark.

"Thrust into hell Satan. And all the evil spirits." She touched her forehead and swiveled again, as if there were spirits around her and she could see them. "Who prowl about the world." Her head going, and he had to look, too, over his shoulder. Seeing the tall shadows thrown onto the buildings on Seventh. Her fear that plain. "Seeking the ruin of souls. Amen."

She turned and saw him then, and he stopped. She looked at his face and moved toward him, and he saw the bulge at her middle then. The stained and ratty jacket stretched over her belly. She started up again, about Saint Michael, but she was searching his face now, and he stood still.

She moved toward him, so that he could smell her, a strange and unexpected sweetness underlain with an odor like wet ashes. She reached out one black hand and patted his bicep, and before he could react she had put her arms around him. "I prayed you would come." He felt the little belly push against his legs, the thin sticks of her arms on his back and her hands patting his shoulder blades. "No wings," she said. "I prayed so hard." She held a hand up, then darted back to get the paper bag. She held it up and smiled, making creases in the dirt on her face. She moved close to him again and opened the bag, and he reared a little, afraid of what might be inside, but she reached in and he got the sweet smell again, stronger.

She came out with a cherry Danish. "They give them away at the Holiday Inn, on Market. Every night they just give them away. But you have to be there right at the exact moment. And they have to like you." She pushed the big pastry toward him, and he put his hand out and took it to keep her from shoving it in his mouth. "I knew it would be you. I kept them for you." She smiled, and tears formed at the corners of her eyes. "For some have entertained angels." She went back in the bag. "I have cherry and I have blueberry," she said. She smiled and wiped at the tears, making white tracks on her dirty face. "Angels unawares."

Orlando sat in the corner of Zoe's hospital room, unable to take his eyes off her, till Kathleen came in and put her hand on his arm. She told him she'd come get him if anything happened and to go get cleaned up. He'd looked at her for a long moment before going into the little bathroom and running the water. The door opened, and she handed him a bag that he opened to find an oversized sweatshirt and a white T-shirt. She told him they were Michael's.

The doctor came in and told them he thought it was something in the heroin. Her lungs had shut down so that there was a terrible hissing machine tied to her mouth and they would have to wait to see if she started breathing on her own again. He went over to the bed, his face still wet from the sink, and bent to her, kissing one hand, seeing the lavender polish on her nails that was chipped and cracked at the edges.

Brendan came in and tapped him on the shoulder. Kathleen watched them as Orlando nodded at his brother, then dropped his head again and whispered something to Zoe. She thought she saw the girl's eyes flicker, but then Orlando was taking

Brendan's hand and pulling him outside. Before he left, Brendan told Kathleen to go home to Michael, who now sometimes woke up in the middle of the night and had to check on Kathleen and Brendan before he could get back to sleep. As if they had been the ones who had been hurt, as if they had been the cause of his worry.

Brendan had a rolled paper bag under his arm, and Orlando followed him to the end of the hall, where his brother set it on a low table next to some couches. He opened the bag and took out Zoe's purse, which Orlando grabbed and shook out on the cheap Formica, spilling out her keys, pens, lipsticks, a wallet made of stamped leather from Mexico, change, a name tag from work that brought back the last, awful moment they were together when they had fought and he had hit her.

He pocketed the razor, her phone, sifted quickly through the wadded Kleenex and rattling boxes of Tic-Tacs until he dropped the tip of a trembling finger on a tiny, waxy bag inked with a design in bright colors. A skull in Day-Glo green, little lightning bolts, a single word from one of those dime-store stamps. RADIOACTIVE.

Orlando stood up and stuffed his shaking hand into his pocket to grip the razor. Brendan touched his rigid arm and looked searchingly into his face and shook his head as if Orlando had spoken aloud, as if they were already arguing.

"Let me get help. Orlando." Hoping the name would make a difference. "I can have a dozen cops on them in ten minutes."

"They tried to kill her. She didn't even do anything. Neither did Michael."

"Why, then? Why did someone do this to Zoe?"

"I asked my friends. My fucking *friends*. About the shooting, about what happened the night the kids were at the dope house. And they tried to shoot me. Down by the El." Tremors passed through him, starting in the bones of his shoulders and rolling out to the edge of his fingers like he was suffering an earthquake only he could feel. He pointed at the table, the little bag of dope, to have something to do with his mutinous hands. "It's all connected, it's all a thing." He picked up the tiny bag and tapped the green design. "Where I saw this before? This place? The guy from this dope house is the guy who tried to shoot me. Maybe the guy who shot Michael and Geo." He wiped at his nose with the back of his wrist.

He's sick, Brendan thought. His brother's body was a collection of leaning sticks, or like something suspended from wires. "I don't understand. Who tried to shoot you?"

Orlando breathed through his mouth, like a dog. "I can't explain it all. It's something with this girl, I don't know. Zoe and me went to a house in Roxborough, around the corner from where Michael and Geo got shot."

"A dope house?"

"No, no. Girls, prostitutes. The boys were there that night. The night they were shot. And they were asking questions about that girl, Sienna." He stepped back. "I gotta go, Brendan. I know I don't make any fucking sense, but I know who did this to Zoe and I gotta go."

"You're sick, I can see it. Let's get help. You can explain it all to that detective. Martinez." He tried to pull his brother closer, hanging on to his sleeve.

Orlando looked at his brother's big hand on his arm. He sagged a little. "Okay," he said, forcing a smile. "Okay, go call somebody. The detective." He looked up and down the hall.

"You're sure?"

"Yeah, go ahead. We'll get this laid out."

Brendan narrowed his eyes, not completely trusting the change of heart, but he turned and pulled the cell phone out of his pocket. A nurse walking from one of the rooms back to the station whispered something to Brendan, and he held up a hand, walked toward the swinging doors to the hall outside the ICU. He had his ear to the phone when he heard a metallic click and turned to see the door to the stairway swinging shut.

He swore and called his brother's name, slapping shut the phone and sticking it in his pocket. He hit the door with both hands and ran down. In the gap through the middle of the stairway he could see his brother, already a level down and moving surprisingly fast for somebody as sick as he was. It should be easy to catch him, but Brendan kept looking over the rail and watching the gap widen between them, hearing the hard bang of his brother's boots hitting the steps going down and the ringing echo in the cinder-block stairway.

Brendan lengthened his stride, letting himself drop to the next landing and feeling the hard jolt to his knees. He almost lost his balance and slid along the rough wall, watching his brother bang through the exit door, hands out in front of him, as Brendan clawed at the railing. He was going too fast and went over hard, sliding down the last flight of stairs on his ass and cracking his head hard against the underside of the metal handrail.

Outside it was dark, and he went through the door limping, cursing. Feeling a hard knot below the skin of his thigh and a throb in his head timed to his racing heart. Orlando was running up Jamestown toward Ridge, his steps erratic, his arms pumping, disjointed, as if he were two separate halves of a human figure, welded together at the waist. Neither he nor his brother was moving fast now, Brendan feeling his legs stiffening, Orlando stopping to heave and spit.

A car moved by Brendan and paused, a colorless old Honda with long scratches and dents in the side panels. He squinted and held a hand up to shade his eyes, but there was too much glare from the streetlights and it was too dark in the car to see anything. The car sped up, coming alongside his brother and slowing again. Orlando was doubled over, one hand pressed to his chest, breathing hard through his mouth. Brendan saw the car drift to a stop and he pushed himself faster, his legs hitting the ground in an uneven lope as if one were shorter than the other.

He saw the driver's side door open and a slight, black-haired guy stood and threw back his coat, bringing a short-barreled police shotgun up and clear of the hood of the car. Brendan's heart flipped in his chest and he pulled his pistol, a blocky .40 caliber Glock, and threw it out in front of his face like he was going to hit somebody with it. He shouted something; it might have been "police," and it might have been his brother's name. The car was maybe thirty yards away, and the guy lifted the gun. He was on the far side of the car, the door open, lights on and the motor running.

Brendan lost sight of his brother, of everything but the man with the gun, sighting down the barrel of his service pistol and locking his arms. Brendan was screaming, his heart going, his eyes dilated. He thought there was a pulse that started behind his eyes and went out through his arms and shook the ground beneath his feet, the street in front of him. The lights overhead dimmed and brightened and dimmed again. He pulled the trigger and the guy kept moving, lifting the shotgun to his shoulder, Brendan firing over and over, shifting himself left to get a clear view, and when he saw the spray of yellow-white sparks from the shotgun barrel, he screamed.

Brendan saw the rear window of the car shatter from the Glock rounds, and the shooter jerked the pump, staggering, and then swung the gun his way so that the end of the barrel was a dark hole under the lights. Brendan fired again and dropped to his knees as the shotgun went off.

CHAPTER

17

Chris looked over at the girl, who said her name was Sienna. She had pulled her legs up onto the seat of the Navigator and hummed to herself, stopping once in a while to say something about Jesus and nod her head. She didn't ask where they were going. She played with the radio, pointed out the window at each of the dots of light that were planes coming into the airport. She said they were angels with a message from God and gave them names.

He reached behind him and pulled the pistol out of his belt and sat it in his lap for a moment. The little black SIG. He remembered when he'd bought it, gave some pimply kid three bills for it, the kid getting to pretend he was dealing iron instead of just some jackass who'd stolen a pistol from his father's locked cabinet. He looked over at the girl again, then opened the compartment between the seats and dropped it in.

The way she was sitting there, her small belly was pushed out between her legs. He'd have to do something with her, and he wasn't going to drop a hammer on a pregnant head case, or whatever the hell she was. He'd done a lot of dumb shit for Asa, but he wasn't doing this. For the first time, he saw more of what was going on, like a door had opened in his head. He was policing up some shit, and the more he thought about it, the more it felt like the last thing he was going to do for Asa Carmody.

What had he wanted? Money, but all he did was hang around the bars and buy jewelry and drinks for girls, and couldn't he have done that working at the refinery like his old man? He'd followed Shannon, that was the truth of it. Followed him into the life. Made the same bad calls and hung with the same dead-end street brawlers, taken up with Asa and done one stupid thing after another because his brother had done it and it was about proving something. Well, hadn't it been settled?

He wasn't as brave as Shannon or Gerry. He wasn't as stupid or as crazy, either. He wasn't a stone killer like Angel Riordan and he wasn't a schemer like Asa Carmody, and he was having trouble remembering when he'd wanted to be those things, like it had all been years in the past. He'd wanted to be somebody, to get respect, but from who? From morons or crazy fuckers who would kill pregnant girls or young kids and think themselves hard.

He thought through his options. He thought a lot about each possibility, making almost random turns around the city. He thought harder than he had in a long time, even when he'd driven away from Gerry and Frank bleeding in the street. He stopped and got the girl takeout from the McDonald's on Girard, near the El. She smiled at him around a mouthful of cheeseburger. He took out a wet wipe from a plastic container, and she closed her eyes and jutted out her chin a little, like a child, and he wiped at her face. She smelled like broiled meat and cherry jelly and lanolin.

She said, "Angels are coming to Philadelphia now. They

found me in the street and they wanted to give me money for the baby. I forget which ones are seraphim and which are cherubim." She pointed at him with a french fry. "Did it hurt? To lose your wings?"

"No," he said. "I never felt a thing."

Orlando got up slowly from the grass, looking off the way the car had gone, its tires smoking and leaving long tails of black in the street as it rocketed out into the traffic on Ridge Avenue, clipping a parked car before straightening out and disappearing east toward Philly.

He looked back down along the front of the hospital and saw his brother curled on the lawn, hat off, trying to lift himself up into a sitting position. He called to him and ran back toward him, seeing a blue-jacketed security man jogging from the main entrance, yelling something into a walkie-talkie.

"Jesus, Bren, are you okay?"

His brother sat back on his haunches, his eyes wide. He unsnapped a clip from his belt and pushed it into his pistol and released the slide, so that it shot forward with a snap. Orlando saw him shiver and wondered what shock looked like.

Brendan smiled. "In case that fucker is just going around the block."

The security guard was waving up a pair of nurses with a gurney. "Let's get him inside."

"I'm okay, I'm okay."

Orlando shook his head and helped him stand upright. He

put his hand on a red hole in Brendan's blues, showing his brother a spot of thick blood. Brendan swore and touched gingerly at the spot, in the meat of his left shoulder just above the collarbone. He grabbed at his brother's sleeve.

"Are you okay? I saw him get a shot off at you, I thought . . ."

"No, I fell on my ass." Orlando pointed back over his shoulder. "All he got was grass and brick."

"I swear to Christ I got him, but he didn't go down." Brendan swayed as the nurses jockeyed the stretcher into place behind him. "Fifteen years I never pointed the gun at anybody. I don't know what happened." His eyes rolled over white and he fainted, guided back onto the white sheets by the nurses and the guard and Orlando, who ripped Brendan's shirt open and ran his hands over his brother's chest and stomach, looking for more holes.

A nurse caught his hand and held it gently. "It's okay. Leave us take him inside and we'll make sure he's okay. All right?"

Orlando nodded, his eyes bright and wide. He helped them spread a blanket over Brendan and then stood at the curb for a moment, watching them go. When they were rounding the corner of the building toward the door, he lifted the pistol he'd taken from his brother's hands and looked at it.

It was big and black and squared-off, the weight in the grip, where he knew the magazine was. He'd just seen his brother load it. He didn't know much about guns. How many bullets were in it? Six, seven? He'd stolen guns and sold them, seen guys wearing them or pointing them, or playing with them like kids, and he'd had no interest. It had little levers, maybe a safety, and a button to press to take the magazine out, but he didn't have any more bullets, so it didn't matter. Whatever was in it would be enough. He turned and walked back up the street.

He crossed the asphalt and looked down at the broken glass and a red shotgun shell, a slightly flattened cylinder with its one yellow brass end. He'd seen the guy's face and knew it was the same guy, the Irish guy who'd come to kill him on Hope Street. There were drops of dark blood, one flattened with a shoe print. So Brendan had hit the fucker. Good. He started walking, then jogging, and stuck the gun into his jacket. Maybe he'd die, the Irishman. Maybe they'd all die. The ones who tried to kill Zoe, who'd killed Geo, shot Michael. The Irishman and his boss, the one who owned the dope house where Zoe scored the poisoned dope. Who'd tried to shoot him and his brother in the street like it was nothing. He came to Ridge, turned left, threaded the traffic moving east.

Benigno sat in the dark at the dope house on Shurs Lane, smoking a joint and watching the street in his underwear. He heard Min shift in her sleep and made a face. It was a mistake to stay in the house. He'd given the girl the smack, like Asa told him, the stuff laced with fentanyl that some of the kids called Murder. They should have left when they turned off the lights, though, not waited around to see if the fucking girl died and if anyone figured out where the dope had come from. Maybe it was a one-in-a-million shot, but it was keeping him up.

Closing shop and moving would mean he'd take a hit. It would take a while to find someplace cool to set up, get his old customers back, or pull new ones in, and fuck that. He'd do that if he had to, he'd done it before, but it sucked, and all for some dumb-ass junkie girl who probably crawled under some porch to die. He told himself, if anyone gave a shit about her, she wouldn't be copping heroin in the middle of the day in his house. It was what he thought about all the gearheads and base-heads and stunned junkies who wandered through the house, leaking money and staggering back out into the night to steal or work or whatever they did to prop up their habits. He'd started to hate them. Thought, *Who gives a shit? Give me your money and get the fuck out.*

He laughed to himself, a little stoned giggle that he was struggling to control when he heard a window break downstairs. He stood up, looked down at Min, and then grabbed the .32 off the nightstand. She was coming awake while he stepped into his shoes, pulling his jersey on and moving toward the door to cock his head and listen.

She sat up, pulling the covers over her. "Bennie?"

He made a frantic gesture for her to shut up, wiping the air with his hands, and mouthed, "Stay put," but she was already spilling out of bed to grab for the shotgun under the mattress. He held up his hands, pleading calm, then slowly opened the door.

Out on the landing he could hear more sounds from downstairs. Something scraping the wood sash of a window. A bottle thrown down a hallway to crack open in the kitchen. Benigno moved to the head of the stairs, the pistol pointed down. He'd taken one step, trying to remember which ones squeaked, when he heard a hissing rush and saw a bloom of orange light reflected along the hallway at the foot of the stairs. He went back into the room and saw Min raise the shotgun and tense her arms.

"It's me, for chrissake!" He crossed the room to pull his pants on while Min twisted the sawed-off gun in her hands. "Get dressed!" He grabbed her purse and swept their keys and phones and everything in with one hand so that pennies and dimes rang on the floor.

"What's going on, Bennie? What's that smell?"

"The fucking place is on fire." He jumped up and took the gun from her. "Come on!"

"Let's go out the window!" They could hear cracking now, a hiss building to a roar. She pulled on a shirt that flapped over open jeans.

"The bars. There are fucking bars on all the windows. We'd have to go out the goddamn attic." He pulled her, one shoe on and one shoe off, out the door and down the first few stairs. He cranked the pump on the shotgun, spitting a live round that plinked down the steps to roll in the empty hallway, now bright with fire from the kitchen.

He craned his neck to see the length of the house through the rails. He screamed warnings and threats to whoever might be downstairs. Min clung to him, off balance and holding one shoe, pulling at him as she struggled not to fall, and he flapped his arm to keep his distance from her as they sidestepped down the stairs.

He called them junkie motherfuckers, racked the slide to scare them, called on whoever was in his house to show themselves and die like men. He popped his bushy head up and down to see over and under the banister, pointing the heavy gun into the shadowed corners and swearing under his breath. Finally, he just ran for the front door and threw it open, his back turned to cover the interior of the house with the wildly swinging shotgun.

He was half out the front door, turning with the gun, when Orlando clocked him hard with the Glock, holding it like a hammer by the barrel and chopping at Bennie's skull. One solid shot, so that the kid squeezed the trigger and discharged the gun with an unholy echoing roar that shattered the door frame. The gun dropped out of his hands and landed on Min's small foot. She screamed and hopped to the side of the door, and Orlando grabbed her and pinned her hard against the porch, then righted the pistol and pushed it into her cheek while Bennie moaned and rocked himself upright, rubbing the side of his head.

"What do you think, you're going to get rich? Dumb junkie fuck. You're going to score off me?"

Orlando said, "You know that's not why I'm here, so don't even start a game with me." The girl moaned, something in Korean, and Orlando breathed hard through his mouth. "I don't know how this gun works. I don't know about guns."

"I'll show you in a minute." Bennie looked at the shotgun at his feet.

"Did you even know who she was, know her name? Was it just being, like, fuck it, who cares about her? Did you just think it didn't matter?"

Bennie watched the fire inside the door, making its way toward where they lay on the porch, his eyes red with the light. "I see all you come here. I used to think it was just partying. This life. People coming and having fun. Then, I don't know. I see you stealing, whoring, fucking each other over. You all come around over and over and just turn to skeletons."

Orlando felt the heat growing on his face. "She protected me. Why would she do that for me?" He held the pistol against the girl's temple, his mind empty, as if the gun were thinking for him, giving shape and volition to his acts. "What do I do without her?"

Bennie held up his hands. "I wouldn't hurt anyone just to do it. I do what I'm told. He sends those big apes around to collect the money, so I do what the fuck I'm told. You think you want to know, you're mad and you want to get at him, but you can't. He's too smart. There are so many people out there who take his money." He leaned forward, his eyes darting back and forth between Orlando's wild eyes and the shotgun on the floor.

Orlando said, "You think I care about living or dying. I don't care. This isn't that. She was perfect. Something has to happen if she dies. The world has to end." He pushed the girl down with the gun at her temple.

Bennie put one hand out slowly, touching the girl's foot. "I can tell you his name. I'll tell you. You think you'll learn something, but you'll just die."

"If you lie to me, I'll know it. I saw the bag. I know every bag stamp in this town. I studied every way people get high." There was a crash inside, things dropping and blowing up. Bottles of liquor, maybe. His hands were cramping, and he turned and breathed through his mouth, trying to keep from getting sick. He sat back, finally, and Min disentangled her hair from his fingers and climbed to Bennie.

Bennie said, "You already know, then why did you come here?"

"I wanted to hear you say it. I wanted to see your face and hear you say his name, tell me where he is."

The heat was getting worse, and Min's hair lifted in little updrafts. She said, "Then what? You can't stop this. You can't stop anything. No one can. Not the police, not anyone."

"No, but I'll get him. I'll get him somehow."

The door swung on its own, as if the fire were a spirit taking control of the house. Bennie made a face. "You're sick. I can see it. Right now, you're sick. Does that gun even work? Is it loaded? You don't know."

Orlando lifted it and they ducked, Bennie and Min. He pointed it at them, his face screwed up in anticipation of the noise. He swung it toward the open door and pulled the trigger, his hand shaking with the effort. There was a pop and Min gave a little shriek. For a while they all looked into the red interior of the house. Watched, fascinated, like animals in the dark for a minute, before Orlando finally got up and they followed him to the curb, to stand and watch the house burn. The house, whatever dope and money there was inside it. They watched expressionless, their thoughts unknowable. The fire trucks appeared at the end of the block, and people began coming out of the other houses to stand blinking with their children, like they had been called against their will.

Benigno said, "His name is Asa Carmody."

Orlando dropped to the curb, exhausted, and folded his legs under him. He saw Bennie holding Min and watching the house as if they were any young couple losing their home, as if they were poor sodbusters watching a grass fire reduce their hovel on some prairie as coyotes circled and whined. He thought about how everyone thought they had the right to do whatever they did. Everything, no matter what. People just built a little bridge of self-justified bullshit over whatever terrible things they did to each other. Orlando saw it all around him, and knew he had done it, too.

He was conscious of them moving, now, Bennie herding Min with furtive movements away from the light and commotion on the street. Orlando got up and followed, all of his body flaring with pain so intense he thought it should be audible, a high whine like a drill. They began to pick up speed, both of them in their underwear, weaving around neighbors and firemen. Orlando caught them at the end of the block, jammed the pistol discreetly in the hollow under Bennie's ribs.

The tall kid sagged. "All right, then." He closed his eyes, said something in Spanish. Crossed himself. A few steps away, Min put her hand across her face, a kid at a scary movie, wanting to see and not see.

"No," Orlando said, "not that."

"What?"

"Can I borrow your car?"

Bennie shook his head, wiped at the tears at the corner of one red eye. "Jesus, I pissed myself."

The bar was loud, the place on South, crowded with young people, and Angel pushed his way slowly to the end of the bar to claim a seat where he could see her. To see Hannah, finally. The sight of her giving him a physical rush of pleasure as if he'd touched her. He'd had to move slowly, one foot in front of the other, concentrating on staying upright, staying awake. It was ending, he knew, and he was glad of it. He hadn't thought he'd be so ready, thought he'd fought it all those years, used his skill to ward it off, but he saw plain that he'd been looking for his own death for a long time.

He held himself erect, watching her take the orders, the way she had of cocking her head, her hair coiled in the braids he liked so much, changing colors under the lights, gold and then red and then gold again. He grabbed a handful of napkins from the bar and stuffed them inside his shirt, trying not to be noticed. The music was going, something he didn't know, but he liked it, about living fast and dying young. The girls moved around him, dancing, looking at each other but doing it for the boys. Their hands up, arms cocked, making circles in the air with their slim hips. Smelling of perfume and sweet drinks and the sweat of dancing.

He'd never danced with Hannah, but watching her work was like that, so he'd take it with him. She was making her way down the bar, grabbing glasses and soda guns, doing her practiced thing, people calling to her and everyone happy, everyone wanting their drinks. Soon she'd turn and see him and then he could relax and sit back and let go. He just needed that one more time, that smile. That crooked line across her broad face, her lips dark. What was that geometry that added up to beauty? Lines, points along a curve. That was all.

It was hard to wait. He wanted to grab her, take her outside, stop traffic, open his coat in the street. Fire his guns at the moon, hold her close while he smiled with blood in his teeth like the dead African boy on Hope Street. This was all right, though. As good as anything, as good as anywhere. Someone slipped behind him; he heard voices, and a girl screamed about blood on the floor. The place was loud, roaring, so nobody noticed, but it was hard to hold his head up, hard to wait for her to see him. His hands were wet from holding himself together, and he was tired.

Finally he had to let his head down on the bar. Somebody's drink was spilled, somebody was touching his arm and wanted to talk, but he was focused on her, and she was turning, finally. Seeing him, and there it was, the smile. He reached up, took his glasses off. Put them on the edge of the bar and smiled back. Closed his eyes. Wondered if he'd dream.

Danny was sitting in his car in the dark in front of Rodi's, drinking Old Grand-Dad from a pint bottle. Officially, he was on leave. There had been some kind of meeting, he knew, between the Captain and Lieutenant Barclay, and then Barclay had called him into the office and told him to take three days. The lieutenant was talking fast, his head down, moving him toward the door as if he were afraid Danny would infect him with something. He'd called Rogan, but the phone just rang through to his voice mail, and Danny had hung up without leaving a message. He'd gone home just long enough to change, then gotten back in the car and started driving. The Grand-Dad had calmed him down, muted the frantic feeling he'd had since seeing Derrick Leon.

His phone rang and it was Brendan, a little wild, a little doped up, telling him about the gunfight and Zoe and his brother out looking for whoever poisoned his girlfriend. He could hear Brendan struggle against whatever they'd given him for pain.

"The kid's all fucked up, I don't know what he'd do. He's got, he's all messed up. And he's sick. Withdrawing, I'm pretty sure."

"He said where the dope came from? That made his girlfriend sick?"

"A place around the corner. Shurs Lane. I don't know the address, but he told me what it looked like."

The house on Shurs was Asa's, he knew that now. He'd cruised it three times, watching the people go in and out, seeing the bars on the windows and the reinforced door. It was in Asa's mother's name. One of the ghosts that held all the paper on Asa's life.

"Who's he looking for, Danny? Do you know?"

"Same person I am."

Danny cranked the ignition on his car and picked up his notebook. He'd been driving by places Asa owned all day long. The places were in other names. His mother's, a brother who'd died when Asa was four. There were three houses in West Philly where people were probably processing or storing dope. The place on Shurs, a small apartment building in Kensington. A couple of bars, a workingman's place down in Chester, and Rodi's, and Danny was cruising them figuring he'd run into Asa at one of them. Now he lifted the notebook and looked at the last place on the list, a garage on North American, up above York.

Danny opened the window and threw the pint hard at the front of the bar so that it broke open on the stucco front. A guy in a Flyers jersey swore and ran over to the car, and Danny opened his coat and pulled his piece. The guy stopped short, and Danny laughed and said, "Yeah, I thought so."

Chris's mother had lived in the same house for fifty-three years, on Tulip Street in Fishtown. The real Fishtown, below Norris Street, not the made-up one going all the way up to Lehigh Avenue. Chris would have to listen to this rant once a week from his mother, about how everybody wanted to be in Fishtown now and they should have seen it twenty years ago, by which she meant forty years ago, when it was just the run-down places and the bars and Goodwill stores, not the galleries and restaurants full of young couples tattooed and pierced, even the women. Chris had to wake her up before he left, show her the girl, who carried the stale pastries with her and sat in the corner of the living room, rocking, doing her prayer, talking to the unborn baby. His mother stood with her hands on her hips, asking what she was supposed to do with her and saying she wasn't the welfare office and then stamping back upstairs to watch her TV shows.

He should be used to it. It had been worse when Shannon was alive. His older brother would come home cut, fucked up from bar fights, running from the cops, asking his mother to sew up a hole in his cheek, asking her to put up some rummy he'd met in a bar, asking her to hide a gun. He'd been her favorite, and when Chris asked for the smallest thing it was a big deal and she whined and started the litany about raising two boys on her own, so he would just pick her up, drop her off, give her money, and keep moving. When Shannon had showed up dead she wailed, tore at her hair, performed the whole opera for her friends, the priest, all the neighborhood people who'd turned out for the funeral, and most of them looking at his body in the casket the way you'd look at a bloodied shark on a dock.

He let the girl hug him one more time before he left, getting something off her small hands on his back, smelling her crazy-girl smell of glazed sugar and cherries and soot, and then went back out and started the Navigator. He pulled the gun out of the console and put it on the seat next to him. He realized there was no one he trusted, and if things had gone different he'd have brought Gerry and Frank with him to go see Asa, and for the first time he missed them.

She stood at the window and watched him, then ran to the door and came out to pull open the back door and climb in.

"Go inside."

"It's okay. I'm not here."

"It's not safe."

"No, she smells bad. The baby doesn't like her. Thy womb Jesus."

"Yeah, she does kind of smell bad, huh? Like I don't know. Cabbage and Bengay or something." He laughed and listened to her settling down onto the floor behind his seat. "Stay down low, okay? You hear me?"

"Defend us in battle. Saint Michael."

"My name is Christopher."

"He's not a real saint."

"No."

CHAPTER
18

Danny crossed Diamond and pulled up half a block from the garage on American, letting his car coast to a stop against the side of a dark job-shop. He got out slow, a little unsteady from the bourbon, though it was burning out of his system quick enough. He took the small H&K pistol out from under his coat, snapped off the safety, and moved through the quiet night, trying to see into each of the few passing cars that went by and staying close to the shadowed and shuttered buildings looming in the dark.

There was a big SUV parked at the curb, and as he got closer a head appeared inside, as if someone had been low in the seat and suddenly popped upright, and Danny froze and watched, halfway across an open area bordered on his right by a chain-link fence. He stood, his hand on the pistol held down behind his thigh, watching the figure in the black SUV. It was a Navigator, the engine loud even when it was just idling, and Danny kept moving forward, his heart kicking up, conscious of the blood moving in his chest and arms.

He got close enough to hear the radio thumping behind the glass, see the silhouette of whoever was at the wheel. It looked like he was talking to himself, shifting his body. Trying to work himself up to something, maybe, or talking to somebody on a cell phone. Danny's breath was loud in his ears, and he flattened himself in the shadow of the garage, just steps away from the Navigator, and he brought the pistol forward and put both hands on it. Another few feet and he'd be on the car, and he hoped it was Asa. He hoped it was Asa and that he'd do something stupid, make some move.

He closed the last few feet as the figure in the car lifted a pistol, barrel up, still not registering that Danny was there next to the car. Danny was hyperventilating, alert, shifting his eyes quick back and forth between the lit windows of the garage and the SUV, watching for movement, trying to see what was going on in the dark car. Danny saw the pistol and raised his, pointing it at the head in the car and screaming to be heard over the thump and rattle of the radio.

The head swung left, then right, and then jumped when he registered Danny just beyond the door, the pistol going out, but he probably never heard what Danny said, identifying himself as a police officer and telling him to freeze. The first thing he probably heard was the shot and the glass breaking as Danny emptied the pistol through the door, aiming each shot, the shots spaced out with a breath after each one. When the window broke, the radio got loud all of a sudden, something Danny knew but couldn't name, and it was one of those songs about being hard, being invulnerable, a badass.

Danny moved around the car, dropping the clip, but got to the driver's side to see Chris Black drop out of the Navigator, a long, slow fall, grabbing at the seat, blood pouring out of him, trying to say something. The gun spun away on the ground, and

Danny stood over him, the kid shaking his head and smiling even as his eyes filled with tears.

He pulled himself up, one arm hanging limp and blood coming out from under his jersey and splattering on the sidewalk, making a noise like rain. "Jesus, that hurts. Is she okay?"

Danny knelt beside him, pulling the cell phone out of his pocket. "Lay still. The medics are coming. Is who okay?"

The door to the garage opened slowly, and Asa stepped out, his eyebrows up as if he was surprised to find visitors this late. He took in Chris on the ground, Danny with his pistol out, the broken glass and blood running into the street.

"What the fuck," he said, and then he laughed. "Jesus, Danny."

Chris Black brought up his dripping hand and pointed. "That's the one. That fucker there. Jesus, I'm feeling bad. Where's the girl?"

Asa lifted one shoulder, let it drop. "Whyn't you shut the fuck up now? Save your strength."

Chris grabbed at Danny's sleeve. "Jesus, I'm dying. I never went anywhere. I never left this fucking place once. Make sure she's okay?" His fingers tightened on Danny's arm. "I shot those kids. Me and Gerry Dunn. He sent us."

Asa stuck his hands in his pockets, rocking on his heels as if he had better things to do somewhere else. "Yeah, good luck proving that. You piece of shit. Your brother would piss on you right now, you know that?"

Chris opened his mouth, baring his teeth and hissing, and it took a minute before Danny figured out he was laughing. "I shot him, too. Shannon. I put two in his head. My brother. Fucking Shannon. I fucking spit on all of you."

"You're not helping your case here, rat. I hear you saying you killed a bunch of people in front of a police officer."

Danny looked up at him. "Shut up, Asa."

"Do you believe this crap, Danny? You know me."

"Yeah, I do. Finally, I do. I know you've been bringing me your competitors for a long time. Instead of killing them yourself. You've just handed them to me. Derrick Leon and Darnell Burns. All those words in my ear. All that bullshit."

"Danny, think about this. You start some shit now it isn't going to stop with me. This looks bad, you know? Not just for me. For you. I go down, what happens to you?"

"I know how it looks."

"Can't you just . . . be smart?" Asa walked to the street, cocking his head as if listening for something. "This was good for both of us, Danny. You got good arrests, right? The promotions, the shield. Got some bad people off the street. You're going to fuck that up? Why?"

Danny got out his cell phone, turning to keep both Asa and Chris in his field of view. He dialed the phone, holding the pistol out and down. "You used me like you used these crazy, fucked-up kids. Those people you put me onto were your competitors in the drug business." Danny pivoted, keeping his back to the street and trying to watch Asa and Chris and the garage. He wasn't thinking clearly, his heart racing from the shooting and confronting Asa. He wasn't controlling the scene.

"Oh, grow the fuck up. You think you know something special? Everybody gets something. Nobody gets out of bed unless they get something. People need shit, and I get it for them, and it doesn't matter. You arrest me, you think what? People are going to stop using?" Asa moved around behind Danny so that he had to shift to keep him in sight, and he saw Asa's eyes go to the ground like he was searching for something.

Danny looked at his own hands, at the pistol that was still locked open and empty. He closed the phone and started fumbling in his pockets, feeling for the other clip. He wished he hadn't had so much to drink. He said, "You sound like Derrick Leon now."

"Then he's smarter than I thought."

"And I know about DeAngelo Barnes. And Darius Williams." Danny became aware of Asa shifting, reaching for something on the ground.

"Who?" Asa stood up, and he had something in his hands. A gun.

Orlando tore up American Street, jamming his foot hard against the floor and banging through the stop signs. Bennie and Min had a CD in and he recognized it, "Modern World," Wolf Parade. About a torch driving savages back to the trees, and that sounded right to him. He swerved around teenagers in the street and actually veered by a cop in the street at Berks, the guy sweeping his arms up like a matador making his veronica as Orlando rocketed by, inches away. The engine roared and thumped, started a rattle that grew as he ran north, until he could actually feel it through the foot plastered to the accelerator by the time he blasted through the light at Diamond. He saw the Navigator at the garage and stood on the brakes, jumped out with Brendan's gun up, and ran toward where the SUV door stood open and shot full of holes, the light inside bright and a chime going because the keys were still in the ignition.

There was somebody slumped against the side of the truck, a big kid he didn't recognize, dark blood moving in a slow current from his legs to the street. The door to the garage stood open, and there was another guy curled in a ball by the door, only this one was still moving, holding a gun up against his chest. He was young, smaller than the hulking guy bleeding out by the SUV and wearing wire-rim glasses. His face was white and he was breathing fast and trying to talk to Orlando, motioning with the gun, his hand red. Orlando moved slowly, hearing sounds from inside the garage and a voice talking, complaining and swearing, and somebody throwing things around.

When he got close the guy by the door reached with one shaking hand into his jacket and brought out a blood-soaked wallet that he tried to open, but he dropped it and Orlando saw the badge and nodded, moving to the left of the door and into the shadow, lifting Brendan's gun to point it at the door.

"I'm a cop," the guy said, panting. "My name is Daniel Martinez. I've been shot by the man inside. His name is Asa Carmody. Just go around the corner." The cop tried to grab Orlando's wrist, his breathing ragged. "He's got a gun. Just go around the corner and you'll be okay." The words slow, spaced by hard breaths. "Take my phone and call the police. I can't get my phone."

Orlando stood up and the cop tried one more time to wave him back, but he moved to the open door. The garage was big inside, and in the center of the floor were two cases, one filled with money and one filled with flat brown bricks of dope. He stood quiet in the shadows by the front door and watched Asa Carmody come down the stairs, favoring one leg. He didn't notice Orlando.

"You shot me, you crazy fuck. You shot me. Why the fuck would you do that?" He dragged one leg, smacking it as if it were a misbehaving child. "Danny?" He dropped his voice, as if talking to himself. "Nobody does a fucking thing I tell them anymore. Not that fucking Chris, not you. Not nobody. Where the fuck is Angel?" He dragged his bleeding leg over to the cases and let himself go down hard on his ass, his legs shaking. He had a book and a pistol, and he was sweating. "Oh, fuck. Not yet, goddammit. I'm not done."

Chris was dying, he knew it, and couldn't lift his arms anymore. There was a shifting inside the truck and the door behind him opened and the girl climbed out. She dropped to one leg and touched his head and he saw glass in her hair like diamonds. Chris licked his lips and they felt thick and dry. He tried to tell her to find a place to hide, but he couldn't say anything and the pain in his side was like a clamp that kept him from talking or breathing right and he felt sick. She got close to him and looked in his eyes and he thought of the first time he'd seen her.

That night on Roxborough Avenue, Frank Dunn at the wheel stomping the accelerator and Gerry in the back, the radio going loud while they'd passed a bottle of Jägermeister back and forth. He'd been half in the bag and it had been so fast, so fast. He remembered more of the getting ready. Fitting the long clip into the handle, his hands pinched in the stiff gloves. Trying to steel himself, Gerry making him nervous, clapping him on the back and giving a whoop like a little kid. Pointing the little blunt machine gun everywhere, making Chris wince to think of him back there drunk with a loaded gun.

Frank had to shout over the music, telling them there it is, and then they had the guns out the window, Gerry opening up first and Chris joining in, his finger already on the trigger before he took in the three people standing on the steps in front of the house. Asa had told them to make sure to get whoever was standing out front. Chris knowing what that meant, but expecting them to be the Dominicans or something. Bulked-up gang-bangers, or the skinny corner runners. Something else, not three young schoolkids all turning to look at them as the car went by. There was more to this than he understood. He got some of it—they were shooting up the Dominicans' place, and they were pinning it all on Darnell Burns. That was why they had the stamp bags. Shoot up the place, drop the bags, and the cops think it's Green Lane trying to kill some Dominicans over turf. But shooting the kids out front? Why would Asa need that?

It was something he couldn't get hold of later. He knew he did it, pulled the trigger and emptied the gun at them, but something about the drinking or his sweating hands inside the gloves or some trick of his mind made it seem like it was something he'd seen, not something he'd done. It should have been loud, but he couldn't remember the sound of the gun as much as seeing the spray of yellow light and the gun bucking in his hands, watching the spent shells spill out and rattle down the street as the car moved. He couldn't have seen that, but he had a memory of it.

Dying now, letting go of everything, it was easier than he'd thought it would be. And he knew why Asa had sent him to kill the girl. She'd been stupid enough to get close to Asa, to get pregnant, and that was a death sentence. For Asa, for whatever Asa was, killing Sienna was the only option. Chris could see that now. Being Asa meant being in a kind of pain all the time. He wasn't a man, Chris knew. He was some kind of dark, vibrating energy that Chris could actually see, now he was dying, his mind a desolate building in the dark, the lights going off one by one.

There were just a few memories he could still get hold of, and they were terrible things. The gun in his hands. The sight of the kids falling on Roxborough Avenue, and his own voice in his head. And maybe he hadn't said it, but he'd thought it, and what he'd thought was *Now I'm going to hell.*

Orlando watched Asa on the floor, sitting in a spreading pool of blood. He was holding the book up and smiling and talking about his plan. Then his hand started shaking and he dropped the book and went back on his elbows. Orlando walked out into the light in the center of the room and knelt down in front of Asa and the cases holding the money and the flat brown bricks of heroin, pain spreading in hard waves from his spine, conducted by his bones to his arms and legs and the top of his head, and there were bursts of light at the corners of his eyes.

He had the gun up, pointing, but Asa's hands were shaking and his face was bloodless, the skin going green. Orlando could see sweat standing out on Asa's forehead, and he had the sad and guilty eyes of a dog.

Asa said, "I can't be here."

"But here you are. Do you know why?"

"The weak always try to stop the strong, but they never can."

Orlando shook his head. "The strong. You tried to have a pregnant girl killed. You sent men to shoot children down in the street, didn't you?"

"Everybody thinks they know my business. What do you think you know, junkie?"

"You sent the Irishman to kill me. Because I was asking questions. I saw you at that dope house on Shurs Lane. You and him together." He remembered the man again, lost in his dope dreams. "We got high together and he told me. About killing people and throwing them in the river. I was high, I didn't put it together at first. It's for you, right? He kills people for you. Then you had that Puerto Rican kid kill my girl." Orlando saw it, saw it the way he sometimes did, like there were lines drawn in the air in front of him. The patterns coming together, the machinery laid bare. Now, though, instead of making him feel powerful and connected to everything, it just made him feel sick and alone.

"So that means it was you who shot the kids. Right? Or you had it done." His hands were shaking so hard the pistol rattled in his fist, and he stopped and held the cool metal of the barrel

317

to his hot forehead. He felt like he was going to pass out and talked fast, wanting to know, to get his questions answered. "Two young boys and that poor, fucked-up girl. The boys were there by accident, but why the girl? Why would you need to kill a pregnant crazy girl?"

"She's a junkie, a whore. I'm going to have that around me? Slowing me down? How the hell did I know there were going to be kids standing there? That's on the fuckups who pulled the trigger. Not me."

"Jesus, it was you. You got her pregnant."

"She asked me to take care of her." Asa's eyes caught pinpoints of light, like an animal caught in headlights on a dark road.

"That boy you killed, he was a good person. He tried to help people. I never did that. He taught someone to read. His name was George Parkman."

"I don't know who that is."

Orlando looked at the gun in his hand and then put it on the floor behind him. He stared at the dope, thought he could smell it, a rich tang like fertile soil that he could taste on the tip of his tongue. Jesus, he was so sick, was he dying? And there it was, all that dope just sitting there, brown and wet-looking, almost black under the hard light of the garage.

A girl came from the dark street and sat by Asa, and Orlando remembered she was important but he couldn't think about it just then. There were things he wanted to say, more questions he wanted to ask but he forgot what they were, and put out one white hand and touched the plastic-wrapped bricks that were dark and swollen and tight like ripe fruit.

The girl sat cross-legged in a rivulet of blood and smiled at them and talked about spirits and saints and children with wings and bread. Orlando rocked on his knees and took a velvet-wrapped bundle out of the lining of his jacket and opened it on the floor, taking out his needles, a bent spoon, a book of matches. The girl was reproving Asa, gently, smoothing his hair back and telling him he could still be saved, they could all be saved. Then she took his hand and put it on her stomach and asked him what they should name the baby. She said she knew he hadn't wanted her to get pregnant, that he had plans, but that was love, and how could love ever be wrong, ever be wasted? Orlando heard Asa talking back to her, telling her about the plan, his plan, about the nature of the universe and the way it could be bent to the will of the determined. He was trying to push a rag against the hole in his leg, but after a little while there was no point in it and he just lay back. Orlando told him, "It's just gravity," and that there wasn't a goddamn thing anyone could do about it.

Orlando lifted one of the bricks of dope and tore at it with his hands and dumped the muddy brown powder out in a pile and sifted it in his fingers. Asa might have said his last words then, "You win, you win," which he thought was something he'd have to remember and tell Zoe. He picked up a purple ribbon that had still held a few errant strands of her hair, then spit into the bowl of the spoon and lit the matches and waited.

The cops came in, guns drawn, and they cleared the rooms and then let the ambulance crews come in. The cops were shouting to each other and the medics, pointing at each body and trying to set priority cases. They moved quick to get the one they knew was a cop up on the stretcher, and two cops in uniform were trying to coax what looked like a homeless pregnant girl onto a gurney when they came across a pale, thin male with blond hair lying on his side on a mattress thrown in the doorway to the garage office. The first cop to see him covered him with his gun, prodding him gently with one boot.

"Another DOA in here, I think." A medic carrying a tackle box with an EMS insignia on the side slid by the cop and knelt down. She took in the bruises and welts, the stitches leaking green fluid. She felt for a pulse, lifted one eyelid.

"Wow, been through the wars, this one." She opened the case and unwrapped a stethoscope from around her neck. "Okay, nah. He's just, I don't know. Passed out or something." She called for a board, then ran her gloved hands along his neck and back. She felt something, gently lifted his black leather jacket and exposed a syringe, the tip glowing wetly. "Oh, okay. Wow."

The cop snorted. "We got a live witness, anyway."

"Yeah, maybe. His pulse is all over the place."

The cop turned to look at the scene again. "What the fuck happened here?" He nodded toward the lightly snoring blond kid. "Maybe he can tell us."

The medic looked up at the cop and waggled her eyebrows. "This kid is so fucked up, he was probably on the nod through the whole thing. He might have just wandered in, saw the dope and fired up, you know?" It had happened before.

The young cop holstered his pistol, reset his cap, and made

a gesture, his hands open and sweeping the scene, taking it all in. Orlando on the floor with his bruises and sputtering heart, the money wet with blood, the drugs, the dead and the dying. "Junkies."

CHAPTER

19

A week later, Brendan met Orlando at the hospital, shook his hand, and followed him to the room where Sienna lay dozing in a patch of sunlight, pale, her eyes set in wells of dark skin. Orlando wore Michael's sweatshirt, and Brendan was still in his blues, coming off his shift working the desk at the Fifth District up on Ridge. Brendan saw that his brother was clean and the cuts on his face were healing, but he was thin and pale and his hands shook. They sat wordlessly until she woke, and seeing Orlando, she smiled and lifted a hand and he took it.

"How's it going today?"

"Okay. Today is okay." She looked at Brendan. "This is your brother?" Closed one eye and squinted at them. "I can see it."

Brendan worked his cap in his hands and smiled. "Then you're the first."

"No, it's something around the eyes."

Brendan looked at Orlando and then the girl, not sure what it was okay to say. He knew his brother had been visiting her, in the week since she'd been brought to the hospital. His brother was on methadone. It kept him from getting sick until they could get him into rehab.

He looked at the girl and wasn't sure what to feel. She'd been the cause of Michael and Geo getting shot, but she hadn't done anything except get pregnant by a man who'd rather have her killed than accept the responsibility, so what did that make her but a victim herself? He said, "So, you're feeling, you know. Better?"

She looked out the window. "I can't remember everything. I still get confused." Her hand went to her throat and she worked a small crucifix there, running it back and forth along a chain. "The doctor told me it was seeing, you know, all of that. The boys. How they were hurt. And the drugs I was taking. I went crazy for a while. They told me what it's called, but . . ." She put a hand across her eyes, and they waited for a minute. Brendan got her a tissue from a box, and she took it and thanked him.

"Fugue." Orlando took her free hand.

"Right. Like in music." She put one hand over her stomach, gingerly patting the hard mound. "I know the things I saw, a lot of them weren't real. I remember touching one of the boys. When he was there, shot. Touching his face." She touched her own face then, her small hands shaking, her eyes wet. "Anyway, it's in my head that I did it. I don't know."

Brendan poured a glass of water for her, and she took it in both hands, like a child.

"Mostly I'm just tired. I sleep a lot. I just pray, I pray so hard that nothing I did hurt the baby. Asa's dead, isn't he?"

Brendan looked at Orlando, who touched her hand again. "Yes. We talked about that, remember?"

She nodded. "Right, that's right. I'm sorry."

"It's okay."

"He tried to kill me. I can't believe it, even if I know it's true. Me and the baby. I thought I could get him to take care of me. I was such an idiot. I knew what kind of man he was when I started seeing him." She laughed. "Listen to me. Seeing him, like in school. He had money and drugs and some kind of power, and I wanted to be around that. That's why this happened, isn't it? So much sin, so much evil. I invited it. That's how it works, you have to invite the devil in."

She held on to Orlando's hand again, her eyes fierce, and he just kept smiling, smiling, hoping she'd feel safe and relax. Telling her it was over, all of her troubles, that she was safe, the baby was safe. After a while, maybe she'd believe it, even if he never would.

Orlando had seen Zoe leave the hospital. He'd been discharged himself, walking back up from the front desk with his papers toward her room, and had caught a glimpse of her at the curb in a wheelchair. He'd stopped and gone to the window, watching her mother holding her hand and talking to her. Zoe looked hunched and small in an oversized sweater. He watched the older woman's lips moving soundlessly. A big old BMW pulled up and Zoe's father got out. Older, his hair thinner, but still a big man, and they were both talking, the father and the mother, getting her out of the chair, helping her sit on the edge of the backseat. She smiled then, at her mother, her lips somehow smaller, bloodless, not the full red he always pictured. Then, released from the effort of holding the smile, her face went slack and empty. She looked right at him, he thought, her eyes pointed toward his face, but there was no sign of recognition. It might have been a trick of sun or shadow that made him invisible to her. Or maybe it was for him, the emptiness in that look, and the thought made him drop his eyes until the car and the girl were gone.

They stood in the hall outside Sienna's room, and Brendan was looking at his watch when George Parkman Sr. came through the door at the end of the hall. He moved slowly, taking in Orlando in his clean new clothes, Brendan in his blues. He moved slowly toward them but his eyes moved fast, back and forth between them and darting into the corners as if he were afraid of being trapped. He didn't offer to shake hands.

"Okay, I'm here."

Orlando looked at Brendan, who fingered his cap and then went to look out a window. Parkman worked the muscles in his jaw. "I'm not paying you anything. Is this why he's here? Is the uniform supposed to scare me?"

Orlando stepped to the side and turned, inclining his head so that Parkman would move forward to the door of Sienna's room. He stopped there, looking in, but Orlando took his arm and guided him in, and he went. She was sleeping, and they stood and looked at her, and Orlando thought Parkman looked in that moment as miserable as anyone he'd ever seen. His face seemed to lengthen with it, his mouth gaping slightly, and his eyes burned red as if he were standing in a column of smoke. The girl shifted, and she put one hand on her swollen belly in her sleep. Parkman took a half step forward, one hand up. He could have wanted to touch her. He might have been shielding himself.

He looked from Orlando to the girl and then back, and his voice was barely audible. "Why is she here?"

Orlando looked to the door and saw Brendan had come back and was standing there, listening. Brendan's eyes were red.

Orlando spoke quietly. "She was there. She was standing with your son and Michael when they were shot. I think the boys were looking for her. I think George Jr. knew. Something. About you and about this girl. I think he saw her at the homeless shelter where he volunteered. Strung out, pregnant. I think he sold some things. The camera. And he found her and he was trying to give her money, or get her help. And while they were standing there some men tried to kill her, and they killed your son instead." Parkman turned suddenly and went to stand facing the far wall. He put one hand out and touched it, gingerly, as if testing its reality.

Orlando said, "I can't figure out how your son knew who she was. I know you . . . saw her. At the house where she worked. The girls there told me you used to come and see her. I think your son found out somehow and he thought if you weren't going to help her, he would. Do you know how he found out about her? Did you keep her name somewhere? Something he might have found?"

Parkman reached out and touched a chair and tried to lower himself into it, but he ended up going to his knees instead. He kept his face turned to the wall. His voice was a whisper, so low Orlando had to lean in to catch it. "He met her. He knew her."

Orlando and Brendan looked at each other, and both took a step toward the chair where Parkman kneeled.

"I was afraid. I was afraid he wasn't . . . normal." He lowered his head and it was even harder to hear him. There was a small noise from the bed. The girl sighing in a dream. "I thought he needed help, maybe. He was so delicate. So strange. I couldn't know him. A father wants things for his son. His mother didn't understand. She babied him and I thought . . . I don't know. Something went wrong." He pointed over his shoulder at the bed. "I sent her. I sent that girl. To him. Gave her money to be with him."

Brendan sighed. "Jesus Christ. Because he didn't what? Act like you? You sent a prostitute to your own son?"

"My father did it. The same thing. It was how I learned. And I did it." His voice was a whisper. "Don't judge me. You can't judge me. I thought, what normal boy wouldn't? What normal boy?"

Parkman got to his feet and walked out to the hallway. His eyes were unfocused, as if he'd gone blind. Brendan and his brother walked out and let the door close softly behind them. Orlando asked Parkman, "Did he have sex with her?"

The voice was almost inaudible. "I don't know. Maybe. He wouldn't talk to me."

Brendan looked at Orlando. "Would he have?"

"He was a good kid, I think. A kid who tried to do the right thing for people. But he was still a sixteen-year-old boy."

"So. He might have. He might have had sex with her, and then when she shows up pregnant . . ." Brendan drew a breath, his face drawn up as if in pain. "Do you think? Do you think he saw her pregnant and thought it was something he'd done?"

"I don't know. I don't know that it mattered to him. He saw somebody who needed help, so he wanted to help her."

Parkman looked at them each in turn, then down at his feet. "What are you going to say? About this?"

Brendan shook his head. "Christ. There's no fucking end to you, is there?"

Orlando lifted his brother's arm and looked at the watch there. "We don't give a shit about anything except that girl gets help."

The door opened at the end of the hall and Francine Parkman stepped through. Orlando looked at his brother, and then back and forth between the advancing woman and Parkman Sr. He nodded, then banged through the stairwell door, leaving them behind.

Parkman put his hand to the side of his face. "What are you going to say?"

Brendan spoke quietly, his mouth close to Parkman's ear. "That this girl needs help. That your son died trying to help her. That's all. If she gets what she needs, that's all."

. . .

The brothers got Cokes at a Burger King drive-through and put the windows down as they rode across town. The streets were clogged with rush hour traffic, everyone abandoning the city for the shore. Orlando held Brendan's cap and fingered the badge as they rode, and they talked about the Parkmans.

Orlando said, "What did you tell Francine Parkman?"

"I just said George Jr. was trying to help Sienna when he was killed, and that she did need a lot of help, and taking care of her might be a way to honor that. I didn't think there was a reason to get into anything. About anything."

"No."

"But to tell the truth, I got the impression she knew more about all of this than she let on."

"That wouldn't surprise me. She knew them both, her husband and her son. Better than anyone."

"Anyway, she'll help or she won't. You did what you could."

Orlando looked down. "What I could." They came off the Parkway near the river, and both of them looked at the skyline. "How's Michael making it?"

"The doctors say he's a hundred percent, but we can see he gets a little hesitant with some things. I guess it's not really his brain or anything, just, you know. Remembering the trauma or whatever. He's a little more thoughtful before he does anything. I guess that's not the end of the world for a teenage boy, huh?"

"No. How's the shoulder?"

"Okay, you know." He shifted, moved his arm to demonstrate.

"It never really hurt, so I did too much and it got infected. Kathleen gave me shit about it, but it's okay."

"Have you talked to Detective Martinez? Is he . . . can he walk?"

"No, he's still in the chair. The bullet's right up against the spine, so I guess they have to figure out whether they can get it out or just let it sit there."

Orlando thought about that. "Jesus. Wouldn't you be afraid to do anything, then? That you'd hurt yourself worse?"

"I guess you deal with it. Don't put yourself in situations where you could get hurt." Brendan thought about the last time he'd seen Danny Martinez, staring out a window at the University of Pennsylvania Hospital and watching earthmoving machines tearing a hole in the ground for some kind of expansion. He'd listened quietly to Brendan tell their side of it, which Danny hadn't known. About the pregnant girl, and Geo trying to help her. Danny'd nodded, distracted, looking at his watch. Brendan asked when Danny thought he'd be able to return to duty, and Danny said he wasn't worried about that. In fact, he said, he wasn't sure he wanted to be a cop anymore, and Brendan didn't know what to say to that. After a few minutes a tall, striking woman had come in and Danny had introduced Brendan to Jelan Williams. He felt suddenly like he was intruding, and said his good-byes. When he left, she was sitting on the bed and touching Danny's hair, saying next time she'd bring her scissors.

· · ·

Brendan slowed at a light, and Orlando pointed to where two kids shook hands, passing something between them.

"Corner runners."

Brendan looked down the blocks at City Hall, its yellow clock like an eye. "Here, too?"

"Here, there, everywhere. Maybe it's why people build cities. So they can have a place to score dope."

"Have you talked to Zoe?"

"Ah, no. I saw her leaving the hospital. Her parents were taking her home. I talked to the nurses and they said she was doing good when she left. I just didn't know, you know. What to say. She's better off. Even with them. Anywhere, with anyone, right?" They stopped at a light, and Brendan put his hand on Orlando's arm while he looked out the window.

"I think she knows you love her. You did the best you could."

"No, I didn't. Not for her, not for anyone." He wiped at his eyes.

"You were trying to do something good."

"Does that even matter? Jesus, Bren. Everyone just ended up dead or fucked up."

"It matters. It matters to me and Kathleen and Michael. I think it matters to Francine Parkman. And Sienna."

Brendan looked at his brother.

"No, listen, it always matters. Everything right that you do, it doesn't always make things better. Sometimes, I don't know. Sometimes it does just hurt everyone, but maybe that's how you know it was the right thing to do." He closed one eye, like he was trying to focus on something. "And you were alone, and that was my fault. I gave up on you, and I shouldn't have."

"I gave up on myself."

"Well, we're neither of us doing that now." They stopped, finally, at a gray building on Thirty-third overlooking the edge of Fairmount Park. There was a small plaque near the door that read SUNRISE DRUG AND ALCOHOL CENTER, and two anxious-looking women standing near the door smoking cigarettes. The brothers both looked up at it, then at each other, and Brendan smiled. "How long are you in for?"

"Thirty days. Thank God for Medicaid, right?"

"That's enough."

"Yeah? What if it doesn't, you know. Take."

"Then we'll do it again, or we'll do something else."

"You sound pretty fucking sure of yourself."

"Yeah, well, I get to sit out here at the curb."

Every day in rehab, Orlando watched an old man tie up a dog in front of the church next door. He'd sit in the window in his room and smoke a cigarette, a habit he'd fixed on after he came out of the detox ward and moved into the small room at the front of the building overlooking the park. Everyone here had a cigarette going. The meetings were blue with smoke, and people went at smoking the way they'd gone at dope on the outside.

The dog was big, with wolfish ears, long haunches, and an arched back, and the old man would tie it up early and leave it there while he went into the church. Sometimes the man would bring cleaning supplies and be inside the place for a while, and Orlando watched people come up and talk to the dog and pat it on the head. Once a little girl gave it a cookie from a plastic bag and screamed with delight as the dog accepted it and sat placidly, its long jaws working.

Orlando was awake at odd hours and would watch people in the park. Girls in tank tops and boys with shaggy hair tossed Frisbees and dumped water over their heads and then threw themselves down on blankets and talked, talked. At night kids ran around in packs, screaming to each other, throwing rocks at the stars. He read, whatever was around. There weren't a lot of books, so he read an old copy of *War of the Worlds* twice. Somehow it suited his mood to read about stunned people drifting through a ruined landscape, wondering whether anyone else had survived.

He had terrible, vivid dreams about fires and wars. People lost and people dying. He drank coffee, though somewhere in the second week he'd switched to decaf. Somehow he had ended up with Zoe's iPod and listened to her music when he was up in the middle of the night. Sufjan Stevens's fluttering clarinets. Neko Case telling him to hold on, hold on.

He walked out August fifth, the day after his birthday, and, standing in the lowering sun, traded phone numbers with a couple of his rehab friends and shook hands with his counselor and his sponsor, Austin, a tall, red-haired guy who clerked at a record store in University City. Austin hugged him hard and told him, "Things go right or things go wrong, call me. Remember, you're not Superman anymore."

Brendan was at work, and Marty was going to pick him up when his shift ended, so he waved off Austin's offer to get a cup of coffee, paced the curb, and stood alone, watching the traffic skirt the park. The dog was sitting at the corner, and he smiled when he saw it, reaching into his pocket for an oatmeal cookie he'd saved from lunch and extending it with his head a little bowed.

The thing went berserk, laid back its ears and charged him, its long head low to the ground and front paws splayed. Now he was close, he could see it had a long black scar, a ridge of dark flesh bisecting one milky eye. It lunged and hit the end of the lead, and the cord made a noise like a plucked string and gave out. Orlando laughed but stepped back, almost lost his footing, and threw his ass onto the hood of a car at the curb. The dog came on, its claws hitting the front panel and scoring the paint, and Orlando pivoted and put his feet down on the street and took off running.

They'd done some exercising every day in rehab, and it felt good to be moving the first twenty yards or thirty yards. It was hot, though the sun was beginning to drop across the river and the shadows were dark blue lines pointing into the city behind him. He turned to see the dog still moving in a fast, uneven lope, its eyes a hard yellow over the black muzzle. He lost momentum in turning and it closed with him, getting a piece of his jeans below his right knee and tearing his skin.

He cut hard and headed north, feeling the fabric give and the heat of the dog's open mouth. Across the park he could see a couple playing tennis and hear cars moving on the river drives.

The dog lost its footing, skidded, but got traction on the asphalt path and shot after him, making a noise deep in its throat that sounded like desire.

He ran hard, past statues and across a wide street, and the dog kept pace. Tongue out, a low modulated whine in its throat like it was trying to communicate something intricate. Orlando panted, openmouthed, crossing lanes and passing strolling couples and people on bikes. The sun was getting lower, and when he tried to cut back east, to circle around toward the rehab again, the dog anticipated him and swung wide to his right, barking and going at his heels, as if it were herding him north and west.

If he kept going that way, he knew, eventually he'd hit the river and then he could swim. Pictured it, broad strokes and white wings of water over his shoulders. Leaving the city behind, heading out toward the Main Line. Toward Zoe, maybe, out there somewhere in the Tudor castle where she'd grown up, behind high walls he'd scale to get to her. Or he could just keep going out of the city, wander south and west into the fields and along farm roads that lead one to the other and where he didn't know anyone.

He looked back and the dog was lagging, so he slowed, and then it wasn't a chase, but something else. Maybe they'd run together until the sun went down, and then they'd walk. Maybe the dog was his now; maybe that was the way it worked and you had to tear at someone a little to belong to them. He could see that and laugh, let everything go and just put one foot down and then another. Cross the fields that smelled like grass, into the shaded cemetery that smelled like stones and water. Keep going, into the woods to get lost among the trees as the world went black. Disappear but for white teeth and yellow eyes. Bay and whine and snap at the dark. Drink from the river and wait for the faint, answering howl.